"Why are you really here, Reed?"

"I wanted to make sure you were all right. I couldn't stop thinking about you. I... Oh, hell."

His mouth covered her, his kiss hungry and hot as he pulled her up against him. Then, just as abruptly as the kiss had begun, it ended. His expression fierce, he looked away. "No. That's not why I came here. Actually, I came to apologize to you."

"Apologize for what?"

"For that. For what happened before."

Ah, now she understood. "You don't have to—"

"I do. You deserve better. Kaitlyn, all your life, men have manipulated you. They wanted to own you. I will not do that to you."

"I think I understand. You want to make sure I don't get the wrong impression just because we..."

"Exactly." He sounded so relieved she nearly smiled.

"No worries, then. We're two adults. Our coming together was completely consensual."

"You came to me for help. Instead, I took advantage of you. And God help me, I still want you."

***

If you're on Twitter, tell us what you think of Harlequin Romantic Suspense!
#harlequinromsuspense

Dear Reader,

I know the people in my latest book, *The Rancher's Return*. I suspect you do, too, or someone like them. Kaitlyn Nuhn is beautiful and sexy. On the outside, she appears to have it all. Except her looks have only been a curse to her. She has recently escaped a rich and powerful man who was holding her prisoner. The experience has scarred her on the inside, and she doesn't know if she will ever be able to love again.

The hero, Reed Westbrook, is also scarred. He was sent to prison for three years for killing his own brother, a crime he did not commit. When he finally gets out on appeal, he tries to build a new life, haunted by the knowledge that his brother's real murderer might never be caught.

And then Kaitlyn shows up on his doorstep telling him she knows who the killer is.

The Rancher's Return is a roller-coaster book of emotion and danger. I enjoyed giving two wounded people their own happily-ever-after. I hope you enjoy reading their story!

Karen Whiddon

THE RANCHER'S RETURN

Karen Whiddon

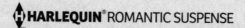

Recycling programs
for this product may
not exist in your area.

ISBN-13: 978-0-373-27911-1

The Rancher's Return

Copyright © 2015 by Karen Whiddon

Printed in U.S.A.

Karen Whiddon started weaving fanciful tales for her younger brothers at eleven. Amid the Catskill Mountains, then the Rocky Mountains, she fueled her imagination with the natural beauty surrounding her. Karen lives in north Texas and shares her life with her hero of a husband and three doting dogs. You can email Karen at KWhiddon1@aol.com or write to her at PO Box 820807, Fort Worth, TX 76182. Fans can also check out her website, karenwhiddon.com.

Books by Karen Whiddon

HARLEQUIN ROMANTIC SUSPENSE

A Secret Colton Baby
Texas Secrets, Lovers' Lies
The Millionaire Cowboy's Secret
The Cop's Missing Child
The CEO's Secret Baby
Colton's Christmas Baby
Profile for Seduction
The Perfect Soldier
Black Sheep P.I.
Bulletproof Marriage

Visit the Author Profile page at Harlequin.com for more titles.

Once again, to the fine folks at Legacy Boxer Rescue, Inc. Volunteering and helping to save dogs' lives, get them healthy and find a forever home is an experience that brings another layer of meaning to my life. Thank you for all you do. (savetheboxers.com)

Chapter 1

Reed Westbrook knew all too well that there were many kinds of torment. Some were subtle, like the way most townsfolk crossed to the other side of the street to avoid having to speak to him, or when salesclerks in the local stores averted their eyes as they reluctantly waited on him.

Reed was pretty damn tired of it.

Judging from the repetitive knocking on Reed's front door—right in the final forty-five seconds of the play-off football game—Deputy Sheriff George Putchinski was at it again.

Reed debated ignoring it, pretending he wasn't home. But since his presence was obvious—with his pickup parked in his driveway and the TV turned up pretty loud—he hefted himself out of his chair and headed toward the door.

The first few times this had happened, when he'd opened the door to see a uniformed Anniversary deputy standing on his step, he'd been flabbergasted. Ten or fifteen instances later, he'd gotten his response down pat.

Swinging open the door, he started his spiel. "I didn't do it. Whatever it was. Now go—"

He stopped. Stared. Not George. No, not even close. The gorgeous woman with the amazing blue eyes definitely wasn't Reed's nemesis. And yet she was.

He knew her instantly. Kaitlyn Nuhn had once been the girlfriend of his brother, Tim. In addition to that, she'd been the only person who'd known the truth, and who could have kept Reed from going to prison for his brother's murder. The fact that she hadn't, and disappeared instead, brought the anger back, full force. He nearly shut the door in her face.

By some instinct, he held back. Because maybe, after all this time, she'd give him a reason, some freaking closure. And possibly even a chance to finally clear his name and find out who had really shot Tim dead.

Heaven help him if she confessed it had been her.

As he stood staring, their gazes locked, he saw a flash of something in her eyes. He recognized it as pain, an emotion he'd felt often during the dark time he'd spent behind bars. If he hadn't gotten out on appeal, he knew he would have gone crazy, locked away in hell for a crime he hadn't committed.

"Kaitlyn Nuhn. I'll be damned," he said softly, raking his gaze over her as if he found her repulsive, when in fact it was the opposite. Just like always, his heart stuttered, his chest felt tight and he couldn't speak. He clenched his fist around the doorknob, frozen with indecision, which pissed him off even more.

When he'd thought of her, which had been more often than he'd like to admit, he'd hoped time hadn't been kind to her. Surely the ugliness inside had to have manifested in her looks, somehow.

Shocked, he now saw that hadn't been the case. She still looked…unreal. Still as stunningly beautiful, as if she'd just stepped from the pages of some glossy magazine ad for women's lingerie. Just as in the old days, the power of that beauty felt like a punch in the gut.

She didn't speak. Just stood staring up at him, a combination of naked fear, sorrow or regret making hollows in her cheeks. He looked past her, noting the sleek silver luxury car. Why had she returned? To make an apology? She was way too late for that. Three years, to be exact. It would have been longer had it not been for his astute lawyer, the prosecution's mistakes and lack of evidence.

But that didn't negate the three years he'd spent in a hellhole, with his brother dead and not knowing who had killed him. Or the way people in this town still treated him like a killer, capable of gunning down his own twin brother.

"What do you want?" he asked, not bothering to be polite. He'd let her say her spiel, nod in response and close the door in her face. Then he'd go back to his football game and his ordinary, quiet life. And try to forget the way seeing her brought the past rushing back up.

"I came to tell you I'm sorry." Her husky voice wavered and she swallowed, continuing to keep her gaze locked on his.

"Sorry?" He spat the word. "Too little, too late. Your apology means nothing to me."

Bowing her head, she nodded, as if she'd expected this. "I'm sorry about what happened to you. That's why

I came back. I wanted you to know the truth, about all of it. I know who murdered Tim." Pausing for breath, she kept her gaze locked on his. "And then he set you up to go to prison for it. He couldn't keep you from filing the appeal or from getting out, but he tried."

Of all the things she could have said, he hadn't expected this. Worse, he didn't believe her. Why should he, after all this time? "You also knew I couldn't have done it. Especially since you'd left me in your bed, waiting for your return."

Unbelievably, she blushed. "That was a mistake."

"You'd better believe it was." He met her gaze full on, letting his loathing show. "You were my only alibi, and you disappeared. And you know what? For the longest time, I thought you might have been who killed Tim."

Recoiling as if he'd stabbed her, she stared at him. He only looked away when her bottom lip started trembling, furious with himself that he could still feel any emotion at all toward her.

"Why are you *really* here?" Reed took a step closer, aware he was clenching his hands into fists.

"I wanted to apologize. For everything. He set it up so that we'd blame each other." She swallowed again, the movement drawing his gaze to her graceful throat. "I came as soon as I learned the truth."

Part of him wanted to believe her. After all, he'd spent years wondering who'd really killed Tim and set Reed up to take the blame. Prison had given him time to burn for revenge.

And now, when Kaitlyn held out the information like a poisoned T-bone in front of a starving dog, he wasn't sure what to believe. The past he'd shared with this woman had proven that she wasn't to be trusted. No matter how great her beauty.

Finally, as he'd known he would, he went for the bone. "Who?" he rasped. "Give me the name."

The fact that she still hesitated made another strike against her.

"The name," he repeated.

She glanced at the doorway, almost as if she expected someone to come charging through and save her. Or knock her down.

Finally, she spoke. "Okay." She met his gaze straight on and lifted her chin. "Alex Ramirez."

At first he didn't recognize the name. When he did, his first impulse was to think she was lying. "*Lieutenant Governor* Ramirez? The same guy who's been talking about making a run for governor?"

"Yes." Though her generous mouth thinned, making her appear miserable, she stood her ground. "That's the one."

He nearly snorted out loud. "Why him? And if you're telling the truth, why didn't you come forward before now?"

Again the hesitation. Just enough to make him question whatever she might say.

"I couldn't."

"Why not?" He fired back.

"Because I've been Alex's prisoner for the last three years." She took a little breath, blowing it back out her nose. "He likes to brutalize wounded things."

Her words made no sense. "Why should I believe anything you have to say?" he said. "Don't show up here and then try to play me for a fool."

"I'm not, believe me." Her chest heaved as she turned

to go, drawing his unwilling gaze. "You know what? You're right. I shouldn't have come. I'm sorry to have bothered you."

Something she'd said haunted him. "Wait," he told her. "What do you mean about him liking to brutalize wounded things?"

Her blue eyes blazed—either with hope or with pain. In his mind, sometimes the two had become indistinguishable.

"Exactly what it sounds like. And now I've escaped. If he finds me, I'm a dead woman. Especially since I know what he's done."

Still not entirely convinced, nonetheless he stepped aside and motioned her into his living room. "Please. Come in."

As she moved past him, he caught a whiff of her scent, which surprisingly reminded him of vanilla rather than the flowery perfume he remembered.

"Have a seat." Though he sounded churlish, he didn't care. Indicating the sofa, he tried not to stare as she sank gracefully onto the leather cushions. She wore a T-shirt and jeans—ordinary clothes that were elevated to an entirely new level by her feminine curves. Her kind of lush, wild beauty would make any red-blooded man break out in a sweat.

And Reed was no exception. The sharp surge of desire he felt when he looked at her was nothing new, though certainly as unwelcome now as it had been before. He'd always had trouble not wanting her, even back then when she'd belonged to his brother. He didn't understand how this could still be so, especially now when he should despise her.

Noise from the television drew his attention. The football game had gone into overtime. Since he no longer cared, Reed grabbed the remote and turned off the TV.

Deciding to continue standing, he crossed his arms and glared at her, deliberately hostile, feeling it was safer this way. "Explain," he ordered, when she showed no sign of elaborating.

She sighed and smoothed back her wealth of golden hair with perfectly manicured fingers, although a few wisps defied her hand and continue to frame her perfect, oval face. Her skin glowed, the flawless alabaster of fine porcelain, beauty personified. Eyeing her he wondered exactly as he'd done in the past, how his brother had been able to get a girl as lovely as her.

Of course neither Reed nor Tim had known her beauty concealed the heart of a snake. Best to remember this now, he knew. Steeling himself, he cocked his head while he waited for her to speak.

"May I please have a glass of water?" she asked. "It's a long drive from Austin. I was afraid to stop more than once." She looked down. "I wasn't sure if I was being followed, so I had to take several evasive precautions."

"Followed?" Shaking his head, he got up, fetched a plastic bottle of spring water from the fridge and handed it to her. "Here you go."

He waited, trying not to stare while she drank, though the movement of her long slender throat drew his eye. He both hated and acknowledged it, aware he could use this edginess to keep him sharp and on his toes.

When she'd finished drinking, she set the bottle down. "Thank you."

"You're welcome." He inclined his head.

"Yes." She sighed. "Before I begin, you should know I can't stay long. This is the first place he'll look. If he finds me, he'll kill me and whoever I'm with. So you're putting yourself in danger by even talking to me."

"A risk I'm willing to take, if what you say is true. Let's hear it."

She winced. "It's a long story."

"No. Make it short and to the point." He went so far as to glance at his watch before meeting her gaze again. "If you plan to lie to me, don't. I've had enough BS from you to last more than a lifetime."

Her amazing eyes widened. "I've never lied to you."

"Really." He couldn't resist. "Since you were my only alibi, I'd say the way you managed to disappear rather than show up in court is falsehood enough. I went to prison—innocent—for the death of my own brother. Because you couldn't take the time to tell the truth." Again, he felt the sharp, burning ache he always felt when he thought of the way his brother had been gunned down in cold blood.

"It's not what you think," she began.

"Be that as it may, Tim's dead." He managed to sound normal. "And you aren't. Now you're going to tell me what proof you have that Alex Ramirez killed him, and how."

Back ramrod straight, Kaitlyn tried to draw on the sense of purpose that had propelled her the entire way to Anniversary. She'd expected hostility, after all.

Still, some tiny, foolish part of her heart had hoped he'd understand. Maybe even be sympathetic, but she could hardly blame him. He'd spent the past three years believing her responsible for what he'd endured. She couldn't expect him to comprehend how badly she'd suffered herself.

She wasn't here for sympathy, or to try and repair the broken pieces of a relationship that had been doomed from the start. She'd come to find justice. For not only Tim's murder and Reed's incarceration, but for what Alex Ramirez had done to her. He'd ruined three lives, as casually as another man would kill a fly. He deserved to pay.

But would Reed believe her? He'd already made it clear what he thought. Worse, she didn't even have proof. Just her word against a powerful lieutenant governor.

Raising her head, she saw Reed watched her, his gaze dark and intent. A shiver ghosted over her skin, making goose bumps rise. Prison had changed him some, sharpened the edges of his profile, and deepened the reserve in his eyes. Still, he was easy on the eyes, despite the hardship he'd endured. She'd always thought him beautiful, even back when she and his twin brother, Tim, had been an item. Though Reed and Tim had the same features, the same shock of thick, dark hair, something in the depths of Reed's hazel eyes had always called to her.

The attraction that had simmered between the two of them had made her feel like a moth circling around a flame.

Finally, unable to resist, she'd given in. And then the one evening of explosive passion they'd shared had been the night Tim had been murdered. She'd spent three years wondering if Reed would always associate her embrace with the brutal death of his brother.

"Well?" he prodded. "If you have something to say, say it."

"When I left you, still asleep in my bed, I knew what I needed to do. So I scribbled a quick note to you and I went to find Tim." She swallowed, her throat suddenly dry. She took a long drink of water, willing her voice to remain steady. "I intended to break it off with him."

Surprise flashed across his rugged features, but he didn't comment.

Briefly, she closed her eyes. Even after all this time, the horrible scene still had the power to paralyze her. "I walked in on him and Alex arguing. Of course, I didn't know who Alex was then." Her throat felt raw. This might be past history, but the memory of it still hurt.

"Go on," he urged.

She tried to speak and couldn't.

"Alex Ramirez and Tim were arguing? And then what?"

"Yes. The instant Tim saw me, he looked afraid. He ordered me to leave, but Alex grabbed me. I knew from the expression on Tim's face that it wasn't good, but I didn't know how bad. Not yet."

She took a deep, shaky breath, aware what she had to tell him next would be painful. Miserable, she tried to find the right words, then decided just to say it.

"Alex killed him." The words came out in a hoarse whisper. "He turned around, pulled out a pistol and shot Tim dead. Right there, right in front of me. And when I freaked out, he told me to calm down or he'd kill me, too."

Reed swore. The dark shadow in his gaze spoke of his contempt for her, of the fact that he disbelieved her story. She told herself that didn't matter, that it was justified. Just like she'd actually come to believe she deserved to be treated the way Alex had abused her.

"And then Alex tied me up, put me in the trunk of his car, and took me back to his mansion." Such a simple sentence could not possibly convey the horror of what had happened. That night and for many days and nights after. Years, actually.

"And no one noticed you were gone?" He couldn't quite hide his disbelief.

"With everything that happened, I think they assumed I fled out of cowardice."

Silence, while he considered this.

"How'd you escape?" Reed asked. "And when?"

Heaven help her, her lower lip started quivering. She coughed, using her hand to try and cover it up. "Just now. Today. Despite knowing Anniversary is the first place Alex will look, I needed to come to you and try to make things right before I go on the run."

The skepticism in his eyes made her feel sick. "I shouldn't have come here. I see that now."

"Then why did you?" he asked quietly. "Really, why did you?"

She shrugged to mask her pain. "You were the only other person I could think of who would care. The only person beside myself who would give a damn about what Alex had done. Not only to Tim, but to you. And me. With all my heart, I believe he should pay."

Clearly not believing her, he didn't speak again, so she collected her purse and turned to go. Head up, shoulders back, hoping like hell she projected an attitude that was different from how broken and defeated she felt inside.

She got half the distance to the door before he stopped her. "Wait."

Though she knew she should have kept moving, she froze. "Yes?"

"All right. I'm still listening. Tell me more, make me believe you. Why would a man as rich and powerful as

Alex Ramirez do such a thing? What was he even doing with my brother?"

Exhaustion made her sag, though the instant she realized this she straightened her shoulders. "Politics isn't the only thing Alex is involved with. He runs a huge drug operation in central Texas. Apparently Tim was working for him."

He knew, she saw. The emotion passing over his face might have been fleeting, but she realized he understood that this at least was the truth.

"You're telling me that you witnessed a politician kill my brother and he let you live."

"Yes. As his prisoner."

"Why? Tell me why he'd do that?"

She looked him in the eye and gave him the truth. "Because he's a sociopath."

Silence while he digested this. Then he asked, "Do you have proof? Something besides your word that this man killed my brother and kept you prisoner?"

"No." She swallowed. "Only my word against his. And I had no idea that he'd framed you and had you sent to prison. You've got to believe me. I just found out the other night when he got drunk and started bragging."

"I'm having trouble with the entire story. If you were his prisoner, how'd you escape now?"

Cheeks burning, she told him her shame. "After three years, he'd loosened his hold on me. I wasn't always kept locked up. I really think he believed I wouldn't go."

"Did he treat you well, then?" He asked the question with deceptive calmness.

"Well? I wouldn't call it that."

Hazel eyes burning, he tilted his head. "Then what would you call it?"

"Reed, he beat and raped me. I was a possession to him, a toy to do with as he wanted." She tried to sound matter-of-fact, even though saying the truth out loud felt both mortifying and painful. "He enjoyed hurting and humiliating me. In the early months, I tried to escape and he blackened my eyes and broke my ribs. If I hadn't figured out a way to get away now, I have no doubt once he got tired of me, he would have eventually killed me."

"Forgive me, but I can't bring myself to feel sorry for you. Your story is far-fetched and bizarre."

"I know." She resisted the urge to hang her head. "Truth is sometimes stranger than fiction."

His features hardened. "I see. Let me ask you something, and I need you to tell me the truth, for once. Even though you claim Alex Ramirez did it, I have to ask. Was it you, all along? Did you kill my brother?"

Stunned, at first she couldn't speak, couldn't respond. She should have expected this. In fact, she probably would have wondered the same thing had their places been reversed.

Finally, she found her voice. "No. I did not."

"Excuse me if I don't take your word for it."

Finally defeated, she straightened her spine and nodded. "I understand. Believe me. I'll leave and let you go back to your life."

"Wait." This time, he stopped her before she turned. "Give me something to help me believe, to make me understand. You've come here with this story, which you have to admit is way out there. You claim you not only witnessed my brother's murder, but you've been kept a prisoner by the killer, who just happens to be the lieutenant governor of Texas, a guy who's considered a front-runner for governor next election. Does that about cover it?"

"Yes."

"Kaitlyn, I want to believe you…."

"But you just can't. I understand."

"Then give me something." The fierceness in his voice made her blink. "You've got to have something, some sort of proof, no matter how small, that would help me accept what you say as truth."

Swallowing, she realized she did. Turning slowly, she lifted her shirt and showed him her back, with its jagged and horrible crisscross web of scars.

Chapter 2

Stunned, Reed couldn't speak. He could only stare. Once upon a time, he'd explored every inch of Kaitlyn's perfect body. He moved forward, reaching out his hand, withdrawing it at the last moment. Some of the red, raised welts were recent, while others bore the whitish appearance of old scars.

"He did this?" he asked, his voice sounding as if he'd swallowed gravel.

"Yes." Dropping her shirt, she turned. Her perfect face appeared expressionless. Except for her eyes. The shadows in them reminded him of prison. "He likes whips. And chains. And other instruments of torture." She shuddered. "And I was his own personal plaything. That's all the proof I have."

"It's enough." Stomach twisting, he tried to find the right words, finally settling on two. "I'm sorry."

"So am I." She dipped her chin, acknowledging the sentiment, though he knew—like her apology—it had come too late. She turned, giving him one last lingering glance. Not imploring. More like resolute. "And now, I've got to go. Once Alex realizes I've escaped, he'll stop at nothing to find me."

He didn't care, he shouldn't have cared, but he couldn't seem to help himself. "Where are you going?"

One delicate shoulder lifted in a shrug. "I don't know. I've got to keep moving. Otherwise, I'm dead."

He thought of his ranch, of the secluded frame house a few hours away, where he'd taken to spending more and more of his time. "I have land my uncle left me about southwest of Mineral Wells," he said. "It's a small, working cattle ranch. I've got livestock there, with hired hands looking after the place. It's really remote and accessible only by a dirt road. It isn't much, but there's running water and electricity. If you don't mind the isolation, you can stay there."

Watching him warily, she nodded. "Thanks. If you want to give me directions, I'll head that way now."

He wasn't sure he wanted her to go alone. "Give me a minute. I need to think."

She seemed to practically vibrate with impatience. "Please don't take too long. I don't have a lot of time. Alex is a powerful man and very successful at getting rid of people. I can't tell you how many times he's bragged about the people he's made disappear. I know too much, therefore I'm a liability he'll need to eliminate. He has people working everywhere. If someone sees my car and reports back to him…"

Refusing to let her rush him, he continued to consider. If he was jumping into this mess, he needed to study all angles.

Finally, he glanced out the window, at the low-slung, glossy car. "That Jaguar won't do well there. Plus, it'll stick out like a sore thumb. Is it his?"

For maybe a second, she looked abashed. "Yes. It's one of many. He'll want it back."

Right then, he decided. "We need to move it. Leave it in a parking lot downtown."

"Then how will I get to your place?"

He hoped he wouldn't regret what he was about to say. "I'll drive you. It's about time for me to run out there and check on things. I can stay out there a little while. And I've got a four-wheel drive pickup that makes the trip perfectly."

After snatching his keys off the counter, he grabbed his laptop and motioned for her to go ahead. Instead, she stood frozen, staring at him.

"But what about this?" she sputtered, gesturing at his house. "I don't want to take you away from your life here in Anniversary. What about your job?"

"My job can be anywhere I want it to be, as long as I have this." He held up the laptop. "Now let's get a move on. Especially since you seem to think Alex or one of his people could show up at any moment."

Still she didn't move. "What about clothes? Food? Medicines? Shouldn't you pack?"

"I have everything I need at the ranch. I go out there all the time. Come on." And he opened the front door and stepped aside so she could pass.

They parked the Jag at the marina. Reed hoped doing so might make anyone in pursuit think maybe Kaitlyn had gone somewhere out on the lake in a boat. This would buy them a bit more time.

Reed watched as Kaitlyn climbed out of the sports car, her long legs glistening in the sun. After removing an overnight bag from the backseat, she strode to the edge of the water, and then tossed the keys in. She then walked over and got into his truck, her expression relieved.

"That felt good," she said. "Like a weight has been lifted off my shoulders."

He moved to adjust her visor and she flinched. More proof, though she probably didn't realize it, of what she'd endured. "Easy," he said. "I'm not going to touch you."

Nodding, she gripped the door handle with one hand as he put the truck in gear and they pulled away.

"I'm a bit on edge," she told him unnecessarily. "So please don't mind if I ask you how you can be sure we won't be followed."

"I'll answer as honestly as I can. I can't, at least not until we leave the cities and the highways behind. It's a lot easier to tell on a two-lane road. We'll be skirting around Dallas on 635 and then picking up 820 to go around Fort Worth. It's a bit of a drive, so you might as well settle in and try and get comfortable."

Though she nodded, he could tell she still felt antsy. That was all right, he didn't blame her. In a way, she'd just gotten out of prison. He remembered how that had felt. For a while, everything in the outside world had seemed surreal.

They were crossing through Irving, former home of the Dallas Cowboys, when she faced him. "Why are you helping me?" she asked. "I'm assuming it's because you're going to try to figure out a way to get Alex arrested for his crime."

"Crimes," he corrected. "Plural. And yes, you are a witness and therefore extremely dangerous to him. So I've got to keep you safe while I get the feds working on this."

"Feds?" She sounded horrified. "You can't… You don't understand. Alex has people working for him everywhere."

"In law enforcement? Even in the FBI?"

She nodded. "Yes. He's not just involved in drugs. He's got his finger in a lot of other things."

"Weird. According to the media, Alex Ramirez is a blasted saint. Every news story about him talks about his good works and generous charitable contributions."

"It's all a front. He uses a lot of the charitable organizations to launder money. You wouldn't believe all the illegal operations Alex is involved with."

"And because you know all this, you're even more dangerous to him."

"Yes. There's no way he's going to allow me to live. We have to be careful about who we approach. Alex has boasted many times about having the FBI and the DEA on his payroll, even people in the governor's office and the Senate. There's no way to know who to trust."

Reed cursed. "If you're telling the truth, this sounds like the mafia or a cartel. Organized crime."

"In a way, it is. Whatever you want to call it, it's dangerous. Getting in his way—protecting me—would be risky. In fact, I'd call it a death sentence. Especially if he thinks you know anything, which he will. Before you decide to help me, I want to make sure you understand."

"I get that." He flashed a grim smile, still not one hundred percent convinced. "I've already given up three years of my life and lost my brother. Damned if I'm letting him get away with anything more."

"Taking him down won't be easy."

"I understand." He shot her another glance, his emotions raw and confused. He'd spent the past three years hating her, and now to learn she'd been just as much of a victim as he? If her story was true, that is.

"Tell me specifically how you escaped," he asked as casually as he could. "If you've been under lock and key as you say, how'd you manage to get away even with his being more permissive?"

"He got drunk and forgot to lock me in my room. Either he thought he did or maybe he believed I was completely brainwashed." She looked down, as if embarrassed. "Stockholm syndrome and all that."

"Were you?"

"In a way." When she raised her chin to meet his gaze, her expression was bleak. "I haven't been allowed off the property in all this time. I wasn't permitted any contact with other people, except for his employees. Even if he let me go outside the house on the grounds, he or one of the men he'd assigned as guards, was with me."

She swallowed, the stiff way she held her shoulders telling him of her tension. "I'd come to believe I deserved to live like that. I came to feel the pain was punishment well deserved. Over time, after hearing the same things repeated over and over, I was beaten, both in body and spirit. He saw this. It made him happy. I believe he didn't think I'd ever have the guts to run."

Her quiet, matter-of-fact tone moved him more than he wanted her to know. Clearing his throat, he swallowed hard. "But you did."

"Yes. He was drunk. For whatever reason, he brought

you and Tim up. He was gloating about sending you to prison and furious that you'd gotten out." A shadow crossed her eyes. "This time, when I heard that, something inside me snapped. After he passed out, I left. No one even tried to stop me."

The more she spoke, the more he believed her. "How long do you think you have until he realizes you're gone?"

"I don't know. Usually, when he drinks like that, he looks for me first thing in the morning when he wakes up."

The grim twist to her lovely mouth told him why.

Drumming his fingers on the steering wheel, he changed the subject. "You really didn't know I was initially convicted of killing Tim?"

"No. I honestly had no idea. I wasn't permitted access to television, internet or even newspapers. I'm sorry."

Which meant he'd spent a lot of time hating her for no valid reason.

That thought so blew his mind he had to think of something else. "I'm pretty sure Alex won't risk searching for you himself. There are too many things that can go wrong. He'll send people. Most likely he'll also use the media. People who have never met you might have your picture."

"What are you suggesting?" She frowned. "That I wear a disguise?"

"More like a complete overhaul. You won't even recognize yourself when you look in the mirror. At least for when you go out. Do you wear contacts?"

"No."

"Okay, then we'll get colored, non-prescription ones and change your eye color. Your blue eyes are very striking. We'll tone that down. I'm thinking a muddy brown."

At first she appeared startled. Then she smiled, sending a jolt of lust straight to his gut. He remembered her smile. Though already beautiful, her smile lent her a sweetness, a girl-next-door look that tugged at his heartstrings. Just like before, when she'd been with his brother and Reed had wanted her so badly he'd burned with it. The times when he'd come across her sitting on the couch in flannel pajamas, without makeup and with her hair in a careless ponytail had been when he'd thought her most irresistible.

Pushing the thoughts away, he studied her. "We're going to cut and color your hair," he announced, wincing inside. "Something matronly."

"Even though I'll be hiding out at your ranch?"

"Even so. You might have to go to town sometime."

"Fine." She exhaled. "Do you have a plan?"

"Not yet. But I will."

"How long are you thinking this is going to take?" she asked, beginning to look concerned.

"I don't know. Since you said he has a bunch of law enforcement people on his payroll, it should just be a matter of seeing who we can trust."

"That could take a while." She sounded glum. He could relate. After all, she'd just gotten out of a prison—of sorts—too.

"Maybe not. You never know. I don't want to make mistakes. When we take him down, I want to make sure he doesn't get off on a technicality."

Slowly, she nodded. "No worries, I'll wear the disguise when I'm out in public. Though I think if I change my haircut and color, I shouldn't need colored contacts."

"Better safe than sorry. I'll order the contacts online and pay extra to have them overnighted," he said. "We'll also find the ugliest, most unflattering clothes we can. That should be a good start."

"I…" Swallowing, she appeared hesitant and uncertain.

"You said you were willing to do whatever it takes," he reminded her. "If you don't want to be found, you're going to have to wear a disguise."

After a moment, she sighed. "True. And you're right. I'll change my appearance however much is necessary."

As for himself, he'd be glad to make her less of a distraction. She'd been in his life for only an hour, and already he found himself wanting her.

Physically, that is. Nothing more. He'd put that down to the way he'd been living life as a semi-hermit. Most of the women in town wanted nothing to do with an ex-con like him. Not that he cared. He was fine living alone.

"How long do you think we have before he starts combing the town?"

"He was passed out when I left." Jiggling her long and coltish legs, she appeared to vibrate with tension. He hated that he had to tear his eyes away, drawn to her again and again, despite his earlier self-admonishment. "It depends on when he wakes up. I'm hoping he stays out until morning."

"That's a long time, considering it just got dark. How long have you been gone?"

Her bright blue gaze locked on his. "Not very long. I drove straight here. A few hours, at most. When he wakes up and goes to my room to find me, all hell will break lose."

"Good thing we hightailed it out of town, then."

"Especially since your house will be the first place he'll look."

Startled, he realized she was right. The history she and his brother had shared made him the obvious choice. "It's okay. We should be safe."

"What about your ranch? If the deed is in your name, it's a matter of public record. Alex will find it."

"Then it's a good thing it's not in my name. Since I was in prison when my uncle learned he had terminal lung cancer, he had his lawyer set up a corporation. Just in case I never got out. So there's no way to trace it to me."

Clearly relieved, she smiled again.

After they passed Fort Worth, she fell asleep, which told him she must have been exhausted. He let her doze, enjoying the time to think.

Once again, everything in his world had been turned upside down. He wasn't sure what to make of any of this and had long ago given up on the idea of knowing who really killed his brother. In prison, he'd had plenty of time to wonder. All signs had pointed to Kaitlyn, for so many reasons.

She'd left Reed in her bed and had gone to Tim. Reed had suspected this, though he hadn't known for certain. Her claim that she'd planned to break things off with his brother made sense, and if things had gone differently, he'd have been overjoyed. And guilty. Especially since he'd been the one in bed with his own brother's girlfriend.

Reed didn't blame her—he knew it took two to tango. He'd let it go on, even though he'd known better. The lingering looks, the electricity that coursed through him with every accidental touch, the way he'd burned for Kaitlyn, despite knowing he had no right.

But somehow he'd gone from sleeping with his brother's girlfriend to being accused of murdering that same brother in cold blood. Kaitlyn had disappeared, despite the fact that she was his only alibi.

He'd been railroaded, he realized that now. The men who'd arrested and questioned him most likely worked for Alex. The district attorney who had indicted him on no evidence had been in Alex's pocket, too. The judge definitely had been.

Reed had spent nearly three years locked away in that horrible place before his lawyer finally filed an appeal and got him a new trial. This time, the judge clearly hadn't been on Alex's payroll since Reed was now a free man.

Though his name had been forever blackened.

When he'd gotten out and returned home to Anniversary, he'd searched for Kaitlyn, of course. He'd intended to make her tell him why she hadn't come forward, why she'd let him rot in prison, why, why, why. So many unanswered questions.

Damn it all to hell. Even though he had to admit her explanation made sense, in a twisted sort of way.

He had to question how Alex had gotten away with keeping a woman hostage for three years. Then he remembered the guy in Ohio or Indiana who'd kept three women prisoners in his basement for far longer than that. Such a thing definitely was possible, especially for a man with lots of money and influence.

As he drove, the land became flatter, the trees more sparse and twisted. He'd always liked the beginning of west Texas, because it was hardscrabble and tough.

The sun sank beneath the horizon, a fiery ball of orange and red, trailing rosy tendrils in its wake. Darkness

settled over the land in increments, deeper and more vel-
vety now that they'd left the city lights behind.

When he left the pavement for the rutted, gravel road
that led to his ranch, Kaitlyn woke up. She yawned and
stretched while he tried not to notice the way her T-shirt
strained against her curves.

"Are we there yet?"

"Just about. We've got a few more miles on this gravel
road and then we go off road and up."

"Off road?" She sounded concerned.

"Yeah. It's a path, sort of. That's why I said that fancy
car you were driving wouldn't do well here. This truck
can make it, no problem. So could a Jeep or an ATV.
That's about it."

Nodding, she squinted into the darkness. "I like that.
It makes me feel safe."

He grinned. "I enjoy coming out here. I always feel
more alive. Like I'm free. I've even been thinking of
selling my house in Anniversary and moving out here
permanently."

"Really?" She didn't sound surprised at all. "I can see
that." Giving him a quizzical look, she appeared to be
considering asking him something.

"Go ahead," he prompted. "We'll be spending a fair
bit of time together, so you might as well ask whatever
it is that's bothering you."

"Okay. I know you said you could work anywhere.
Back before all this craziness happened, you were VP
at the bank. What do you do now?"

"The bank didn't want me back," he said quietly. "And
who could blame them? Not many people are willing
to hire a felon, even though my murder conviction was

overturned. The ranch brings in a nice income, which I supplement with my own business."

"Which is?"

He found himself hesitating, not sure exactly why. He was proud of what he'd accomplished, and the way his orders had grown so much he'd had to hire a couple of guys to help him out, precutting forms in bulk. "I make custom bird feeders and birdhouses. I sell them from my website."

"Really?" The surprised pleasure in her voice washed over him. "That's amazing. You'll have to show me the website later, assuming you have internet way out here."

"We do. I purchased mobile Wi-Fi, so I'm never without internet access." Slowing the truck down, he squinted into the darkness. "Brace yourself. We're fixing to go off road."

There—the fence post with the three boards nailed to it, making a small triangle, with a letter *W* in the middle. Putting on the brakes, he let his headlights point out the marker. "See that? Pyramid W Ranch."

"*W* for Westbrook?"

He grinned, pleased. "Yep. Are you ready?"

At her nod, he turned the truck toward the gap in the fence. "Hang on." The tires rattled as they crossed the metal crossing guard. "The road's kind of rutted in places, so get ready to bounce."

He'd barely gotten the last word out when they hit the first of many crevices. Once they were over, he turned to glance at her. "Are you all right?"

"Yes." One hand gripped the door handle, the other the dashboard in front of her. "My teeth are clattering, but I'll be fine."

"Good. Because we've still got a ways to go."

By the time they reached the turnoff that wound up the hill to his small ranch house, Kaitlyn appeared weary.

"We're almost there," he told her. "And my driveway is much better, I promise."

She nodded. "Great."

Finally, they crested the hill and his headlights illuminated the frame building. It was small, but he'd always found it homey, especially since he and Tim had come here often as kids to visit his uncle. He supposed the memories of his childhood here made the ranch feel more like home than anywhere else.

"Very nice," Kaitlyn commented. "It looks like you keep it up well. Or do you have a ranch foreman or someone living there while you're gone?"

"My ranch foreman has a mobile home on the other side of the property. I try to come out here at least once a month. Sometimes more."

She turned and touched his arm, surprising him. "Are you sure no one in town knows about this place?"

"I have a friend or two," he replied. "Brock McCauley and his wife Zoe. But they won't say anything without checking with me first."

"Zoe?" Kaitlyn appeared surprised. "Brock and Zoe finally got together?"

"Yes." He couldn't help but smile. "They're among a handful of people who don't treat me like a leper, as though serving time tainted me with poison."

He knew he sounded bitter but he didn't care.

"I'm sorry," Kaitlyn said, touching him again. He had to force himself not to twist away.

"Come on." Killing the engine, he left the headlights on so they could see the front door. "I'll turn them off once I can get the porch light on."

"You should get a motion-sensor light," she said.

"I'd thought about that, except then any critter crossing my yard would activate it."

"Good point."

He got out and crossed around to her side, intending to open her door for her. The manners his mama had taught him ran deep, but Kaitlyn had already gotten out by the time he reached her.

"Come on," he said, leading the way to the front door. "I've put in one of those locks where you just enter a code." That said, he punched it in, waiting until the dead bolt had turned before pushing the door open and flicking the light switch to On.

"Here we go." He couldn't keep the pride from his voice. Inside were oak hardwood floors, with matching baseboards. The furniture looked comfortably worn, a sort of cowboy shabby chic.

"Wow." She walked around the living room, examining the display of Western art he'd carefully displayed. "Nice."

"Thank you."

He showed her the guest room, which did double duty as his office, along with the hall bathroom. "It's only a two-bedroom house. That couch makes out into a bed."

She nodded, her expression pensive. "If you don't mind, I'm going to freshen up and then turn in. It's been a long day and it's late. I'm exhausted."

"I understand." He pointed the way to his linen closet, where he kept extra towels as well as linens to make up the sofa sleeper. "If you're thirsty or get hungry, help yourself to anything in the fridge. I keep it well stocked."

Her tired smile underscored her earlier statement. "Thank you."

He wasn't sure how to reply, so he settled on a nod. A moment later, she quietly closed the door, shutting him out.

Which was good, he told himself, turning to head back to his kitchen. He needed to do some thinking so he could formulate some sort of plan.

Chapter 3

Despite the prominent hump in the middle of the sofa bed, Kaitlyn slept deeply. More deeply than she had in a long time. She was free, and she'd finally taken charge of her destiny. If everything worked out, Alex would finally face justice and Reed's name would be cleared once and for all.

Sunlight streamed through the blinds covering the window. She jumped up, turned the blinds to open, and peered outside, squinting into the brightness. She couldn't see much, just a medium-sized, live oak tree.

Fine. She'd explore the ranch after she'd had a shower and breakfast.

Reed. Just the thought of him, broad-shouldered and muscular, had her heart skipping a beat. There was a new edginess to him that he didn't have before, a darkness lurking in his eyes. Oddly enough, this only made him more attractive.

No, she reminded herself. Reed was part of the past, the past she wanted to forget. As soon as she was free, she planned to make a new future, as far away from Texas as she could get.

Later, with her hair still damp from the shower, wearing a clean T-shirt and jeans, she emerged from her room, following the tantalizing scent of coffee to the kitchen. Reed sat at the kitchen table, his laptop open before him. He looked up as she entered, and smiled absently.

His masculine confidence made him beautiful. Mesmerized, she froze. Only when she reminded herself to stop being foolish was she able to move forward. "The coffee smells wonderful."

"I hope you like it strong." He pointed to a cup he'd set out on the counter for her. "There's some powdered creamer, too, and sugar if you need it."

"I do and I do." She took a deep breath and told herself to relax. Preparing her coffee helped, since the relatively normal act was something she'd had no control over for the past three years. If she got coffee, she'd had to drink it black, and Alex had seemed to delight in making it as bitter as possible.

Her first sip of Reed's brew had her humming with pleasure. "It's good. I like it."

Nodding, he barely looked up from his computer.

She took her mug, crossed over to the table and pulled out the chair across from him, even though this meant she faced the back of his computer. "Are you working on birdhouse orders?"

He shook his head, still not looking at her. "Not right now. I'm trying to get down some sort of basic plan. I've been outlining what we might try. I confess, what you said about Alex having people everywhere is hampering my efforts to plan. It's not like I can just approach anyone in law enforcement. Especially since, as far as they'll be concerned, I'm an ex-con."

At his words, her insides twisted. "We'll figure something out." She waited until he finally looked up and met her gaze before continuing. "I want to thank you for taking a chance and helping me."

Staring at her, he didn't reply at first. When he did, his serious expression told her he meant his words. "Kaitlyn, I'll do my best to keep you safe. You've offered me something I thought I'd never have—the chance to avenge my brother's murder. For that, I owe you."

Relieved, she started to respond, but realized he hadn't finished, so she took a deep drink of her coffee instead.

"One thing you need to know," he told her. "What happened between us before was a mistake, and I've spent the past three years regretting it. You were Tim's girlfriend and we betrayed him."

Harsh words, but she deserved them. Dipping her head, she knew she couldn't tell him how many times she'd tried to break things off with Tim, and how badly Tim had reacted. She'd realized early into the relationship that it wasn't working, and not just because of Tim's substance abuse issues. Because all along she'd wanted someone else.

She'd wanted Reed. From the instant she first laid eyes on him she'd realized she'd chosen the wrong brother. She'd believed they were meant to be together forever. What a foolish, naive woman she'd been.

She'd paid penance for that indiscretion during her captivity. She'd survived what Alex did to her body, but she knew it would be a long time before she could let anyone touch her that way again. Even Reed. Especially Reed.

"Go ahead and get settled," he said.

"Thank you." She exhaled, for what felt like the first time in years. "This is very nice."

"I'm glad you like it." Looking satisfied, he snatched his truck keys up off the coffee table. "I'll be right back. This place is pretty isolated, so I'm going to run into Breckenridge and hit up the Walmart there. Wait here."

"I'd like to go with you."

"You can't. I'm sorry, but we haven't got your disguise yet. We can't take the chance that you'll be seen." He pointed in the direction of the kitchen. "Make yourself at home. There's plenty to eat and drink, if you're hungry. I'll be back as quickly as I can."

Defeated, she nodded quickly. She couldn't fault him for being thorough. Even though the chance of running into one of Alex's people might be virtually nonexistent out here, as long as a possibility existed, they couldn't risk it. She'd have to wear a disguise when she wanted to leave, and she would.

One last quick glance to make sure she understood, and Reed left. He locked the door behind him on the way out. The sound of the dead bolt turning made Kaitlyn tense up again. She was all too familiar with that sound.

More shaken than she cared to admit, she began exploring. Though she didn't want to be intrusive, she couldn't help but check out the place where she'd be staying for a little while. Hopefully not too long. She knew she couldn't really begin healing until she'd left everyone and everything from her past behind.

Trying to settle her tension, she wandered the compact house. She wasn't hungry—her nerves had taken care of that—so she once again checked out the other rooms.

The guest room where she'd spent the night looked a

bit utilitarian, with the sofa sleeper for a bed and a small dresser. It had the look of never having been used, as if Reed didn't have a lot of visitors out here in the back of beyond. She guessed she might have been the first to stay there.

In the guest room, she inspected the wide oak desk and computer and wall-to-wall bookshelves, packed floor to ceiling with books. She moved closer, checking them out. Everything from classics to modern thrillers, non-fiction to horror stories by *New York Times* bestselling authors.

Thrilled despite herself, she found several titles she'd been meaning to read and, eyeing the overstuffed chair in one corner, knew she'd spend a lot of time in this room during her stay. She'd never pegged Reed as a reader, but then she'd never really gotten to know him.

Except for that one night, when passion had exploded between them and they'd made a mistake that would impact both of their lives forever.

Again, the past. Resolutely, she pushed the memories away.

Next she moved down the hallway toward what had to be the master bedroom. She felt oddly nervous about venturing in there, but also felt Reed's most personal space might give her the most insight into the man she'd just agreed to trust with her safety.

After all, she'd already made enough missteps to last a lifetime.

At the doorway to his bedroom, she paused, taking it all in. In typical masculine fashion, the comforter was dark, a pleasing combination of browns and maroon. Several framed photographs hung on the wall, black-

and-white landscapes, making her wonder if he'd taken them himself or simply purchased them.

Either way, they were beautiful, in an eerie, haunting way. She stood, absorbing each one before moving on to the other. Something about them called to her, and for a brief, glorious second she felt connected to the man who'd hung them. Her chest tightened and her throat stung, even as she realized her own foolishness. She could no more afford to indulge in romantic fantasies about Reed than she could expect to emerge from a confrontation with Alex unscathed.

And then she saw it. A familiar sight, as Alex had several in various locations all over his house. A gun safe, one of the larger ones, with a keypad locked entry.

Stunned, she stared. A rancher would need guns, right? Just because Alex had used his for nefarious purposes, didn't mean Reed did.

Still, she backed away from the gun safe, her heart pounding.

Back in the living room, trying to calm her pulse, she clicked on the television. The five o'clock news had just begun, and she was startled to see a photo of herself, with the words *Possible Abduction* underneath. Listening in disbelief, she realized Alex had made up a story about an intruder, and even doctored surveillance video to show her—actually someone playing the part of her—being taken forcibly from her bed, clearly unconscious, and carried out the side door.

"Authorities are on the lookout for a woman matching this description—five-two, 110 pounds, long blond hair and blue eyes. Caution is advised since the man who took her may be considered armed and dangerous. If seen, please contact your local authorities."

She stared at the screen, not even noticing that the program switched to another story. When she finally roused herself to click the off button on the remote, her fingers were shaking and she couldn't catch her breath.

Aware that if she kept hyperventilating she'd pass out, she forced herself to slowly inhale and then exhale. Deeply, striving for calm. While she'd known Alex would go on the offensive, she hadn't expected him to take it public right off the bat. In her mind, she'd guessed he'd send a few of his goons out snooping around before taking a chance with the media.

Proof she'd been wrong. How could she have forgotten the rock-solid confidence Alex placed in his ability to manipulate everyone and everything?

Still feeling dizzy and jittery, she pushed to her feet and began to pace. The sooner Reed returned with her disguise, the better she'd feel. Or so she hoped. Good thing she'd listened and hadn't gone with him to the store.

Her stomach growled. She remembered Reed telling her to make herself something to eat. Even though she wasn't sure she could, she welcomed the distraction. A quick search of the refrigerator revealed nothing she could use to put together a salad, but a loaf of bread, sliced cheese and cold cuts would enable her to make a sandwich.

She checked the cupboards and found a can of creamy tomato soup—her favorite. As soon as the soup was hot, she ladled out a bowl and carried it to the table to eat with her sandwich. The announcer's words kept playing over and over inside her head: *armed and dangerous.* Which made it even worse for Reed. A crooked law enforcement officer like George could say he felt justified for shooting Reed on the spot. Thank goodness they'd gotten out of Anniversary.

Still, she'd never intended to put Reed's life in danger. She needed to make sure he understood the risk. Despite what she'd told him about Alex, she wasn't sure he did.

After eating, she'd just finished washing out the dishes when she heard the sound of a vehicle in the drive. Despite being ninety percent sure it was Reed, she ran to the window and peered out.

Alex had surprised her with his first move. She didn't want to take a chance on being surprised with a second.

Of course it was only Reed returning from his brief shopping expedition. She still started trembling. She took several deep breaths and tried to think calming thoughts before greeting him. She didn't want him to see how rattled she'd gotten.

He walked in the doorway, his shoulders reassuringly broad. Glancing at her, he smiled as he placed two plastic bags on the kitchen counter. "I got most of your disguise," he said. "Except for the colored contacts. I'll order those on the internet, but they'll take a few days to get here."

Though she managed to nod, she didn't immediately reply.

He went still when he caught sight of her face. "What's wrong?"

"Alex," she said, and then told him what she'd seen on the news.

After she'd finished, he simply nodded. His strong profile spoke of strength. His broad shoulders and muscular arms should have made her feel safe. Instead, she felt uneasy.

"That's all right," he reassured her. "Don't worry. No

one will recognize you once we're finished. Here." He handed her a box of hair color in a shade that could only be described as mousy brown. "After I cut your hair, you can get started on this."

"*You're* cutting my hair?" The thought made her nervous again, not because of vanity, but because the act would be far too intimate. She eyed his big hands, and his fingers, long and strong, and shivered.

"Yep. It might not look like it was done by a professional, but that's kind of the point."

Trying for resigned, she only managed to squash down nervous anticipation, even though the thought of his hands on her head made her entire body quiver. She really needed to get this attraction from the past under control.

"Let's get it cut so I can color it," she said, managing to sound completely normal. "The sooner I can change my appearance, the better."

Handsome face expressionless, he nodded and then reached into a kitchen drawer for scissors. "Take a seat." He indicated a chair at the table. "Remember, the goal is to make you look as unattractive as possible."

Was it her, or did he sound as if he might be enjoying this a bit too much?

"Just don't go so overboard that it's obvious," she warned, dropping into a chair. "If you give me a mullet or something, it's not going to be believable."

He laughed, the rich sound rolling over her like a velvet blanket. "Take it easy. I promise not to give you a mullet or a burr."

As he walked up behind her, she stiffened. "Have you ever cut hair before?"

"A long time ago. Tim and I used to trim each other's

hair when we were kids." When he lifted her heavy hair up from her back, a wisp of air hit the back of her neck, making her shiver again.

He went still. "Are you all right?"

"Yes," she lied. "I'm fine. Just do it before I lose my nerve."

Without saying anything else, he cut. And cut. The long, silken strands dropped to the kitchen floor. After the first stunned look, she closed her eyes, refusing to watch, shocked at the depth of her vanity. Even though she'd always considered her hair her best feature, vanity had no place in her life now.

The light touch of his hands on her scalp, the steady snip-snip of the scissors…if she tried hard enough, she could almost pretend she was in a pricey beauty salon. But then his muscular arm brushed her shoulder, and she caught a whiff of his masculine scent, and her attempt to disassociate herself from him failed.

"Okay," he finally said. "You can look."

Though she really didn't want to see, she opened her eyes, accepting the hand mirror he gave her. "Bangs?" she squeaked. "You gave me bangs?" Not just any bangs, but a thick fringe cut straight across halfway up her forehead. As for the rest—she looked like he'd put a bowl over her head and started cutting.

Of course, the more she thought about it, the cut was perfect. No one would ever suspect she was the same woman they'd shown on the television.

"Thank you," she said quietly. "It's exactly right. I can't wait to see what it looks like once it's brown."

He grinned, softening the hard ridges of his face. "Not just brown. The most boring, dullest brown I could find."

She made a face. "I guess I should be glad you didn't go with gray."

"I almost did. But then I worried it would look too good on you."

Though she squinted at him, trying to determine if he'd made a joke—he sounded serious. She worked up a smile and met his gaze. "Well. Anyway, thank you."

The amused expression vanished and he gave her a hard look. "We need to get one thing straight. I'm going to avenge my brother's death and make sure Alex Ramirez is punished. Understood?"

"Understood," she said, matching her brusque tone to his. "We both want the same thing."

"Good."

Shortly after sunset, Reed's cell phone rang. Caller ID showed Anniversary Sheriff's Department. Of course. Since he wasn't home, George had decided to try and reach him by cell.

"What now?" he asked, trying to sound bored and irritated all at once.

"I'm at your front door," George told him. "I need you to come home so we can talk."

"Sorry, I'm out of town. Any talking we do will have to be on the phone."

Silence for a moment while the deputy considered Reed's words. "How long are you going to be gone?"

Though Reed wanted to tell him it was none of his business, he held his tongue. "I'm not sure. Why? What's up?"

"I'm looking for Kaitlyn Nuhn." George finally drawled. "No doubt you've seen on the news that she's been abducted. Since she used to live here in town, we're going door to door to check and see if anyone has spotted her."

"Kaitlyn Nuhn?" Reed didn't have to feign his shock. "Tim's old girlfriend? Why in the hell would you think I'd have anything to do with her?"

At the bitterness in Reed's tone, George's chuckled, a smug sound. Hearing that, Reed clenched his hand into a fist. He wanted to punch something. Someone.

The flash of violence startled him. Though George had managed to get under his skin over time, Reed had never wanted to actually hit the guy. Now... The knowledge that not only was the deputy on Alex Ramirez's payroll but had known all along who'd killed Tim, made Reed want to smash his fist in the other man's face.

There was nothing Reed hated more than a liar. Nothing.

Blood boiling, Reed swallowed back his rage. "I haven't seen her," he said. "Now, if you don't need anything else—"

"Not so fast." Making every syllable count, as if he thought Reed might not be able to follow, George gave an overly forced chuckle. "Since you're not here, I'm going to have to break into your house. I'd like to take a look inside, if you don't mind."

"No. That's taking this harassment to a whole new level, isn't it, George?"

"The only reason I can come up with why you'd object would be that you have something to hide." The taunt fell flat.

"Really?" Sarcasm dripped from Reed's voice. "What about invasion of privacy? As well as the harassment I mentioned earlier. This is getting really old, George. You're going to have to get a search warrant."

At those words, the deputy sheriff dropped all pretense of pleasantry. "You know, since you're out of town, you have no way of knowing what I do." With that, George ended the call.

As Reed stood there, heart pounding from an excess of adrenaline, he wondered exactly how stupid the other man might be. He knew if George did break into his house, he'd make sure and destroy as much as possible. After all, what could Reed do? Call the police?

Furious, he paced from the living room to the kitchen, trying to get himself under control.

"So it begins." Kaitlyn's voice washed over him like a soothing salve over a festering wound. "Though I hate it, I'm glad you got me this disguise."

"Yeah." Looking at her, with her ridiculously awful hairdo and frumpy, oversize clothes, he felt some of the tightness leave him. "Though George has been hassling me ever since I got out. I imagine he's thrilled to have a new reason."

She nodded, her expression serious. "What else did he say?"

"They're looking for you. You were right about Anniversary being the first place Alex would look." Clenching his jaw, he glanced away. "George is a bumbling idiot and he doesn't really suspect anything. Even if he did, no one in town knows about this place, so we ought to be safe for now."

"Then maybe this disguise isn't really necessary."

She sounded so hopeful he almost smiled. "Better safe than sorry. And I'll tell you honestly, from that news story he's put out about you being abducted, the FBI is probably already working the case."

Her eyes went wide. "Crap."

This time, he nearly laughed out loud. "It's okay. That's why you look nothing like yourself." He'd never tell her, but he'd been stunned to realize that, despite everything he'd done to make her appear ordinary, he still found her shockingly beautiful. "Except of course, you still have those blue eyes."

"We need to get those colored contacts," she said. "I don't want to take a chance on them recognizing me."

"I agree." Even with the awful haircut and the dull hair color, her amazing cornflower-blue eyes still blazed from her heart-shaped face. That and her creamy skin, high cheekbones and a mouth made for kissing.

No. Time to cut those thoughts off immediately. Apparently, he couldn't keep from finding her attractive, but he did have enough willpower to keep from acting on it.

Or so he hoped.

His cell phone rang again. Brock McCauley, his old high school buddy and one of the few people who'd not only visited him in prison, but had stood by him ever since he'd been out.

"Did you see the news?" Brock asked. "Tim's old girlfriend has been abducted. I didn't even know she'd taken up with Alex Ramirez, of all people."

Before he could help himself, Reed snorted. "I saw that. I'm not surprised. Kaitlyn Nuhn was nothing but trouble."

Next to him, Kaitlyn made a soft sound of protest, which Reed ignored.

"Maybe," Brock conceded. "But she always was pleasant to me. Zoe liked her, too.

"And she never cheated on Tim," Brock continued. "Even though he was always fooling around behind her back and bragging about it."

Reed refused to acknowledge the slow flush of guilt. He'd had three long years to regret what he and Kaitlyn had done. Somehow he'd managed to forget the way Tim always managed to have a girlfriend on the side.

"Do you think she knew?" Eyeing the subject of their discussion, Reed was suddenly glad she couldn't hear both sides of the conversation.

"About Tim? I doubt it." Brock sounded contemplative.

"Hey, I really called to see if you wanted to come to dinner tomorrow night. Zoe's making lasagna, and she knows how much you like it."

"Like it? That's the understatement of the year." Grimacing, Reed declined. "But I can't. I'm not in town. I'm out at the ranch right now."

"Even better," Brock laughed. "You know I've been wanting to show Zoe that place. How about we drive up there tomorrow after I close the feed store? We can bring the lasagna, too. We could spend the night."

Reed winced. Not only was Brock one of the only people who knew about the ranch, they were good enough friends that he didn't think twice about inviting himself over.

"Not right now," Reed said. "I have company."

"Company?" Brock's voice sounded surprised, and Reed couldn't blame him. Brock knew Reed didn't socialize much. Brock also knew that Reed didn't lie.

"Yeah." Taking a deep breath, Reed braced himself for his friend's reaction. "I have, er...a lady friend with me."

"That's great!" Brock plowed on. "We'd love to meet her. Unless it's a first date?"

The question sort of hung there, waiting to be answered. Reed inwardly cursed as he sorted through a possible response that wouldn't be an outright lie. "It's too early for anyone to be meeting her. It's not a date at all, actually. We're just…hanging out."

"Well, then, what's the problem?" One thing about Brock, he'd never been good at taking a hint.

Crap. "I don't think that's a good idea."

"Why not?" Brock actually sounded puzzled. "Are you ashamed of her or something?"

"Hell, no." Reed didn't even have to think. "It's not that. It's…"

"So you're ashamed of us, then?" From the slight lilt in his voice, Reed realized Brock just might be enjoying this.

"You know better. It's just too early. Next time, maybe."

"Okay." Brock laughed. "It's incredibly promising that you know there will be a next time. I can't wait to meet her." Brock ended the call before Reed could respond.

Slowly, Reed replaced the receiver, startled to realize his palms were sweating. Eyeing Kaitlyn, he shook his head. "That was Brock McCauley," he said.

Her smile lit up her entire face. Trying to ignore the way that smile affected him, he scratched his head. "He just invited us to dinner tomorrow night. And when I told him I was at the ranch, he wanted to drive on out."

Her grimace told him what she thought of that. "That's what you meant when you said you didn't think that was a good idea."

"Yep."

She froze. "Are they coming here? Because even with this disguise, one or both of them is bound to recognize me. I've known them for years."

"I agree. But no worries. I told him now wasn't a good time. I think he'll respect that."

"You think?" Eyes huge, she appeared visibly shaken. "Just in case, maybe you should call him back and tell him you're sick, or I'm sick. Both of us, with something contagious, like the flu."

Slowly, he shook his head. "I don't lie."

Her eyes widened even more. "Ever?"

"Ever. Not if I can help it."

He wondered if she knew how kissable she looked like that, with her face tilted up and her mouth pursed in mutiny. As his body reacted, he turned away. "Get some rest. I'll talk to you in the morning."

Reed didn't think he'd sleep much, but the instant his head hit the pillow, he was out. Sunlight streaming through his window woke him. Stretching, he wondered why he felt uneasy, especially since he didn't recall any of his dreams. And then he remembered.

Kaitlyn. Alex Ramirez, Tim's death, and the way the past had managed to catch up with him. Ignoring his arousal, he pushed back the sheet, got to his feet and padded into his bathroom. From past experience he knew a shower, fresh clothes and a cup of steaming hot coffee would do wonders to help him think.

Chapter 4

For a man used to living alone, it was a shock to get out of the shower and step into your kitchen to find one of the most beautiful women in the world sitting at your table, reading a book and drinking coffee. The baggy T-shirt hinted at the luxuriant curves underneath and the short, shaggy hairdo only enhanced her perfect features and lush lips. It didn't help that Reed was still half-asleep despite the hot shower, or that he'd woken aroused. Desire slammed into him like a sucker punch to the gut.

He stopped, rubbing the sleep out of his eyes, and wished there was a way to grab his cup of coffee without having to speak.

He made it halfway to the coffeemaker when she looked up from her book and smiled. That smile stopped him dead in his tracks.

"Good morning," she said. "I hope you don't mind, but I made coffee."

Mouth dry, he struggled to speak. "Thanks. I thought you'd be sleeping in."

"Nope. I never do. I'm a morning person," she said. "In case you can't tell."

Clearing his throat, he settled on a brusque nod and went past her. Hopefully, the awkwardness would fade with time. With time? How long did he expect her to stay with him anyway?

"What's on the agenda for today?" she asked, her voice far too cheerful for so early in the day. He had to wonder if her relentless happiness was a coping mechanism of sorts. After all, she'd just escaped her own prison. Maybe she was afraid if she let go and thought about it, she'd lose control and reveal exactly how much trauma she was dealing with.

Or perhaps he just overanalyzed everything.

He shrugged and took a long drink of his coffee, hoping the caffeine would send a jolt and help with his brain fog. "I've got to talk to my foreman and get an update. I also want to take a quick drive around the surrounding area and see if anything looks out of the ordinary. After I get back, I thought I might take a ride around the ranch."

She nodded. "A ride as in horses? Or in your truck?"

"Horses." And just like that, a memory came slamming into him. Tim and Kaitlyn and Brock had gone riding, out on Brock's family land. Tim and Brock had gone on ahead, leaving Reed and Kaitlyn to bring up the rear.

She'd chattered happily and he'd listened, too enthralled by the way the sun lit up her beautiful blond hair, and the gentle sway of her body with the horse's movements to pay much attention to anything she'd said.

The tug of attraction hadn't been new. The emotion attached to it had shocked him. He'd realized in that instant that she could be the ruin of him, which would destroy him and his brother's relationship. As soon as the thought hit him, he'd spurred his horse ahead to catch up with the other men, leaving Kaitlyn alone behind him.

After that, he'd taken great pains to avoid her. Until he hadn't, and wound up in prison with his brother dead. Those internet pundits hadn't been kidding. Karma really was a bitch.

"Horses?" Kaitlyn asked, her husky voice full of quiet wonder, bringing him back to the present. "Do you mind if I come along? Riding was one of the things I missed most when I was locked up."

Her choice of words brought him another realization. In a way, they'd both done time. While her cell might have been more luxurious, the other things she'd endured made her imprisonment a whole lot worse.

"Sure," he managed, hoping like hell no sympathy showed on his face. He was better off if he considered Kaitlyn a predator of sorts. As in, if he displayed the slightest weakness, she'd pounce.

"Thank you," she said quietly, a marked difference to the squeal of excitement he'd half expected. Of course, that would have been the Kaitlyn of the past.

They'd both changed. Circumstances and life had forged new personalities.

"Are you okay?" She tilted her head, the thick fringe of her bangs shifting with the move. Mentally, he swore, thinking he should have given her a more masculine cut or something. Anything, to stop the embers that ignited inside him every time he looked at her.

He grimaced. Who was he kidding? With her bone structure, she'd probably look even more beautiful with her head shaved.

"I'm looking forward to it," she said. "Eventually, maybe you can take me into town and show me around the area. I don't want to become a prisoner here, like I was with Alex."

Though even hearing the other man's name made him clench his teeth, he managed to keep his tone civil. "You haven't been here long enough to consider yourself a prisoner," he replied.

"And yes, that is the point of your disguise, but I'm not taking chances. The nearest town is about the same size as Anniversary, and people talk. Once I know the situation in town, I can make a better decision."

She eyed him in silence, considering. "I have to admit you make sense. Hopefully, we'll figure out a way to get Alex arrested so I can get out of your hair." She pushed herself up from her chair and headed to the coffeepot for another cup. He couldn't help but watch the enticing sway of her hips as she moved.

Furious with himself, Reed took that opportunity to beat a hasty exit back to his room.

Later, having showered and dressed, he decided to return to the kitchen for a second cup of coffee. As he opened his door, he inhaled the mouthwatering scent of bacon. In the kitchen, Kaitlyn still sat in the same chair, finishing up a plate of scrambled eggs and bacon.

"I made you some, too," she said, pointing toward the counter, where she'd covered a plate with a paper towel. "If it's cooled off too much, you can warm it in the microwave."

The small kindness surprised him. "Thanks," he said, pushing away the tangle of emotions swirling inside him.

Shoveling the food into his mouth so he didn't have to

talk, he knew he'd have to figure out a way to convince himself he no longer craved her.

Only he'd be lying to himself. And since he didn't believe in lies…

After cleaning his plate, he carried the dish to the sink. "Thanks again," he said, managing a smile. "I'll be back in a few hours and then we'll go for a ride."

Unsmiling, she nodded. "While you're gone, do you mind if I wander around, maybe check out a few of the horses?" She bit her lip, drawing his gaze to her lush mouth.

"How long has it been since you've ridden?" he asked.

Her gaze darkened to midnight. "Years."

"Are you sure you remember how?" Dragging his hand through his hair, he forced himself to meet her gaze directly. "I don't want you to take a chance and get hurt."

"It's like riding a bicycle." She shrugged, a thread of anger running through her voice. "It's just something I looked forward to every single day while I was his captive."

Her flippant tone did little to disguise her pain. Studying her, he realized her wounds ran deep, too. As deep as his, or maybe even more.

"Where is it?" He should have asked this question before. "Alex's place, where he kept you locked up?"

"Near Austin. Maybe an hour's drive west from there."

"Good to know." He thought hard, swallowed and then gave her the truth. "I'm glad you made it out safely."

"Thank you. I was very lucky. No matter what you see on TV, Alex Ramirez is a horrible man," she told him. "But then again, I guess most psychopaths are. If he finds out you helped me, he won't just kill you. That'd be too merciful. He'll torture you, make sure you suffer before you die." Her blue eyes had gone cloudy, full of miserable memories. He had a flash of an urge to comfort her somehow, but managed to push it away. Somewhat.

"Don't worry," he heard himself say. "He won't find out. And if he does, I won't get caught."

"You don't know that." Anguish rang in her voice. "He has a lot of enemies. Several of them have tried to get to him. So far, no one has succeeded and a few have ended up dead."

He shrugged. "Then I'll be the first. We'll work out a plan. Meanwhile, for now, stay off the horses. We'll ride together when I have time." And then, without waiting for an answer, he took off before he got himself into any more trouble.

The meeting with his ranch foreman Boyd, an older, taciturn man Reed had known all his life, went exactly the same way it had every other time Reed had come out to the ranch.

"Everything's fine," Boyd drawled, just as he always did. "We got plenty of hay and the new crop of cattle should fetch a pretty penny. No one's quit, and I've even had to hire a new hand."

Reed nodded. "If there's anything you need…"

"I won't hesitate to let you know." Grinning, Boyd slapped him on the back and sauntered off. Reed shook his head and watched him go.

As he walked to his pickup, he found himself wondering how Boyd and the other ranch hands would react to Kaitlyn. He had a pretty good idea. If he wasn't careful, she'd be a major distraction.

As she had already become for him.

On the drive into town, he called himself all kinds of fool. Having her at his farm could be a colossal, mistake.

Of course, he'd be damned before he'd let Alex Ramirez harm one hair on her pretty little head.

He'd been to Breckenridge when he'd gone to Walmart to pick up Kaitlyn's disguise. There were no other large- or even medium-sized towns close to the ranch, so he drove about ten miles out and rode the dirt roads. This part of West Texas, with its dry, arid landscape and twisted trees, called to him even more than the treed, more scenic area of Anniversary. Hardscrabble, he thought. Like him.

After a good forty-five minutes of driving, he headed home, satisfied that no one suspicious had come to this part of the state.

Yet.

When he passed a little barbecue joint, he impulsively pulled in and got a couple of chopped beef sandwiches.

As he pulled from the dirt road into the long drive leading toward his ranch, he felt confident. Kaitlyn wouldn't be discovered here. There were no strange vehicles anywhere to be seen and the house looked exactly the same as it had when he'd left it.

Safe. A perfect hiding place. He smiled as he parked his truck. But the instant he killed the engine, the back door flew open. Kaitlyn hurried over, visibly shaken.

His stomach clenched. "What's wrong?"

Running a shaky hand through that awful haircut of hers, she inhaled. "I just watched the afternoon news. Now Alex is claiming that my supposed kidnapper has sent him a ransom request."

Again suppressing the urge to comfort her, Reed shook his head. "It'll be okay." Handing her the two foam boxes, he got out.

"What's this?" she asked, sniffing. "Whatever it is, it smells wonderful."

"I picked up lunch. Barbecue."

At first her eyes narrowed. He could have sworn a flash of suspicion crossed her face. Holy hell. He realized maybe Alex Ramirez had even used food as a form of torture.

"It's just a sandwich." He held it out, careful to hide his anger. "No strings. I remember you used to like it."

Finally, she rewarded him with a wobbly smile and accepted the bag. "I do. Thank you."

"You're welcome." Chest a bit too tight, he followed her into the house. He realized that although she'd escaped, she wasn't entirely free. Nor would she be, not until she learned to deal with her inner demons. One more crime for which Alex would need to pay.

"What about Alex?" Kaitlyn asked, almost as if he'd spoken the name out loud. "What do you think he's doing? Why make up a story as elaborate as that?"

"I don't know. I'm guessing he thinks if he can get everyone stirred up and have not only the FBI but the general public help him hunt you, he'll find you that much easier."

"Even if his story is proven to be false."

"Right. I'm guessing whatever friends he has inside will make sure that story dies a quiet death after he finds you."

Panic flashed in her eyes. "Don't say it like that. As though him finding me is a given."

"Sorry. You know what I mean. Come on," he prodded gently. "Sit. Let's eat."

She took a seat at the kitchen table and opened the bag. Head bent, she removed the wrapped sandwiches, bags of chips, plastic cutlery and napkins. Crossing to the refrigerator, he snagged a couple of cans of cola for them.

"There." He dropped into his chair, wishing he could figure out a way to stop feeling a weird sort of kinship with her. "We're all set."

Though messy, the barbecue tasted delicious. They ate in companionable silence, which made him feel a bit restless.

Since he finished before her, he sat quietly and watched her while she ate. Instead of picking up the sandwich and taking bites, she attacked her food, using her plastic fork and knife with gusto. Only when she'd cut several small pieces did she eat a few. After that, she ate a couple of chips and took a sip of cola. And then she started the process all over again, focused and intent. As if by regulating this, she regained some measure of control over her world, however small.

Again the twinge of sympathy. He'd caught himself doing similar things when he'd been in prison.

Finally she finished, and looked up. "That was wonderful," she sighed. "Thanks again."

He nodded, turning away so she wouldn't see desire or warmth or whatever the hell it was he was feeling on his face. "No problem." He gathered up the wrappings and chip bags and carried them to the trash. Once he had his expression and his body under control, he turned to face her. "Now tell me exactly what you saw on the news earlier."

Just like that, her expression changed, making him realize she'd relaxed and he'd unthinkingly ruined it. With the tension back in her posture, even her features seemed sharper.

"Basically, what I said. It was the opening story for the noon newscast. Prominent and respected politician Alex Ramirez has now been contacted by the kidnappers who abducted his girlfriend. According to Alex, they're demanding a ransom of several million dollars."

He frowned. "That doesn't make sense. The feds are going to be all over this now. Why would he do that?"

"I'm sure his inside people are helping him." The bitterness in her voice matched her flat expression. "He probably plans to pay himself and use this as a way to launder money or something. He's always talking about having to find creative ways to do that without anyone catching on."

Astounded, Reed swallowed. "You know a lot about his business, don't you?"

Her chin went up. "Yes. Even if I didn't know about the murder, I know enough to put him away for a long, long time."

"So it's not just that you witnessed him kill Tim that makes you valuable to him. It's all the other information you could use against him."

"Exactly." She looked down at her hands, which she'd begun wringing.

"But now that everyone knows about you, if he got you back, he could no longer keep you locked away."

"No." She never looked up. "Which is why he won't stop until I'm dead."

The bleak despair in her voice made him ache to comfort her. "You don't need to worry about that. He isn't going to find you. Plus, he's going to dig his own grave with these lies," he said. "Sooner or later, someone's going to catch on and his honesty will be called into question."

"Since he has a lot of law enforcement people on his payroll, I doubt it."

Reed considered his next words carefully. "I'm guessing he's doing this to keep the case fresh in the public's eye. The more people hear about you, the more likely someone will spot you and report to the FBI."

"And then to him." She grimaced. "Anything's possible, where Alex is concerned. It even makes a kind of twisted sense, though I don't like it."

"Of course not." Again he had to fight the urge to touch her. "Me, either. That settles one thing, though. Until I have a handle on who we can and cannot trust, you're definitely going to have to keep a low profile. Even though we're out in the middle of nowhere."

"Thank you again for helping me."

He waved her thanks away. "Do you still want to go riding?"

"Yes."

"Great." Considering her shapeless dress, he carefully avoided meeting her gaze. "Why don't you put on some jeans and meet me at the barn? I'll get the horses saddled and ready."

Without waiting for her to answer, he grabbed his cowboy hat and headed outside.

Watching out the window as Reed sauntered down to the barn, Kaitlyn tried to get a handle on the complicated emotions roiling inside her. She'd known she'd have some lingering trauma after what she'd been through with Alex, but she hadn't expected to cringe every time he moved too fast. Luckily, so far she'd managed to keep all her flinching inside. As far as she could tell, Reed had no idea.

Which was good. The last thing she wanted from him was pity.

Despite the abuse she'd suffered, being around Reed

again, even after all these years, made her want things she'd never thought she'd be able to want again. In fact, after the way she'd been treated, she'd come to believe she'd never feel attracted toward a man again.

She'd been wrong. Very wrong. Disgusted with herself, she ran her fingers through her ugly haircut and grimaced. All along in the back of her mind, she'd known her old crush on him might make her uncomfortable, but she'd thought she could deal with it. Right. What she hadn't expected was this full-blown craving. Though she thought she'd been successful at hiding it, she trembled with the urge to get close to him every time they were in the same room.

She had to get past this. Her life was at stake after all. Since Reed had made it perfectly clear he didn't feel the same way about her—how could he—she'd rely on him to keep her safe and help bring Alex to justice. Nothing more.

In fact, she wanted this over and done with so that she could move on to the next chapter of her life. So they both could.

Restless and unsettled inside her own body, she pushed through the kitchen door and headed down toward the barn. Dusk had settled on the landscape, though darkness had yet to envelope the farm. Nevertheless, a bright spotlight on the outside of the barn illuminated not only the yard, but the corrals. Reed stood inside a round pen, lifting a Western saddle up onto a beautiful gray horse.

A few feet away, she stopped. Her mouth went dry as she stood and watched, admiring the way the muscles in his arms worked while he hefted the bags. Again the desire, the raw urge, stunning her, shocking her. Once more, she managed to push it away.

He turned and faced her, dipping his chin in acknowledgment. "I got this gelding ready for you. He's docile and well trained. You shouldn't have any trouble with him."

"Thank you." Making her feet propel her forward, she took the reins. "Where's your horse?"

"Inside the barn." He held out his cupped hands for her to step into. "Let me give you a leg up."

Just like that, her heart began hammering in her throat. She wasn't sure she could bear his touch. As she stood staring at him, feeling foolish, she forced herself to move forward. Using his hands as a springboard, she jumped up into the saddle. Only when she'd gotten settled did Reed go and retrieve his own mount.

The sun felt warm, the horse's gait smooth, and as they rode up a winding dirt road, Kaitlyn finally began to relax. She wished she could stop having the need to keep reminding herself she was safe here, and hated also the expectation that at any moment, she'd find out she wasn't.

Maybe after she'd been free awhile she'd stop jumping at every shadow and her neck wouldn't hurt from constantly looking over her shoulder.

This person she'd become, the woman Alex had turned her into, wasn't who she wanted to be. But she wasn't sure she even knew how to get back to her old self. Or even if she wanted to.

"Nice, isn't it?" Reed rode up alongside her, sitting as easily on the saddle as if he'd been born on horseback.

Despite her sudden melancholy, she gave him her brightest smile. He had no need to know how damaged she'd become inside. "More than nice. This is exactly what I needed. I'd forgotten what it feels like to be this free."

His expression changed, just a minuscule amount, but enough to remind her she'd again managed to bring her past in and ruin the moment. "I'm sorry," she muttered, hating that she felt she had to apologize. "I've only been away a day. I'm trying to get used to the idea."

"No need to be sorry." Despite the kind words, Reed sounded grim. "Believe me, I remember how it feels. As if the sky is too big, too open, and you wonder if you could be crushed to death under the vastness of it all."

Her heart leaped at his words. Of course he understood, and he didn't appear to be ashamed to speak it out loud. "You're exactly right."

One quick jerk of his chin was his only response. As he spurred his horse into a jog, then a lope, he called back over his shoulder at her. "Come on, let's ride."

The afternoon passed much too quickly as far as she was concerned. They rode and rested, Reed taking time to point out various landmarks. She was glad the sky turned cloudy as she hadn't thought to locate sunscreen.

"I think it's time to head back toward the ranch," Reed said.

Kaitlyn sighed. "Thank you again. I haven't had such a nice afternoon in years."

He barely glanced at her, his attention focused on the darkening sky. "We need to ride faster," he said. "That storm out west is heading this way."

When she looked where he'd pointed, she realized he was right. And now that he'd mentioned it, she could smell the hint of the coming rain on the breeze.

"Let's go." He slapped her horse on the rear before urging his own mount into a gallop.

Without looking she could feel the storm gaining on them. The wind picked up, carrying moisture. Thunder boomed, still off in the distance, but gaining.

Finally, they rode up a hill and she could see the ranch spread out below them. Her horse seemed winded, so she slowed the animal to a walk. Ahead of her, when Reed realized what she'd done, he turned and rode back to her.

Just as he reached her, thunder cracked right on top of him, spooking her mount. The immediate flash of lightning meant they were all in danger.

What happened next seemed in slow motion. Kaitlyn's horse bucked and reared up. She almost fell, but held on to the saddle horn and managed to keep her seat.

"Good job," Reed said. "Now ride!"

This time, she didn't wait for him to slap her horse. She dug her heels into the animal's side and took off. As they raced for the barn, thunder booming and rain pelting them, she knew she wore a grin a mile wide. Aware Reed would think she was crazy if he saw it, she restrained herself from shouting with joy into the wind.

She felt more alive in this instant than she could ever remember feeling. Exhilarated, energized and oddly defiant.

With more thunder, the boom was so loud it shook the earth. The air around them sizzled with electricity, which meant lightning had hit nearby.

Fifty feet away the sky opened up. The wind lashed the rain sideways, whipping her with her own wet hair. She knew she looked like a crazy woman, but she couldn't stop laughing as she rode into the barn.

Maybe Reed understood or perhaps he just didn't want to know, but he said nothing as he swung down from his soaked horse. He crossed to her and held out his hand, as if he thought she'd need help dismounting.

Instead, she waved him away. Pushing her drenched and tangled hair away from her face, she slid from the saddle.

Turning, she nearly crashed into him.

He reached out to steady her and just like that, her smile vanished and she froze.

Hands on her upper arms, he stared. "Are you…are you all right?"

Heaven help her, she tried to nod, but her breath caught in her throat and it was all she could do to breathe. Wrenching away, she sucked in air and tried to regain her equilibrium.

While Reed stood watching, clearly not understanding what was wrong.

"Kaitlyn. I'm sorry." His deep voice revealed his confusion. "I'll ask you again. Are you okay?"

"Maybe." Keeping her back to him, wondering. "And maybe not. I think I might be going crazy. One minute, I'm thrilled to be alive, and the next, I'm…" She stopped, unable to finish.

"Well, if you're able, unsaddle your horse. We need to get the saddles off and the horse brushed down. At least the rain should have cooled them off so we won't need to walk them."

More grateful than she could articulate at the return to normalcy, she got busy doing exactly what he'd said.

Chapter 5

Reed knew enough about post-traumatic stress disorder to understand what had happened. His touch had sent Kaitlyn back. Back to that awful place where a touch had meant torture, a beating or rape. He clenched his jaw and seethed with anger at the man who'd done this to her.

One thing he remembered about Kaitlyn Nuhn was the way she'd always been brimming with life. Even alone, her positive energy brightened the room. He'd seen her joy in the race against the storm; hell, he'd caught some of the excitement, too.

And then to see it all quashed by a casual touch... He shook his head. Stuff like that made it difficult to focus.

After helping Kaitlyn remove the saddle from her horse, he carried it into the tack room and set it on the wooden tree, drying it off with a towel. Then he did the same with his and grabbed a couple more towels from the small stack and two curry brushes. Handing one of each to Kaitlyn, he returned to his mare and began drying her coat before he started brushing out the sweat. The rhythmic sounds as he brushed never failed to soothe him.

Except now, he felt overly aware of the woman next to him, doing the same thing. He hoped the simple repetitive motion might bring her some peace.

His cell phone rang. "Hey, Brock," he answered. "What's up?"

"Someone broke into your house." Brock sounded pissed. "I just left there. The police are still there. And they assigned that idiot George to investigate."

Reed swore. "He's probably the one who broke in. He called me wanting to search my house. I told him to get a warrant."

"Search for what?"

"Tim's old girlfriend." In his peripheral vision, he saw Kaitlyn flinch.

"He's trying to pin that on you?" Brock's incredulous tone made Reed smile.

"Probably. You know how he's always trying to find something to arrest me for. Did they let you inside my place? Were you able to tell what's missing?"

"Yeah, they let me in until George showed up. I tell you, it didn't look like your typical robbery. Your big screen is still there, so are all your other electronics. I'm assuming you have your laptop with you."

"I do." Reed glanced at Kaitlyn, who continued to brush her horse while watching him.

"Maybe you could take a quick trip home?" Brock suggested. "If you can tear yourself away from your lady friend."

Reed's face heated as he remembered what he'd told his

pal. "I think I will." He glanced at his watch. "I'll come first thing in the morning. Though I know that's what George wants."

"Great." Brock's tone seemed a bit more cheerful. "And bring that lady friend of yours if you want. I'd love to meet her."

Brock hung up before Reed could figure out an excuse.

As he slipped his phone back into his pocket, he sighed. "Brock says my place has been broken into. I'm betting it was George, but I'm going to have to drive back to Anniversary and check it out. I need to secure the house and see if anything is missing."

Eyes wide, she nodded. "I know it's not safe for me to go with you, but please, if you come back here, make sure no one follows you."

If? If he came back? Did she really think he wouldn't? "I'm leaving in the morning and will be back tomorrow night. It's about a two-and-a-half-hour drive each way." Instinctively, he reached to squeeze her shoulder in reassurance. Her instant recoil made him wince.

"I'm not going to hurt you," he told her.

"I know." Though her color appeared high, she held his gaze. "I don't do it intentionally. It's instinctive, like a rescue dog that's been beaten. I imagine I'll get better over time."

A dog? The fact that she compared herself to a dog made his chest tight.

"I like dogs," she said as if something had shown on his face. "In my opinion, they're more faithful and loving than most people. I plan to get my own someday."

At least she felt secure enough to consider the future. That meant something. "I'll be back," he repeated. "Stay close to the house."

* * *

During the drive east, he wondered how he'd gone so quickly from outright hostility to sympathy.

As soon as he drove to town, he headed directly toward his house. Someone—Brock, most likely—had locked the place back up and even nailed a piece of plywood over the broken window. In his mind's eye, Reed could picture George after hanging up the phone, using the butt end of his gun to break the glass in the door and then reach through and unlock it.

The idea that George had acted so illegally and brazenly, didn't shock him. Instead, he worried about the possibility that George, if remaining unchecked, would continue to step up his harassment. What next? Setting fire to the house?

Reed's living room and bedroom had been trashed. Sofa cushions torn, curtains sliced, clothes pulled from the dresser and tossed all over the room. This gave Reed pause. If someone had broken in looking for hints of Kaitlyn's presence, the wanton destruction didn't fit. Unless of course, George had decided to wreck the place just because he felt like it.

As far as Reed could tell, nothing had been taken. He put a few more nails to secure the plywood over his window, locked the place up tight, and headed downtown to talk to Brock.

The feed store sat on the south end of Main Street. Brock and his new wife, Zoe, had just returned from their honeymoon. As far as Reed could tell, the two lovebirds appeared to be drifting along on a cloud of bliss.

Reed really appreciated them. Not only had they grown up together, but Brock and Zoe were among the few people in town who didn't treat Reed as if being an ex-con meant he had some sort of nasty, communicable disease.

Once inside, he headed toward the back, where the checkout counter was located. Zoe McCauley stood there, her long dark hair gleaming as she pored over a catalog.

"Hey, there," Reed said.

"Reed!" Lifting her head, Zoe smiled, her eyes lighting up. She practically glowed with happiness. Rushing up, she hugged him and kissed his cheek. "You look fabulous. How are you?"

"I'm good. How's life treating you?" he asked, smiling back. While Zoe was lovely, her beauty couldn't hold a candle to Kaitlyn.

"Great, wonderful and fantastic," Zoe replied. "I'm so happy I feel like I've died and gone to heaven." She beamed at him, as if inviting him to share in her joy.

He managed to smile back. "Someone broke into my place."

Instantly, her smile disappeared. "I heard. Was anything taken?"

"Not as far as I can tell. Right now, it seems more like harassment than theft."

She sighed. "I'd tell you to give it more time, but some of these people…" She shook her head. "What's this I hear about you having a new lady friend?"

Jeezus. Dragging a hand through his hair, he tried to find the right words. "It's not what you think," he began.

Her smile came back. "Sure," she said easily. "Whatever you say."

He refused to show his discomfort. "Uh, is Brock around?"

"Sure." She glanced toward the back, over her shoulder. "Just a second, he's around here somewhere."

As if summoned by the lilt of her voice, Brock came around the corner. He grinned at Reed and winked at Zoe. "Reed." The two men shook hands and clapped each other's backs.

"You were right," Reed said. "I checked out the house. Nothing has been taken, at least as far as I can tell."

Brock nodded. "That's what I thought." He made a show of looking past Reed, pretending to check every aisle of the store. "Where's your friend? I thought you were bringing her with you."

"She couldn't make it." Not a lie, though if the conversation kept going in this direction, things could get tricky.

The store phone rang and Brock answered it. Moving away, he grabbed a pen and paper and began jotting down an order.

Zoe watched him, her expression full of love.

Despite himself, Reed felt a twinge of envy.

"You sure do look happy," he observed.

"I am." She grinned at him. "Beyond my wildest dreams. Love is…well, there aren't enough words. You should try it."

Though he tried like hell to keep his expression neutral, Zoe knew him pretty well. "It's okay," she said, leaning over the counter and patting his arm. "You'll meet someone someday. Who knows—" her expression turned mischievous "—maybe your new friend is The One."

His heart actually stuttered in his chest.

"I doubt it." He glanced around the store, glad there were no other customers at the moment. "I haven't made it into town in a while. Any other news?"

"Oh, yeah." She exhaled, her smile fading. "Remember Kaitlyn Nuhn?"

"Yeah," he answered. "Tim's former girlfriend. She

was abducted. Brock mentioned it when he called me and then I saw it on the news last night."

"Yep." Zoe shook her head. "And now we've got FBI agents in town. The very same ones I couldn't get to even talk to me when Shayna disappeared. The FBI thinks her abductor might be from around these parts."

"No way." He feigned surprise, reflecting he was getting pretty good at this. "Did they say who they suspect?"

She shook her head. "Nope. I don't think they know. They said they're talking to everyone in town, so if they haven't made it out to your place yet, they will."

"I'm not going to be there," he said. "I'm staying out at the ranch for a while."

Zoe's eyes narrowed. "Really?" Head tilted, she waited for him to elaborate. When he didn't reply, she gave up. "The sheriff's office is supposedly helping them," Zoe continued.

"George already paid me a visit. Last night. He called from my front doorstep."

She shook her head. "George is a bumbling idiot. I don't know why Roger ever hired him."

Since he'd often wondered the same thing, Reed agreed. And then, remembering how Kaitlyn had said George was on Alex's payroll, he wondered if the sheriff was, too. Now he understood what Kaitlyn had meant. It was impossible to tell who was a good guy and who wasn't.

The bell on the front door jingled. A moment later, Lila Fowlkes headed toward the counter. She stopped short when she spied Reed. Averting her face to avoid meeting his gaze, she focused on Zoe. "When you have a chance, I could use some help in the dog section."

"I'll be with you in a minute," Zoe replied, her voice

reserved. As Lila sailed away with her nose in the air, Zoe shook her head. "She breeds Yorkies. You know, those long-haired, yippy little dogs."

Though Reed nodded, he couldn't banish the leaden feeling that had settled in his chest. "Some people apparently prefer dogs to people," he said, aware he didn't hide his bitterness.

"I'm sorry." Zoe touched his arm. "She has no reason to treat you that way.

He shrugged. "I'm used to it."

"That doesn't make it right." She glared in the other woman's direction as if she intended to storm over there and make her feelings known.

"Don't," he cautioned. "She's a paying customer and it's not your battle."

She sighed. "You're right. But I'm still sorry."

"You shouldn't be. It's not your fault." He looked around for Brock, who'd wandered into the back office and still appeared to be on the phone.

Reed thanked Zoe, giving her a quick hug. He waved goodbye to Zoe, taking care to include Lila, who turned her head and pretended not to see. After leaving the feed store, he took a turn up Main Street as he usually did, driving slowly down the center of his hometown before beginning the long drive back to the ranch.

Seeing two black, clearly government-issue cars parked in front of Sue's Catfish Hut brought a sobering reminder of what he and Kaitlyn were up against.

Alex Ramirez had to be brought down. Since they didn't know who they could trust, Reed would have to figure out a way to take care of it himself.

The closer he drew to the ranch, the more anticipation filled him at the thought of seeing her. He knew she'd have cabin fever from staying in the house most of the day, so he thought maybe he'd take her riding again. To his surprise, he'd enjoyed their ride yesterday.

After he parked, he headed into the house, eager to tell her everything. Though he knew in the abstract this should bother him, he put it down to having been alone so long. He kind of enjoyed having company.

But Kaitlyn was nowhere to be found. A thorough search of the house showed nothing out of place and since she didn't have a car, he knew she couldn't have gone far.

Surely she hadn't gone riding alone? He hurried out to the barn, noting the same gray gelding she'd ridden the day before was gone. So was the saddle and bridle.

He swore. Though Kaitlyn was a native Texan, west Texas and east Texas were like opposite sides of the country. Out here were scorpions and rattlesnakes, wolves and coyotes.

Moving fast, he saddled his horse and headed out to search for her.

His horse was skittish, no doubt sensing Reed's foul mood. Somehow he got the animal under control and rode down to the river, letting his mount pick her way over the rocks. This was one of his favorite places, where a huge and ancient willow tree trailed branches in the water and the cattle often came to drink. Now, with the drought keeping things arid, this part of the river seemed more like a creek, but he considered it a blessing it hadn't gone completely dry.

Reining his horse to a halt, he inhaled deeply, trying to find the usual feeling of satisfaction this spot brought him. The light breeze stirred the branches of the tree, and the tall grass on the other side of the river appeared to undulate in the sun. He'd moved his cattle to one of the other areas, and this pasture would stay empty for a few weeks, maybe even a month.

As he sat there, tall in the saddle and wondering why he felt out of place for the first time ever, a faint scream drifted toward him on the air. He cocked his head, listening. When it didn't repeat, he relaxed again. Sometimes the wind and the rocks played tricks out here. And his mount didn't appear alarmed, so he decided to move on, continuing his ride until he reached the fence that contained this particular area.

The tall grass near the creek could be dangerous. Cottonmouths and water moccasins hid there, emerging to sun themselves on the rocks.

Another sound, even fainter. He reined to a stop and swiveled in his saddle, looking in all directions. He saw nothing. As the sound grew louder, he realized it was a horse or cow running. Which meant something chased it. Even more perplexing since he'd moved all his livestock out of this area weeks ago.

Urging his mount on, he rode to the top of a small hill. One of his horses ran below, saddled but without a rider, headed hell-bent for leather back to the barn.

Kaitlyn. It had to be. His heart stopped. She must have ridden out after him. Had she fallen? Was she hurt?

He took off in a gallop, heading toward where the riderless horse had come from.

As he rode, full of an odd combination of worry and terror and fury, he thought of the tongue-lashing he'd give Kaitlyn once he found her. Assuming she was unharmed. She had to be unharmed.

For once, he wished this part of his land was flat. But the hills and the trees, and the underbrush that grew near the river, made it difficult to see too far.

He prayed she'd shout out again, or scream, or make some sort of sound to help him find her.

A moment later, his prayer was answered. Another scream had him turning in that direction. He rode hard, up one hill and down another. In the distance he saw her, backed up against some of the rock formations that formed the cliffs—bluffs that overlooked the river. Four or five coyotes had cornered her, which was odd as they usually ran from humans. As he rode closer he saw why.

She held what appeared to be a coyote pup in her arms, a bit of cloth tied around one of its tiny legs. It was still, so still he figured it was dead. Otherwise, there was no way something that wild would allow itself to be held.

He rode at them hard, coming in close and scattering the pack, though they didn't disperse.

They simply circled and reformed, this time including Reed and his horse in their circle.

"Kaitlyn," he said, cautioning her not to move.

"Help me." Wide-eyed, clearly terrified, Kaitlyn stared up at him. "Please, can you chase them off?"

"Listen to me." He kept his voice slow and deliberate. "Put their puppy down and ease over here. I'm gonna grab you up on my horse and we'll make a run for it. The coyotes will be distracted by their pup."

To his disbelief, she shook her head. "No. He's not their pup. And he's almost dead. I found him in the mud near the river. I think something bit him, like a snake. I think there's a chance we can save him, if we can get him to a vet on time."

"Put the animal down. That's his pack and they want him. They'll kill you if they think you want to harm him."

To his disbelief, she slowly shook her head. "No. This

is a dog, Reed. A puppy. Looks like a cross between a sheltie and a schnauzer. If they don't kill him, he'll die if I let him go. I'm his only chance."

His heart felt about to pound right out of his chest. Still, out of necessity, he kept his voice level and calm. "Don't you understand? You'll die if you don't, and then what kind of chance will he have?"

Chin up, she met his gaze. "I have faith in you. You'll think of a way to save us."

The three coyotes leading the others, growled low in their throats. One bared its teeth. Reed suspected they were about to make a move to take Kaitlyn down.

Teeth clenched, he used his heels to make his horse move, even though the terrified gelding wanted nothing more than to get the hell away from here. Despite Kaitlyn's misplaced faith in him, he could see no way to swing her up with the wounded—and probably dying— puppy. This would take two steps. He rode close, keeping the horse in between her and the pack of coyotes.

"Hand me the dog."

For a split second, she eyed him as though uncertain, and then passed the small bundle of fluff up. Briefly it registered that the tiny thing weighed next to nothing and then he shifted it between the horn of his saddle and him, praying it would stay in place. Reaching out to Kaitlyn, he grasped hold of her hands, and pulled.

Jumping at the exact same moment, and demonstrating an astounding amount of grace considering the circumstances, she swung her leg up and over his horse's back. As soon as she was secure, he passed the limp body of the puppy back to her and kicked his horse into motion.

The gelding needed no further urging. He tore off, snarling coyotes hot on his heels.

They followed for a good distance, not wanting to give up their…what? Prey? Adopted offspring? Until finally, they fell back, vocalizing their displeasure.

Seething now that they were safe, Reed didn't speak until they reached the barn. The horse Kaitlyn had taken earlier grazed nearby, empty saddle on his back.

"Thank you," she said, her voice not the least bit contrite, despite the fact that she'd almost been killed.

He dismounted and then held out his hand to assist Kaitlyn. Instead, she handed him down the puppy, so still it might have already expired.

He took a good look at the limp and swollen bag of fluff and grimaced. "I think you might be too late."

"No." Kaitlyn let out a cry and slid down from the horse. "Let me see him," she said, a tear sliding down her cheek. "He was still breathing a minute ago." Wordlessly, he passed over the puppy. She accepted it, burying her face in its fur and going completely still.

"He's still alive," she breathed a moment later. When she raised her face to his, her cheeks were wet with tears. Over an animal she'd never seen before until a short while ago.

While he stared in disbelief, she pointed toward his truck. "How far away is the nearest vet? We need to try and get this baby some help."

All the words he'd been about to say—berating her for risking her life so carelessly—stuck in his throat. The hope shining in her eyes made him want to do anything to keep it from fading.

"I use Dr. Preek," he told her. "He's a large-animal vet and he makes house calls."

"Will you get ahold of him for me, please? See if he'll make a trip out to save this pup's life."

Though he had no idea if Dr. Preek even worked on dogs, Reed dug out his cell phone, located the number, and made the call. To his relief, the vet said he was only a few miles away and would be there in fifteen minutes.

When Reed relayed this information to Kaitlyn, she only nodded. With her head bent, with the sunlight putting reddish gold streaks in her newly dark hair, she took his breath away.

Not good. Not good at all.

"You need to put your contacts in," he said. "Just in case my vet watches the news." It was a good thing they'd arrived the other day.

Still crying, she turned to go and do as he asked.

"I'll go unsaddle and brush down the horses," he said, glad he didn't sound as unsteady as he felt, already moving away. Keeping busy was a necessary distraction because he sure didn't need to keep standing there mooning over her like a damn fool.

Once inside the barn, he tied his horse and went back outside to retrieve hers. He faltered when he saw her, sitting cross-legged on the ground, weeping over a tiny pup that was most likely a lost cause.

Still, her despair made his heart ache. Somehow, he managed to keep walking past her and gather up the horse and lead it back to the barn.

He'd gotten both animals unsaddled and was finishing up brushing the second one when he heard the sound of Dr. Preek's ancient pickup rattling up the drive.

Hoping like hell the brusque veterinarian would let her down gently, Reed put down the curry brush and hurried outside.

Kaitlyn rushed outside as soon as the pickup pulled up, still cradling the pup. To Reed's relief, she'd put on one of her shapeless dresses. As soon as Dr. Preek coasted to a stop, she hurried over, shifting her feet from side to side while waiting for him to open his door.

Chest tight, Reed crossed to her, going up behind her and putting his hand on her shoulder. Damned if he'd ever understand her risking her life to save an animal she didn't even know, one that was probably too far gone anyway, but he'd support her any way he could. He knew she wouldn't take it well if the vet declared the puppy was beyond help.

"What happened?" Dr. Preek asked, inclining his head at Reed in greeting. He listened while Kaitlyn explained everything, and then asked Reed if they could take the pup into the kitchen so they could examine it.

Reed hurried ahead, grabbed a couple of old towels from his laundry room and spread them on the kitchen table.

After taking the pup from Kaitlyn, the vet gently placed it down and removed the sock-tourniquet to begin examining it.

"Looks like a snake got it," he said. "See here." He showed them a puncture wound on the dog's leg. "But tying that sock like you did could have cost him his leg."

Kaitlyn sucked in her breath. "I didn't know."

To Reed's surprise, Dr. Preek smiled. "It's okay. We'll see what we can do. He's not actually a puppy, and I think he'll do fine."

"Then can you help him?" Tears trembled on the edge of her wobbly voice.

Looking from her to Reed and back again, the vet nodded. "Well, I don't know. I've got a snake bite kit with me. We use that to draw out the venom right after the animal's been bit. I think it's too late for that."

Swiping at her eyes, Kaitlyn's lush mouth trembled. "Surely there's something you can do."

Glancing at Reed, Dr. Preek scratched his closely shorn gray head. "We can try aspirin and Benadryl. I'll need to find out the right size dosage to give to a tiny pup like your pet."

"Thank you," Kaitlyn said, a wealth of gratitude in her words. Her muddy eyes practically glowed as she gazed up at the vet.

Glancing at Reed, the vet grinned. On his way past, he clapped his hand on Reed's shoulder. "You picked a good one," he said, apparently believing Kaitlyn was Reed's girlfriend. "She's got a big heart."

Chapter 6

That night, Kaitlyn stayed closeted in her room with the drugged and sleeping dog. Dr. Preek had given her a plastic syringe and told her to try to give him mouthfuls of water every hour.

She'd agreed gladly, while Reed merely looked on, his expression dark and forbidding. She knew he didn't understand, hell she barely understood herself how much this tiny animal moved her. Of course the timing was all wrong. She'd always wanted a dog, though. She hadn't named him, afraid he wouldn't make it, but now alone with him, she felt she owed him the respect of having a name of his own.

So she called him Bentley because his little face appeared so dignified and solemn. And lovable, she just knew. For so long she'd had nothing and no one, and now at least she had him.

Her own dog, and her only family. She'd nurse him through this, she vowed, and help him grow big and strong. He'd always know he was loved, too. And safe and protected.

She fell asleep dreaming of buying him his own bed and toys.

Sometime in the dark of night, a snuffling sound woke her. Blinking, she sat up and clicked on her lamp. Bentley had gotten up and appeared to be checking out her room. His stubby legs were wobbly and weak, but he was standing. He located the small bowl of water she'd put out and lapped eagerly. Her heart felt full as she watched him.

When he finished she realized she probably should take him outside and see if he needed to take care of business. Glancing at the nightstand clock, she saw it was nearly 4:00 a.m. Good. That meant Reed would be asleep.

She scooped up her pet and carried him down the hall and outside. Once she'd placed him in the grass, she watched him as he sniffed around, gathering confidence with each step. Inexplicably, her throat felt tight—as if she might be about to cry. Again.

Enough of that. Wiping at her eyes, she watched as Bentley completed his mission, then picked him up. As she turned to go back inside, she nearly collided with Reed.

He put his hands on her arms to steady her. As usual, she instinctively froze and stared at him as he clicked on a flashlight, blinding her in a quick beam before he pointed it at the ground.

"Oh." Her breath came out in a puff. She couldn't make herself tear her eyes away from the way his bare chest gleamed, right in front of her. Even stranger, her first reaction wasn't fear. Instead, a stab of pure desire clutched her low in the belly.

Shocked, she didn't move. Reed looked…unbelievable. He wore a pair of boxer shorts, nothing else. "What are you doing out here?" she managed to ask.

"I saw movement," he said easily, which calmed her. "After what happened to my house in town, I thought I'd better check."

She nodded, clasping Bentley close to her chest. "He had to go out."

"He appears improved." The husky edge to his voice wrapped around her like a silken scarf, dusting over her nerve endings and bringing them fully awake. Though this frightened her, exhilaration also zinged through her veins.

Fighting panic, she attempted a smile, even though he probably couldn't see in the darkness. "Here." She held out Bentley like a peace offering. "Would you like to hold him?"

"No." He stepped aside to let her pass, shining his beam of light to make a path back to the house. "Maybe another time."

Other than to bring Bentley back in close to her chest, she didn't move. "You don't like dogs?"

"I like dogs just fine. I even used to have one." He turned and began moving away. "But it's the middle of the night and I'm tired."

Tired. Now she was anything but. Following him back to the house, her sleepy pet cradled in her arms, she tried like hell to figure out how Reed could still affect her like this. After all she'd gone through, how she could even think of touching a man in that way astounded her.

Still, she couldn't help but wonder how he'd react if

she gave in to impulse and trailed her fingers down his back. Luckily, she wouldn't dare. The intimacy of such an act would terrify her.

The instant they stepped inside, she set down the dog. Bentley toddled off and collapsed in an uncoordinated heap a few feet away. With a huge sigh, he closed his eyes and slipped into sleep.

Smiling shyly at Reed, she picked her pet up and carried him to her room.

The next morning, Kaitlyn opened her eyes and realized she'd overslept. The bedside clock showed ten-fifteen. Groaning, she tossed back the covers and jumped out of bed, just about positive she'd find a canine mess.

But Bentley raised his head and regarded her solemnly from his position on her bed. Praising him, she hurried him outside. Once he'd done his business, she took a shower and dried her hair. She still hadn't gotten used to the color or the length, though she supposed she would in time. In fact, it had begun to grow on her. She regarded it as a symbol of change.

Carrying Bentley with her, into the kitchen, she realized she needed to figure out something to feed him. She found a couple of cans of dog food in the pantry, which surprised her and made her wonder how long it had been since Reed had had a dog. Clearly, not long since they weren't expired.

She dished some up in a bowl and once her new pet had eaten, she poured a cup of coffee and sat down at the table to enjoy it. The house was quiet, making her wonder if Reed had gone out riding. She'd have to remember to ask him if he had any dog toys or a bed or something. She'd also need to get Bentley more dog food.

"There you are." Reed came around the corner, smiling.

She jumped, unable to help it, and managed to smile back.

"I see you found something to feed him," he said, indicating the half-full can she'd left on the counter.

"Yes. I hope you don't mind, but—"

A knock on the front door startled them both. Little Bentley ran toward the entrance, barking.

"Shhh." Chasing him down, Kaitlyn picked him up. He immediately quieted. "I'll go wait in my room," she whispered. "Were you expecting visitors?"

He shook his head. "Stay hidden until I ask you to come out." He too kept his voice low. "And just in case, put on one of those ugly dresses and the contacts, okay?"

On her way down the hall, she nodded. Heart pounding, she hustled into her room and closed the door behind her.

After placing Bentley on the bed, she went to the closet and pulled out the most hideous thing she could find. It looked like it was supposed to be a dress, though why anyone would make a dress out of sweatshirt material, she didn't know. When she put it on, it hung baggy and shapeless. If she were trying to look halfway decent, she'd try pairing it with a wide belt and leggings. Instead, she decided to wear it over the pair of high-waisted, stretchy jeans Reed had purchased. They were two sizes too big, so she cinched them with a belt, slipped her feet in the ugly, imitation leather black shoes, and took one final look at herself in the mirror.

Perfect. Even she didn't recognize herself. She sat down on the edge of the bed and began patting Bentley, glad to have something to do with her hands. Once she stopped moving, she wasn't surprised to realize how badly she was shaking.

* * *

Taking a deep breath, Reed squared his shoulders and opened the front door. Brock and Zoe stood on his front porch, both of them grinning happily.

"Surprise!" Zoe squealed, launching herself at him for a hug. Behind her, Brock held up two overnight bags.

"What's this?" Reed asked, hoping he appeared perfectly normal.

"We decided to surprise you with a visit. We thought we'd stay the weekend." At Reed's lack of response, Zoe frowned. "What's wrong? Aren't you going to invite us in?"

"Of course." Stepping aside, Reed ushered them into his living room. He couldn't help but wonder if they'd been followed. "It's great to see you, of course. But now might not be the best time…."

At his words, Zoe's smile faded. "You must be really serious about this lady friend of yours. I'm sorry. Don't blame Brock. This was all my idea. I thought you'd be glad to have some company out here in the boonies."

"You also thought you'd meet this woman Reed's been so secretive about," Brock put in, pulling his wife in for a hug.

"True." Zoe's crestfallen expression made Reed feel horrible. "I didn't think we'd really be intruding, since we're all such good friends. But if we are, do you want us to go?"

One look at his two best friends in the entire world was enough to help Reed decide. "No, have a seat. I'm sorry. There's something I need to tell you. I confess, I'm hesitant to do so because I don't want to put you in danger."

Instantly, all the laughter vanished from their faces.

"Are you all right, buddy?" Brock asked. "You're not in some kind of trouble, are you?"

"No, nothing like that." He pointed toward the couch. "Sit. I'll just be a minute."

As he hurried down the hall it occurred to him to wonder if Kaitlyn would share his belief that they could let two more people in on their secret.

Tapping lightly on her door, he smiled as she opened it the tiniest crack. "May I come in?" he asked.

Eyes huge, she stepped back and let him in. He saw she'd put on one of her shapeless dresses and the brown contacts. Bentley slept all curled up in the middle of her bed.

"It's Brock and Zoe," he told her. "I think it's safe to let them in on the truth."

Gaze locked on his, she finally nodded. "Just a minute, then." She crossed over to the dresser and popped out the contacts. Blinking, she sighed. "Much better. I'm still trying to get used to those. Now turn your back."

Startled, he did as she requested.

"I just need a minute to change."

The rustle of cloth as she pulled off the dress had him battling the urge to turn. Instead, he clenched his jaw and called himself every kind of fool for his out of place and utterly ridiculous erotic thoughts.

"Okay," she said, sounding nervous. She'd changed into a pair of well-worn jeans and a T-shirt. Other than her hair, she looked just like herself.

He almost reached for her hand, but stopped himself just in time.

Brock and Zoe sat on the couch, shoulders touching. Reed watched his friend's face as he and Kaitlyn stepped into the room.

"Kaitlyn?" Zoe jumped to her feet, her expression shocked. "What on earth are you doing here?"

"It's a long story."

"I'd really like to hear it." Brock looked about ready to explode. "Alex Ramirez claimed you were abducted. And that the man who kidnapped you was armed and dangerous." He shot Reed a look. "Finding you here makes no sense."

"Before we begin, I'd like to ask you both to give me your word that you'll keep this between us. Kaitlyn's life depends on it."

Zoe stood, too, glaring at him. "Come on, Reed. We're your friends. I can't believe you don't think you can trust us."

Reed swallowed hard. "I do, you know that. But I didn't tell you because the fewer people who know, the better."

Moving over to Kaitlyn and putting her arm around her, Zoe narrowed her gaze on Reed. "We want to know everything. And I think we'd better let Kaitlyn tell us."

Chapter 7

As Kaitlyn told her story once more, the tight ball of tension knotted in her chest began to unravel. Both Zoe and Brock listened without interruption, their rapt attention and sympathetic expressions boosting Kaitlyn's confidence. She skimmed over most of the really bad stuff, and she certainly didn't show either of them her scarred back.

When Kaitlyn finished, Zoe hugged her. "Oh, honey. I'm so sorry. Honestly, when you up and disappeared we had no idea."

Stricken, Kaitlyn gazed at her old high school friend. "Please tell me you didn't think I was the one who killed Tim."

"Of course not." Zoe's prompt response left no doubt. "We knew you'd broken up with him. We even thought—" she gave a sidelong glance toward Reed "—that you and

Reed were together. Especially since he kept expecting you to show up at his trial, though he'd never say why."

Kaitlyn bit her lip, not daring to look at Reed.

"And then when we saw Alex Ramirez on TV..." Zoe shook her head. "We had to wonder what on earth you'd gotten yourself into."

"Not by choice," Kaitlyn replied. "Believe me."

"You know you can trust us," Zoe continued. "And Brock and I will do anything we can to help you. Either of you. Just say the word."

Brock nodded. "Agreed."

Touched, Kaitlyn nodded. "Thank you."

Glancing from Reed to Kaitlyn and back again, Brock rubbed his hands together. "If what you say is true, you can have this man arrested for Tim's murder as well as Reed's wrongful imprisonment."

"Closure." Zoe flashed everyone a soft smile. "And maybe this will bring both of you a chance at happiness."

Kaitlyn's face heated. She pretended not to get that Zoe apparently hoped for a little matchmaking.

"Buddy." Brock clapped Reed on the back. "Seriously, if there's anything I can do to help, just say the word."

"The best way you can help," Reed said, "is for neither of you to say a word about this to anyone."

"Of course we won't." Brock shot his friend a wry smile. "Next time, maybe try trusting us a little."

"Both of you, sit." With his arms crossed, unsmiling, Reed waited until they'd complied. "Alex Ramirez is a powerful man," he began. "George works for him and I don't know who else in the sheriff's department might, as well. Kaitlyn tells me Alex has a number of people on his payroll. That's the main reason I brought Kaitlyn out here to the ranch. No one knows about this place, except you two."

"And it will stay that way," Brock promised.

"Just be careful." Kaitlyn clasped her hands tightly together to keep from fidgeting. "You have no idea what he's capable of."

From down the hall, Bentley began barking.

"I guess he just woke up and realized we had company," Kaitlyn explained.

Zoe grinned. "You have a dog. That's great. I love dogs. Can I meet him?"

"Of course." Kaitlyn hurried to fetch him, grinning as Zoe cooed over him. As she'd expected, Bentley rolled over for a belly rub and basked in all the attention.

Zoe had brought lasagna and two bottles of wine. Feeling the need to contribute, Kaitlyn rustled up enough ingredients to make brownies. She wondered about the stash of chocolate chips she found in the cupboard, but went ahead and made the one thing she could bake successfully.

While the meal was reheating and the brownies baking, Reed opened a bottle of wine. They sat around and talked, almost like old times. For the first time, Kaitlyn felt able to put the past three years away and not let what had happened to her guide her every action and reaction. It was remarkably liberating.

The lasagna was delicious, the conversation flowed along with the wine, and Kaitlyn finally began to relax. By the time she cut into the perfectly cooked brownies, she felt like another person.

When everyone had finished, Kaitlyn shooed them into the living room. "I'll do the dishes," she said, refusing Zoe's offer to help. "Ya'll go and relax. I'll join you in a few minutes."

"I don't think—" Zoe began, laughing when Kaitlyn chased her off. "All right. If you insist."

Alone in the kitchen, Kaitlyn listened to the happy chatter from the other room. She caught herself humming as she rinsed the plates before putting them in the dishwasher.

"Kaitlyn, you'd better come here." Something in Reed's voice.

She put down her plate and rushed into the living room, Bentley right on her heels.

"Alex is going to be on," Reed said. "Maybe you'd better sit down."

The segment was just beginning. Instead of sitting, Kaitlyn stood off to one side, her arms crossed, hating the way all the tension had returned to her body.

The host introduced Alex Ramirez, lieutenant governor of the state of Texas. Despite his tailored, custommade suit and perfect hair, Alex looked exhausted.

"Wow," Brock said. "Either Alex took pains to make sure he looked like he hadn't been able to sleep or he really is taking Kaitlyn's disappearance badly."

"Considering Kaitlyn has enough information to completely shut down his political career, it's probably a little of both," Reed interjected.

The hostess began by asking him to describe his emotions since he hadn't gotten a single lead on where Kaitlyn might be.

Alex leaned forward. He was a rugged-looking guy, despite his obvious wealth. He looked the part of a politician perfectly, and nothing at all like the mobster/criminal Kaitlyn knew him to be.

"Destroyed," Alex answered, his cultured voice bleak. "I can't eat, can't sleep. All the joy has been taken out of my life."

Zoe shot Kaitlyn a look. "I know you were his prisoner, but did he actually have *feelings* for you?"

As if that excused what he'd done to her. But then, Kaitlyn had glossed over the details about that. "In his own twisted way, he does," Kaitlyn admitted. "Though those feelings come and go depending on his mood and how much he's had to drink."

Brock and Reed remained riveted on the screen.

"I need her back. To that end," Alex continued, "I've decided to offer a reward. Ten thousand dollars to anyone with information that leads to my fiancée's safe return."

"Fiancée?" Zoe, Brock and Reed all swiveled to stare at her. "Is that true?"

"Of course not." Kaitlyn felt sick. "Another lie."

"I'm wondering about the reward," Reed said. "What happened to the supposed ransom call?"

Frowning, the television reporter echoed Reed's question.

"That turned out to be a hoax, some criminal's attempt to extort money, nothing more." Alex's quick response indicated he'd anticipated this inquiry.

Kaitlyn's stomach turned. The lovely dinner she'd just shared now threatened to come back up.

Still eyeing the television, where Alex had now begun accepting questions from the audience, she watched as Alex answered increasingly random questions with an air of dignified suffering.

"He's good," Reed grudgingly muttered. "Damn good."

"Of course he is. That's why he's in politics."

"What are you going to do?" Brock asked. "Seriously, I don't understand why you haven't gone to the police."

"Or the media," Zoe put in. "Why are you hiding here and letting him get away with this?"

As they all stared at her, Kaitlyn fought the urge to shrink back. She reminded herself she was no longer that person. "I'd say it's complicated, but that sounds like an excuse."

To Kaitlyn's surprise, Reed got up and came to stand next to her. "We've discussed what we want to do. Since Kaitlyn is a witness to Tim's murder, she feels Alex would have her killed before he'd ever let her go to trial."

"What about the witness protection program?" Brock asked. "Just go to the feds, tell them what you know, and let them protect you."

Unexpectedly, Kaitlyn found herself blinking back tears. "I'd love for it to be that easy, but it's not."

Reed chimed in. "Apparently Alex has several feds on his payroll as well as various local law enforcement personnel, including George. We don't know who we can trust. Until we find out, we're going to have to be very careful."

"They're wrapping it up," Zoe pointed out. A toll-free number flashed up on the screen. Underneath, it claimed to be a direct link to Alex's people and by default, to the man himself.

Reed grabbed a pen and jotted it down.

"What are you doing?" Kaitlyn asked.

"I'm working on a plan," he said, setting the paper aside.

Immediately, everyone went quiet. Brock even grabbed the remote and turned the TV off. "Let me hear what you've come up with," Brock said. "If there's any way I can help, I will."

"Thanks, buddy." Reed clapped him on the shoulder. "As soon as I work out the details, we'll talk."

Kaitlyn struggled not to show her disappointment. The sooner they could devise a plan, the sooner she and Reed could move on with their lives.

"Thanks for a great night." Brock stood, glancing at his watch. "I think we're going to be heading back home."

"You're welcome to stay the night," Reed said. "If Kaitlyn wouldn't mind sleeping on the couch, you can have the guest room."

"No, that's okay," Zoe answered before Kaitlyn could speak. "We really shouldn't have shown up here un-invited." She hugged Reed, then Kaitlyn. "But I'm nosy, so we did. And I'm glad. It's good to see you again."

Kaitlyn found herself wiping away tears at the simple human contact, so kind and unthinkingly honest. "Same here," she managed, turning away out of embarrassment. "You have no idea how nice."

She managed to compose herself enough to scoop up Bentley and walk with Reed to the door. She watched as Brock and Zoe got in his truck and drove off. The oddly couple-like feeling of this made her feel even more con-fused and sad.

Reed waited until they were gone before speaking. "I really didn't want to involve them. It's too dangerous and I don't want them to get hurt."

Defeated, Kaitlyn let her shoulders sag. "You're right. Maybe it would have been better if I'd have kept running and left you out of it, too."

"Don't say that." He turned to face her, his voice

fierce. "Don't even think it. Alex deserves to pay for what he's done. He killed my brother and ruined both of our lives. He's not going to get away with it this time, do you understand?"

"Yes," she replied, moving past him and stepping inside.

Suddenly exhausted, still shaky and on the verge of tears, she knew she needed to be alone. Before she reached the corner that lead to the long hallway, she turned around. "Good night," she told him. "I know it's only a little after nine, but I'm tired. I'm going to go to bed."

He nodded, watching her silently, his broad-shouldered silhouette oddly reassuring.

Once in her own private sanctuary, she washed her face and brushed her teeth. After donning an old sleep T-shirt, she climbed into bed and clicked off the light, praying sleep would come quickly so she didn't have to think.

The sound of tires on the gravel road woke her from a restless sleep. She glanced at the clock on her night-stand—2:08 a.m.

Not sure if she'd imagined it, she lay still and listened. No more gravel. This time, she heard the distinct thud of a car door closing.

Visitors? Had Brock and Zoe returned? Or had Reed taken off while she'd been asleep and just now was re-turning?

Grabbing her robe from the end of the bed, she padded over and opened her bedroom door. When she stepped into the still-dark hallway, she almost collided with Reed. He wore boxer shorts and a T-shirt and a battered pair of flip-flops.

"Careful," he murmured, steadying her with his hand on her shoulder.

"You heard it, too?"

He nodded, steering her toward the kitchen. "I'm going out there. Wait here."

"No." Clutching at his arm, she tried to keep the desperation from her voice. "Don't leave me here alone. Take me with you. Please."

"Kaitlyn." Gently, he removed her hand. "I don't know who's trespassing on my property, or for what reason, but it can't be good. They could be looking for you."

She blinked. "But no one knows I'm here."

"That we know of." He moved away, crossing to the blinds covering the window in the back door. He peered out, tension radiating from him. "Whoever it is, they're heading for the barn."

Grabbing his cell phone from the kitchen counter, he punched in 9-1-1. Nothing happened at first. "It has to go all the way to the dispatch in the nearest town," he told her.

Finally, someone answered. "Intruders," he said, and then rattled off his address. "Send police right away. I'm heading out now."

Before he punched the off button, Kaitlyn heard the squawk of the operator's voice as she asked him not to do that.

He dropped his phone back on the counter, and then went back toward his room. When he emerged, he carried a rifle.

"What are you going to do with that?" she asked. "Wouldn't a shotgun be better?"

Though he gave her an odd look, he shook his head.

"I don't plan on getting too close. Plus, I'm a helluva good shot."

"I am, too," she said, glad that she'd taken Tim's shooting lessons seriously back in the day. "Give me a gun and let me back you up."

"No." Already moving forward, he didn't even look at her. Promise me you'll stay here."

Without waiting for her promise, he slipped out the back door.

She watched him for a moment, until the darkness swallowed him. Frustrated, she paced, then headed toward his room. As she'd suspected, he'd left the gun safe open.

There was another rifle and a couple of shotguns, but Kaitlyn was most familiar with the .38. She picked it up, liking the heft and feel of it in her hand. Checking the chamber, she saw it wasn't loaded, but she spotted the stacked boxes of ammunition and took care of that easily.

Then, pistol in hand, she headed out the door in Reed's footsteps.

Reed saw them long before he reached the barn, thanks to the nearly full moon and the spotlight he'd installed a few months ago. George Putchinski and a couple of his buddies. Drunk, from the sound of it. They'd abandoned any attempt at stealth and were arguing in front of the big barn door.

Careful to stay in the shadows, Reed paused and listened.

"I ain't hurting any horses," one of the men insisted, slurring his words.

"Me, neither," the second man agreed, stumbling

slightly as he moved forward. "Come on, George. You're a cop. We shouldn't even be here."

How on earth had George found this place? And even more, why had he driven two and a half hours to get here?

"Deputy Sheriff," George corrected sharply. "There's a difference. But I'm off duty right now. And it's high time we teach this low-life ex-con a lesson."

"How'd you even know where to find this place?"

"I've got my ways." George sounded smug.

Guy number one giggled, a high-pitched, nervous sound.

"Shut up," George ordered. "If you don't have the stomach for this, then you can wait in the truck."

"What do you have in mind?" the second man asked. "How about we just let his horses loose? He'll be pissed in the morning when he has to go round them up."

For some reason, guy number one found this hilarious. He laughed so hard he doubled over and nearly fell. Apparently he'd had a lot more to drink than the other two.

"Not good enough." George again. "That's why I brought my livestock trailer. We're gonna take his animals to my cousin's place. That'll teach him a lesson."

Reed had had enough. "Horse rustling used to be a hanging offense," he called out, keeping the corner pole of one of his three-sided sheds in between them just in case they carried flashlights.

The three would-be troublemakers froze.

"Who's there?" drunk guy one called out.

"Reed?" Apparently George recognized his voice. "We don't want any trouble."

"Really? Trespassing on my land, talking about stealing my horses? Sounds like trouble to me. In fact, I'm within my rights of shooting to protect myself." He took a deep breath, raising his voice. "I'm warning you. Get off my property."

Hearing the seriousness of the warning in Reed's tone, the other two moved back, edging away from the barn. George however, held his ground, his wide-legged stance belligerent. He had a flashlight, Reed saw, but the kind that was only powerful enough to illuminate a few feet away.

"Or what?" he shouted, withdrawing a pistol. "Do you really want to go to jail for attempting to shoot an officer of the law?"

At this, the first man took off, all trace of inebriation gone judging from his single-minded sprint, flashlight beam bobbing ahead of him as he ran. The second man started to follow, and then stopped, apparently torn between his buddy's good sense and his need to try and save George.

Praying Kaitlyn had stayed hidden as he'd asked, Reed stayed hidden. "I've called 9-1-1. Since I'm sure you don't have a warrant, I can't wait to see how you're going to explain to your coworkers exactly what you're doing here."

George snarled a curse. "Come out where I can see you, you coward."

"So you can shoot me and then claim I drew on you first?" Reed made sure George could hear his contempt and amusement. "No, thanks."

Way off in the distance, the sound of a siren approached. Given how far the ranch sat from the main road, everyone knew they still had a few minutes before law enforcement arrived.

"George, come on," the second man urged. "We need to get the hell out of here."

Though George hesitated, even he knew when it was time to retreat. "Don't think I will forget this, Westbrook," he threatened, enough rage in his voice to let Reed know he meant what he said. As if Reed had been the one guilty of wrongdoing.

"I think you have that mixed up." Unable to resist one final taunt, Reed took care to stay hidden, just in case George decided to be stupid and run toward his voice, trying to use the flashlight to flush him out. "I'm the one who now has something to remember."

"Come on, man," again the second man urged, backing away as he spoke. "I don't want to be here when the state police arrive."

Squinting, Reed tried to place the voice. He recognized the man from somewhere, he just couldn't remember exactly where.

The wail of the siren grew closer. "I think they've turned off the main road," Guy Two urged. "Let's go, George. Now."

Finally, George gave in to common sense and holstered his weapon. "This isn't over," he shouted, before taking off for his pickup. Since there was only one way in and out of the farm, he had to drive his truck pulling a livestock trailer down the same long and winding drive the sheriff's cruiser would take. Right now it would be a toss-up as to whether they'd make it out before the law arrived.

Reed really, really hoped they wouldn't.

He waited until George's taillights vanished before turning around to head back toward the house. He'd barely taken a step when something moved in the darkness, cutting off the back porch light for a second.

Instinctively tensing, he raised his rifle.

"Don't shoot." Kaitlyn's voice, shaky and breathless, stopped him. As he lowered the gun, she materialized out of the dark to stand in front of him. Stunned, he realized she carried his .38.

"What are you doing?" he asked, struggling to contain his anger and terror at what had nearly just happened. "I asked you to wait in the house."

"I came out here in case you needed backup," she said, her confident tone at odds with her stunned expression. "I'm a damn good shot. You just never know."

Hands shaking, he tried to remain calm. Didn't she understand that he could have shot her? Someone from the sheriff's office would be here any minute. If he'd had more time, he'd have let her know what he thought about her blatant disregard for her own safety. Now, though, he needed to get her back inside the house safely.

"Hear that," he said, his voice barely controlled as the siren's wail grew louder. "They'll be here any minute. Get back in your room. Run. If they see you like that, they'll definitely recognize you."

She froze, indecisive. Though he tried not to look, the sleep shirt she wore clung lovingly to her curves.

"Oh, crud." Handing him the pistol, she took off running for the house. He watched her, walking slowly toward the porch light, aware he wanted to meet the sheriff outside.

A moment later, the cruiser came into sight, lights flashing. As it approached, the siren whooped once more, and then cut off as the vehicle stopped.

Though the state trooper killed the engine, he left the lights flashing. The driver's door opened and he emerged.

"Evening," he said, inclining his blond head. He was

middle-aged and had the weary air of one who's seen too much. "What's going on?"

Reed recapped everything since the sound of someone coming down his driveway at 2:00 a.m, including giving George Putchinski's name and the fact that he was a deputy sheriff from a town over two hours away.

The trooper looked at him with a mixture of wariness and disbelief. "Have you been drinking, sir?"

It took everything Reed had to keep from rolling his eyes. "No. I swear to you. George Putchinski has had it in for me ever since I came back home. He and a couple of his buddies—"

"I think I've heard enough." To give him credit, the trooper gave all the appearance of taking the information and writing up a report. "I promise you I'll investigate this fully. I'll call the sheriff of that town—Anniversary, you say?—and speak to him as soon as he gets in tomorrow morning."

"And if George denies everything?" Which Reed knew he would.

The other man gave him a tight smile. "Well, then, without any other witnesses, it's your word against his. And since no damage was actually done..."

"Then as far as you're concerned, no crime has been committed."

"Exactly." Eyeing him carefully, the Trooper stowed his pad and pen in his shirt pocket. "Now, if there's not anything else, I'll go."

Reed nodded. He wished like hell Kaitlyn could come out and tell the sheriff what she'd seen and corroborate his story. But since she couldn't, he had no choice but to stand silently and watch as the state trooper got in the cruiser and pulled away.

Then he went into the house. Kaitlyn waited in the kitchen, watching him expectantly. She fairly vibrated with nervous energy.

"They know how to find me," he told her, not bothering to elaborate on who "they" were.

Eyes wide, she stared. "How?"

"I'm wondering if George put a trace on Brock's truck. I just can't believe he drove two and a half hours just to make trouble."

"If he knows, that means Alex does, too. I need to leave." The panicked defeat in her voice almost had him reaching for her. Almost, except he knew if he did, she'd likely recoil and right now he didn't think he could take that.

"Not yet," he said. "Judging from George's actions tonight, he hasn't told whoever he reports to anything. The state trooper is going to call Roger Giles—our sheriff—tomorrow and talk to him about this. I might even press charges."

She made a soft sound of distress. "That's asking for trouble, wouldn't you say?"

"Is it?" Jaw clenched with the effort of holding himself in, he turned away. "At some point I have to stop the harassment. And that's what this was, plain and simple. Next he's going to start hurting my livestock."

"Why does he hate you so much?" she asked.

"I have no idea." He forced himself to look back at her. "I almost shot you tonight. Don't ever do that again, understand?"

Slowly she nodded. "I'm sorry," she whispered. "I just wanted to help. I'm tired of being a victim."

Though her words stunned him, he refused to show

any reaction. "Good night," he said, and left her standing there without another glance.

Once in his room, he closed the door, sat down on the edge of the bed and wondered how the hell he could possibly go back to sleep. Short answer, he couldn't.

Yanking his door open again, he padded down the hall, past the now-empty kitchen, and retrieved his bottle of whiskey and a glass from the den. He carried those back to his room, well aware he would need at least one drink if he'd have the slightest prayer of sleeping.

Chapter 8

After Reed left, Kaitlyn rushed to her room and tried to get a handle on the breath-choking panic. They knew how to find Reed's ranch. Which meant soon enough, they'd come here looking for her.

She'd rather die than let Alex get his hands on her again. Even though she knew he'd eventually kill her, the things he'd already done to her made her shake.

Not only that, but her mere presence had placed Brock and Zoe and Reed in danger. She couldn't bear it if they were hurt because of her.

Clearly, she'd been wrong. Wrong to believe Reed could help bring Alex to justice. Alex was just too powerful, too well connected. Nothing they could do would bring him down.

Her only other option would be to run.

Fueled by fear, she began tossing her meagre belongings in her duffel bag. Before she'd even finished, she realized she didn't have a car and couldn't walk the distance to town. Even if she could, what then? She had a little cash, maybe enough to buy a used car, but where would she go? How would she survive?

Squaring her shoulders, she finished packing. She'd figure something out. Better a life on the run than endangering everyone who tried to help her.

She'd just zipped up the zipper when Reed knocked on her door. Without waiting for her to answer, he opened it and came in.

"I saw your light. You couldn't sleep, either," he began, but stopping when he saw her packed bag. "What are you doing?"

"I was…" At a loss for words she stared up at him. "I was packing."

"You can't. We're in this together, remember? For Tim and for the years of our lives Alex took from us."

"I can't risk…" She swallowed, unable to finish. He'd taken a step toward her. If she dared, she could reach out and touch him, he'd moved that close. Then, as his gaze shifted to her mouth, she understood something else.

He was going to kiss her. Immediately her pulse began to beat a rapid-fire tattoo. Oh. Once, thoughts of him had been all that kept Alex from breaking her. Eventually, she'd lost that battle.

Now fear warred with desire. Unfortunately for them both, fear won. Her body vibrating like a hummingbird's wings, she took a step back, until the back of her legs butted up against her bed.

Frozen, she stared up at him, unable to catch her breath.

"I won't hurt you," he promised, his voice washing

over her like velvet. She believed him, honestly she did, yet she couldn't seem to stop her body's trembling.

He moved closer, his eyes dark and unfathomable. Moving slowly, deliberately, he cupped her chin. His gentleness felt completely at odds with the fierceness of the desire simmering like banked coal inside the depths of his eyes.

And then…he bent his head and gently touched his lips to hers. She hadn't expected this, the tenderness, the slow and thoughtful movement of his mouth.

Just when she finally began to relax, he broke away and brushed a soft kiss against her forehead. "I will never hurt you, understand?"

Slowly she nodded, her heart beating against her rib cage like a trapped butterfly. "What about…" Her voice broke. "What about this?" She waved her hand vaguely. "This place. It's no longer safe."

"So we'll go somewhere else. Together. Somewhere they won't find us. I've talked to Brock and let him know what happened. He suggested a place—without actually saying the words. Last season he bought a hunting cabin and some land southwest of here. He leases most of it out as deer leases, but he kept the cabin for himself. He took me there last deer season and I know where they keep the key. So go ahead and finish packing. I'll do the same. We'll head out first thing in the morning."

She nodded, unable to tear her gaze away from him. "Is it safe?"

"About as safe as you can get. The cabin sits in some trees on top of a hill. There's only one road in, like this place, but it's more easily defended due to location. Plus, not too many people know about it. Just Brock, Zoe and me."

"How long do you think we'll have to keep running?"

Some of the defeat inside her must have come through in her voice. "We'll figure something out, I promise," he said.

"I have an idea." She lifted her chin. "How about we go back to Anniversary? Now that they've already searched your house, they know you're not harboring me there."

Reed stared. "I don't know if that's a good idea. You'd be a sitting duck if they found you."

"I'll be a sitting duck anywhere. At least in town, we'd have people to help us."

"I don't want to put Brock and Zoe in danger," he said.

"Me, neither." Still holding his gaze, she took a deep breath. "But I'm tired of hiding."

"How about this? We stay at the cabin for a few days while I fine-tune my plan. Then we can reconsider going home."

Home. A word she wondered if she'd ever know again. Right now, it seemed doubtful but she agreed wearily. "Fine. I'm looking forward to hearing your plan."

"I think you'll like it."

As Reed turned to go, she reached out and grabbed his arm. Electricity zinged through her at the contact. Ignoring this, she exhaled. "I'm sorry I'm putting you through all this."

"It's okay." His grin just about stopped her heart. "In the end, all of this will be worth it. Plus, the cabin is closer to Alex's place. That just might come in handy. Now go get some rest."

After tossing and turning, Kaitlyn gave up and got up before dawn. Since she wasn't sure if Reed was awake yet, she took care to move quietly, hurrying while showering and getting dressed.

Through it all, panic thrummed through her veins. Only by really concentrating was she able to keep it at bay. The sooner they were out of here the better.

She wondered what time she should wake Reed. And then she heard the sound of his shower starting and knew he was up. Feeling more relieved than she should have, she headed to the kitchen where she measured coffee grounds, added water and turned on the coffee brewer. A moment later, the mouthwatering smell of Kona filled the room.

She decided they could eat on the road. Coffee however, was a necessity. Too restless to sit still, she got up from the kitchen table and took Bentley outside. The sun had just begun to rise, coloring the sky in pink and purples. Marveling, she let the beauty calm her, unable to keep from wishing she was free to relax and enjoy it.

Something caught her attention. Despite the early hour, a cloud of dust seemed to be moving up the long drive. Not again. Surely George hadn't come back to finish what he'd started. Her heartbeat stuttered as she watched. The instant she saw the black, state police car come around the curve, she knew the occupants were law enforcement and possibly a couple of Alex's cronies. Of course, since Alex had a long reach, they could be both.

Trying to rein in her panic, she grabbed up her little dog and ran for Reed.

In the back of the house, the sound of the shower still running told her he hadn't finished. No matter, this was urgent. Taking a deep breath, she yanked open his bathroom door.

"Reed!"

"Kaitlyn? What the hell—" He moved part of the shower curtain aside to peer out and glared at her.

"Someone's here," she yelped, desperately averting her eyes. "A police car. It's either the government or one of Alex's thugs."

"It's barely sunrise. Damn." He shut the water off, just as someone rang the doorbell. "Wait in your room," he barked. "Do not answer the door, understand?"

His arm snaked out from behind the curtain and he snagged a towel. "Go!" he ordered as he moved from the tub. She spun on her heels and ran for her room, her entire body burning. Reed was right behind her, heading in the opposite direction, no doubt dripping water on the floor.

Once in her space, she closed the door and stood absolutely still, listening. Straining to hear, the sound of Reed's voice reached her. He sounded calm, relaxed even, though she couldn't make out all the words. A few minutes later, nothing. And then she heard the sound of a car starting, and the crunch of gravel as it drove away.

A moment later, Reed tapped on her bedroom door. Bentley barked, just once, until Kaitlyn partially opened the door. Once Bentley spotted Reed, he began wagging his tail.

"All clear," Reed said. "It was the state police following up. No idea why they're here this early, unless they took a page from George's playbook and came early just to hassle me."

"What'd they say?"

"Once they realized I'd just gotten out of the shower, the guy told me the investigation was still ongoing. He promised to call if he had any news. He's gone."

Part of her didn't want to fully open her door. Part of her did. Really, really, badly.

The image of him emerging semi-naked from his shower had been burned on her retinas, seared into her memory. Her entire body flushed hot at the thought. "Meet me in the kitchen once you're dressed," she told him, mentally berating herself for being such a chicken. "I made coffee. I figured we could grab breakfast on the road."

He made a sound that might have been assent and moved away. She counted to ten, then five more just to be safe, giving him plenty long enough to get back to his room, before heading into the kitchen to finish her coffee and feed her dog.

They were on the highway just after the sun had fully risen. Reed checked in with his foreman and let him know he was leaving. They saw no other vehicles on the drive out and even the main road appeared deserted, most likely due to the still-early hour.

Though she would never have believed it possible, Kaitlyn fell asleep with Bentley snoozing in her lap.

Watching as Kaitlyn and her pet slipped off into dreamland, Reed smiled. He hadn't been able to stop thinking about that kiss, that single, sensuous touch of his lips on hers. For once, the stark fear that always haunted her eyes had disappeared. That's when he'd known that someday, Kaitlyn would be okay. Alex hadn't completely ruined her for another man.

Another man. Odd how the thought rankled. Though their past relationship had been nothing but trouble for them both, he found himself remembering how passion-ate and carefree she'd once been. He'd actually fallen half in love with her back then. That mistake would be one he wouldn't repeat.

When they finally turned off the paved road to head to the cabin, he wondered if his truck would make it. The last time he'd been here, he and Brock had parked and ridden an old ATV up the hill. If he remembered right, the drive was uneven and pitted with potholes and washed-out dirt.

Hands tight on the steering wheel, he glanced at Kaitlyn and decided to try it. At the first bump, both she and Bentley had come awake.

"Are we there yet?" she asked, her voice groggy, those lovely blue eyes dazed with sleep.

"Almost. We've got to navigate this drive."

She sat up straight, taking in the landscape. "You're right," she said, bracing one hand on the steering wheel and wincing at the next bounce. "Regular vehicles won't be able to make it up here."

"Let's just hope this truck can. I don't want to get stuck." Slowing to a crawl, he carefully tried to steer around the larger holes.

Somehow, miraculously, they made it to the top. Here, the dirt road evened out for the last five hundred yards before they reached the cabin.

Shaking his head, Reed parked the truck. "I think you'll feel safe here."

"I agree." She gave him a sleepy smile. "But you're going to have to come up with an easier way to get up and down the drive."

He pointed to an ATV parked near the cabin. "Once I make sure that has plenty of gas, I'll use it. I'll take my truck to the bottom and park it. I'll try to hide it the best I can."

She'd already turned away from him and appeared to be studying the cabin. Wincing, he suddenly saw it through her eyes.

"It's a guy's hunting retreat," he said, slightly apologetic. "No frills. Nothing fancy. Though it's two rooms, there's an old kitchen, a separate bathroom with a shower, and a couple of bunk beds."

"One room."

He could have dealt with shock or anger or even fear. But the flatness of her tone told him what she expected to happen.

"Two beds," he said, careful to keep his own voice neutral. "No worries."

She nodded and began moving toward the cabin without glancing back in his direction. Placing Bentley on the ground, she watched as the little dog began exploring, sniffing the various bushes before christening them.

"Be careful and watch for snakes," he said. "This area is known for them."

"Bentley!" she called, snatching up her pet so quickly he had to smile. "Let's go inside."

"The door is unlocked," he called after her before grabbing their supplies out of the truck.

Following her into the cabin, he set their bags down on the foldout cot, which stirred up a cloud of dust.

"Sorry." He shrugged. "We're guys. No one cleans the place when we're not here."

"That's okay." Her smile seemed genuine. "I like it. It's cozy and most important, I feel safe here."

"I'm glad," he told her, meaning it.

"You said you were working on a plan. Why don't you tell me what you've come up with so far? I can help you brainstorm, if you'd like."

Debating silently, he reached a decision. "Hear me out, okay?"

Slowly, she nodded.

"It might sound crazy, but I'm going to go to Alex and offer my assistance to help him find you."

She narrowed her eyes as if not quite sure if he was serious. "That's either the most ridiculous thing I've ever heard, or the most brilliant. I assume there's more?"

He dipped his chin in acknowledgment. "Once I do that, I need to gain his trust. Maybe I can learn exactly who is on his payroll. That way, we know who will help us."

"It's a thought," she said. "But there's only one problem. What if you get caught? He'll destroy you."

"That's the chance I have to take." Crossing his arms, he waited. "Unless you have a better idea."

"I don't. But why would Alex accept your help? He has people—lots of them—on his payroll. Law enforcement, attorneys, thugs, you name it. Why would he need you?"

"Because I'm Tim's brother. You were Tim's girlfriend before. He'll think I have connections and that I'm after the reward money. He might even believe I know something."

"You're probably right." She considered him, her gaze thoughtful and far too beautiful. "Okay. Bentley and I will stay hidden here."

"I won't be able to make contact, you know. Too much risk."

"But I'll have a cell phone, won't I?"

Hiding a smile, he nodded. "Yes. I bought a couple of throwaway phones. I'll leave you with one of those. Just don't call me. If you do, you could be traced."

"I won't." She held out her hand for the phone. Once

he'd given it to her, she attempted a smile. "I don't even know your number."

He considered. "I'm not going to give it to you. I want you to call Brock or Zoe at the feed store if there's an emergency. But only then. Otherwise, don't take the risk."

"I won't." She checked out the phone. "Either write their number down or program it in here. You have one week. If you're not back by then, I'll assume the worst."

He grinned, liking the fact that she thought she could give him a deadline. Despite himself, despite everything she'd done—or hadn't done—he couldn't help liking her. Which stunned him. He'd always found her sexy, but never knew her well enough to *like* her. "Sounds reasonable," he drawled, trying not to laugh. "I'll start working on that today."

"Thank you." Expression earnest, she glanced away. "I spent three years locked up away from the world because of Alex. Even now that I've escaped, I'm still in prison."

He shook his head. "I know you've been through hell, but you have no idea what prison is like." Even saying the word brought the darkness back. Even after all this time, he hadn't been able to shake the oppressive weight of those years he'd lost behind bars.

"I'm sorry," she said. "Bad analogy."

He tried to wave away her apology. Tried, too, to slough off the black mood.

"Maybe talking about it would help. It was bad, wasn't it?"

Talking about it? He *never* talked about it. But this time, he wanted to try.

"I don't think unless you've been there, you can imagine what it's like." No emotion there. Just fact. "What made it worse was that I hadn't done the crime. And after the first few attempts to make that known, I realized every other inmate had the same story. No one believed me. No one gave a damn." He shrugged. "I shouldn't have been so surprised."

"I'm sorry." Her expression told him she knew the words were inadequate.

"Don't be." He tried to sound normal. "I'm free. I'm trying to get my life back the way it used to be."

Except it wasn't. Not only had his brother been killed, but despite his acquittal, a lot of people still thought he'd done it. He'd already told her how most of the people in town treated him like a pariah.

"What about you?" he asked, clearly trying to change the subject. "Do you want to talk about what it was like being held captive by a megalomaniac?"

She gave him a long look and then slowly nodded. "I was terrified. I thought he was going to kill me since I'd witnessed him murdering Tim. Instead, he kept me locked up 24/7. Sure, it was a luxurious room, with my own bath. But there were bars on the windows and I couldn't leave. My food was brought to me.

"I refused to eat at first, but after two days, I was weak and starving. So I ate. Turned out, he'd drugged the food."

Reed opened his mouth to speak, but decided not to. Her prison, while cleaner and more luxurious, was horrible in a different way.

"I don't know how long he kept me drugged. I lost track of time."

Though Reed figured he already knew the answer, he asked anyway. "That was when he raped you, wasn't it?"

She jerked her head in a quick nod. "Yes. That was

the first time. He enjoyed…violence. It never stopped, even after he no longer kept me drugged."

Reed had to look away. "I promise you. He'll pay."

"I hope so," she said briskly, rubbing her hands together as if they were suddenly cold. "Excuse me. I've got to go freshen up." And she hurried into the tiny bathroom, closing the door behind her.

When Kaitlyn had begun talking about her life as Alex Ramirez's captive, at first Reed had been stunned. She'd been drugged, she'd been abused and she'd been conditioned. Yet despite all that, she'd somehow managed to rise above the subservient shadow of her true self, and flee. Reed was humbled that she'd chosen to come to him for help.

But now that she'd bared her innermost self to him, she expected Reed to do the same. He supposed this was a female thing, but he'd never discussed his time in prison with anyone. And he certainly didn't intend to start now.

A few minutes later, Kaitlyn emerged. As he gazed at her, his chest felt tight. She didn't seem to know she had the kind of beauty that started wars. This was why men were driven to possess her. Not because of who she was as a person, but because of the way she looked.

Raw emotion filled him. In that instant, he realized he more than liked her. He still wanted her. He always had, even back when she'd belonged to his brother. Because in all the time he'd known her, she had been treated as a piece of property, and he couldn't act on his desire. The greatest gift he could give her was her freedom.

He'd make sure she never knew the depths of his craving. When this was all over, she'd finally be free.

"Are you all right?"

He blinked, coming out of his thoughts to see her

frowning at him. "Sure." He managed a smile. Remembering what she'd said about baring her soul to him and getting nothing in return, he felt a flush of guilt. Because she was right.

It occurred to him if he told her about his time in prison, this would further serve to help her distance herself from him.

No one could love the man he'd become during his time spent behind bars.

"Shortly after I was incarcerated," he began, "I learned the prison had a definite hierarchy. It helped who you aligned yourself with, but in the end it came down to every man for himself."

His rough voice came out overly loud in the small room, even to himself. She glanced at him, her amazing blue eyes full of guilt.

"I don't blame you," he said, deciding if he was going with total honesty, then he might as well start immediately.

"Part of you does." Her expression sorrowful, she sighed. "Once again, I'm sorry."

He grimaced, wondering if maybe, after all, he should wait until another time. But if he did, his courage might desert him. Maybe he should get it over with, even if making her hate him made for an uncomfortable afternoon.

"You know, everyone has standards. I did. And you'd like to think you'd be able to hold on to your ideals no matter the circumstances."

Seeing the question in her face, he forestalled her with a slight shake of his head. "I told myself I'd maintain my integrity. What a laugh."

Hearing the bitterness in his own voice, he made himself continue. "I got beat up a lot the first weeks I was there. Nearly killed. I kept trying to believe they'd eventually tire of tormenting me and leave me alone, but part of me knew that wasn't going to happen.

"One day two of them cornered me." He swallowed hard, feeling his face heat. "I think they intended to rape me. I fought them. And I turned into someone else."

Still, the shame scarred his soul. Not for defending himself, but for what he'd done after.

Glancing at her, he saw she didn't understand. And he realized he couldn't do it, couldn't tell her all the gory details. "When it was over and the guards put me in isolation, I didn't remember what had happened. I've looked it up since then, and what I did is similar to a berserker of old Norse legend. I'd fought in a trance, with uncontrollable fury and rage."

"Did you…kill them?" she asked, making him wonder if she felt as hollow as her voice sounded.

"No. Though when they got out of the infirmary, someone else did. Most likely punishment by the person who'd sent them after me. It didn't matter. Once I was released from solitary back to the general population, I had become someone to be feared."

When her chin came up, he knew she was going to demand more.

"Don't sweat the small details," he said. "In the end, I became worse than any of the men who'd tormented me. I was a bully, a beast, and the worst thing of all is that I began to actually enjoy it."

For a long moment he only watched out the window, not wanting to see the condemnation on her face, and trying like hell not to shudder at the memory of what he'd become.

Kaitlyn broke the silence first. "How did you find your way back to yourself?"

The insight displayed by that question moved him. Deeply thankful, and grateful, and yes…angry. He wanted her to hate him. To despise him as much as he despised himself.

Maybe he should have told her all the details, about the broken bones, the tortures, the way he'd preyed on men weaker than himself. But even contemplating this made him feel sick and he knew he couldn't.

Then she touched him, leaving her hand on his shoulder. Her touch burned. He should have jerked away, refused her small offer of comfort, but once again he searched his soul and knew he was weak.

"I'm so sorry you had to go through that," she said, her voice breaking in pain. "I'd do anything to go back in time and change things, to have been strong enough to have broken free of Alex and testified. If I had, I could have spared you all that."

How like her, to try and take his suffering into herself and absorb it. Once, he might have agreed with her. Not now, not when he knew she'd been as much a victim as he.

Raising his head, he faced her. The softness in her gaze nearly undid him.

"Enough of this," he said, trying for lightness. "We've both been through hell. Let's focus on the future, on bringing that bastard down."

"I agree. But first, won't you at least accept my apology?" Her eyes were huge in her heart-shaped face.

Exasperated, he grabbed hold of both of her shoulders. "You have nothing to apologize for. Now that I know the circumstances, I completely understand why you couldn't contact the police or testify."

"But I—"

"Was drugged and kept locked up. A prisoner. As much of one as I was. I get it."

Though she nodded, she still looked miserable. "But—"

He did the only thing he could to silence her. Put his mouth on hers and kissed her. Long and hard and deep, until both of them had trouble catching their breaths.

When he pulled away, fighting the temptation to linger, he forced himself to move away, toward the bathroom. "When I get back, let's find something to eat. Then I'm going to call Alex."

"Let's do that first," she said. "I'd like to get it over with."

He decided to humor her and picked up the phone. As he'd expected, the toll-free number went to an anonymous-sounding answering service. Refusing to give the operator any information, he simply asked to leave a message for Alex, consisting of his name, phone number and the fact that he believed he could help.

"There," he said. "I'm not sure how long it will be until I hear from someone." He'd no sooner finished speaking when the phone rang. Caller ID showed Unknown Number.

Before he had time to think, he answered. The voice on the other end was young and female. "Mr. Ramirez would like to request a meeting," she said. And then she rattled out a location, date and time, disconnecting the call without giving Reed a chance to say he'd be there or not.

"Damn," he swore softly. "That guy sure is overly confident. He expects me to meet him tomorrow at ten in the morning."

Slowly, she nodded. "He's moving fast. That's how he is. He never hesitates. You need to remember that when you're dealing with him."

Chapter 9

Though Kaitlyn's stomach had twisted in knots when Reed had called Alex, Reed's kiss had rocked her to her core. As had Reed's confession. She hadn't expected him to open himself up as much as she had. Reed had shared his innermost secret and the source of all his pain. Ironically, this only made her want him more.

Imagine that. How could she desire a man after all she'd been through? This made no sense to her. They were both damaged, maybe beyond repair. Scarred. And intellectually she knew she needed to try and experience life on her own, without a man—or anyone else—controlling things.

Yet her sudden craving for Reed was as deep, as visceral, as her need to breathe.

Dangerous. She should be glad he planned to leave for Alex's house that afternoon. Maybe once she was alone, she could get a grip on herself.

Bentley barked, letting her know he wanted to go outside. Smiling at him, proud he was such a smart little dog, she opened the door and followed him out.

The stunning view helped boost her mood. Despite the twisted, hunched-over trees, the rolling hills and gullies, the pitted landscape spoke of hard times and endurance. It wasn't difficult to see this as a metaphor for her own life.

Behind her, the cabin door slammed. Reed grinned at her as he tossed his bag in the truck. "Before I leave, I'll make sure that ATV is running and has plenty of gas."

She nodded, aching again. Bentley's low growl had her spinning around.

A giant, hairy spider the size of her fist had faced off with her pet. Heart in her throat, Kaitlyn hurried over and scooped her dog up.

"Tarantula," Reed said. "They're common out here."

She shuddered. "Do they bite?"

"They can. My advice is to avoid them when you can. The cabin is pretty tight and I doubt they'll come inside." He squeezed her shoulder lightly as he went past. "You'll be all right."

Somehow, she managed to nod, even though the simple touch had sent a shock straight to her core. The idea of Reed around Alex and his people made her feel sick.

"I'll be fine," he told her, making her realize her thoughts must have shown on her face.

"Just be successful," she replied. "And careful. Remember there are layers under layers in Alex's world."

He nodded, turning to mess with the ATV, which started immediately. "You're good." He sounded pleased. "You also need to be careful. You can hurt yourself on these things."

"I know." She'd grown up riding four-wheelers. "As

long as Bentley and I have plenty of food and water, we'll manage."

"Okay, then." Wiping his hands down the front of his jeans, he faced her. "I'm going to take off."

Stunned, though she knew she shouldn't have been, she managed a nod. "Okay." She had the strangest urge to wrap her arms around him in farewell. Because she honestly wasn't sure she'd ever see him again.

As if she'd spoken out loud, he didn't move. "Come here," he said, his voice rough. Without hesitation, she moved forward, walking right into his open arms. She buried her face against the corded muscles of his chest, inhaling his masculine scent deeply so she could commit it to memory. Sadness warred with a flicker of desire as she tried to relax into his embrace.

"Look at me," he rasped. "Kaitlyn, this isn't goodbye forever. I'll be back and when I am, I'll have enough information to lock that bastard away forever."

Slowly, battling both hope and fear, she raised her head. As their gazes locked, she felt more of the ice inside her melt.

And when his mouth covered hers hungrily, instead of panic, she felt need. Heat blazed between them and her entire body tingled, head to toe, a fire beginning low in her belly.

He pressed against her, and she felt the strength of his arousal. Reeling, she pushed away the initial twinge of fear due to her past and gave herself to sensation. She arched her body toward him, in invitation, in welcome, in farewell.

For a moment, for one heady split second in time, she thought he might take her up on her daring offer of herself. Her knees trembled, her stomach quivered and blood pounded in her veins.

But he cursed and wrenched away. "We. Can't. Do. This." Breathing hard, he turned from her, as if he thought to shield his aroused body from hers.

Of course. Ashamed and perilously close to tears, she bowed her head and wrapped her arms around her own body, both to shield and to comfort. She knew she was damaged goods. Of course no one would ever want her again.

"Kaitlyn…" A plea. It sounded as if her name had been ripped from his throat.

"No. You're right," she managed. "I completely understand."

With a groan, he hauled her up against him. Then he kissed her again, slanting his mouth over hers, hard and punishing. Demanding, possessive, heady.

She drank him in, desperately needing more to chase away the shame.

Somehow, they ended up near the kitchen table. He unsnapped her jeans, slipping his hand under the silky lace of her panties.

Melting, burning, she tugged at his clothes with fumbling fingers, needing them off, willing to tear them if necessary. His gaze blazing, he helped her, making short work of the offending cloth that separated them. She barely registered the size and strength of his arousal, before he lifted her up. Placing her on the tabletop, he pushed into her.

The pleasure was explosive. She barely had time to wonder how Reed, in that moment, had almost managed to erase years of pain, before she trembled, nearly undone before he even began to move. Half ice, half flame, and completely senseless, she clutched him close and let him take her to heaven.

As her tremors began, he slowed his movements, prolonging her ecstasy, even though he shook from the effort of keeping himself under control.

Gasping, her heart bursting, she kissed him deep and long, moving her body again to let him know he could let himself go.

With a low moan, he went wild, pounding into her with a fierceness that ignited another spark low in her belly. Desire flared again, threatening to consume her. She met him thrust for thrust, and finally he gave a strangled cry and shuddered inside her.

Her own passion peaked again, and she cried out too, her mouth on his, tasting the metallic sharpness of his release.

As he held her, their breathing harsh, she realized exactly what they'd done. They'd had no protection, taken no precautions. Even when Alex had raped her, he'd always worn a condom.

Tears stung the backs of her eyes and she silently sent a prayer winging skyward. The last thing either of them needed would be repercussions from a single act of passion, no matter how healing and wonderful it had been.

She didn't know if Reed realized it, too, but when he moved off her, he averted his gaze. Helping her off the table, he silently bent and handed her all of her clothing. Refusing to feel ashamed, she dressed, watching silently as he did the same.

Finally, when they were both fully clothed, he faced her.

"That should never have happened." Though he spoke

in a gentle tone, a tinge of bitterness colored his voice. "And we both need to make sure it doesn't happen again."

Since she agreed, she nodded. "You're right."

He froze. He opened his mouth as if he had more to say, but finally shook his head. "Stay safe," he said.

"You, too," she replied. And then she watched, her heart in her throat, as Reed grabbed his cowboy hat and, without another word to her, slammed out of the house. Hurrying to the window, she stood still as a statue as he climbed into his truck and drove away.

Driving toward Austin, Reed called himself a hundred kinds of fool. He knew better. What he and Kaitlyn had done had been a huge mistake, a colossal error in judgment. She'd seemed so wounded, completely unaware of how irresistible he found her. He'd given in to his base desires and exhibited an appalling lack of self-control. They'd made love, which was so much more than mere sex. A dangerous distinction.

At the thought, his body stirred, causing him to curse again. He wanted her, plain and simple, and now that he'd actually had a taste of her, he craved her even more. Stupid, stupid, stupid.

That can't happen again, he'd told her. Problem was, he wanted it to. Every time he so much as looked at her, he felt a jolt of pure desire. Worse, now that he'd had a taste of her, he wanted to plunge himself into her again and again. More than that—he wanted to hold her in his arms and never, ever let her go.

A sentiment which he had no doubt she didn't share. He couldn't say he blamed her. After all, as far as he could tell, her entire life she'd only known men who wanted to possess and own her. He couldn't be like that—

he wouldn't. He wanted to give her the world, which was ironic considering he had nothing. Still, more than once he'd caught himself daydreaming about the places he'd like to show her. Places he'd always longed to go, but hadn't wanted to see alone.

With Kaitlyn, Reed could actually imagine a future.

And that—that he could even think such a possibility might exist—had him calling himself every kind of fool.

Truth was, he didn't know why she'd even wanted him at all to begin with. And he sure as hell didn't plan to let her know how much the pleasure and unabashed joy she'd taken in his body had meant to him, how far it had gone toward healing his wounded spirit.

She didn't treat him as if he was trash, a low-life ex-con. In fact, she acted as if she found him as breathtakingly beautiful as he found her.

Stupid. He'd never been the kind of man given to flights of fancy. Why start now?

Circumstances had forced them to be together. He felt pretty sure if things were different, if Kaitlyn didn't need his help, she'd never look twice at him.

Therefore, the logical conclusion would be to stop all this nonsense and try to focus only on what mattered— avenging his brother's death and clearing his own name.

He found a hotel on the outskirts of Austin and booked a room. Once inside, he snagged a drink from his cooler and sat down on the sagging sofa, aware he had to have a semi-organized approach to his meeting with Alex. He had to be extremely careful. He didn't want to give away too much too fast, but he had to make sure to pique the other man's interest.

Later that night, so restless he couldn't stand it, he finally gave up and went to bed early. To his surprise, he slept well, without any dreams, and woke up focused and determined.

He showered and dressed, had a couple of cups of bitter coffee from the small room coffeepot. Every time Kaitlyn came to mind, he resolutely turned his thoughts to the task at hand. Not only would he avenge his brother's death, but his own wrongful incarceration. Freeing Kaitlyn was an incidental bonus.

Arriving early at the coffee shop, Reed found a booth near the back of the room and took a seat with a full view of the front door.

The instant Alex Ramirez strode in, Reed's every sense rang an alert. He'd seen the man on TV of course, but on the flat screen he hadn't been able to get a sense of the man's energy. Alex fairly vibrated with authority. Power mingled with something darker, dangerous.

Suppressing an instinctive shudder of distaste, Reed stood as Alex approached the booth and held out his hand. Alex's grip was firm and brief. At least the politician had a decent handshake.

They sat, and the waitress immediately hurried over to take their order.

Alex ordered a regular coffee, black, and the combo breakfast. Reed already had his coffee, but he did the same.

"Have we met before?" Alex asked. "You look awfully familiar."

"No, we haven't met." From somewhere, Reed mustered a casual smile. "But my brother and I looked like identical twins. A lot of people had trouble telling us apart."

Alex acknowledged that statement with a dip of his chin. Reed concealed his bitterness that the other man didn't even acknowledge Tim, especially since Alex had shot Tim in cold blood.

To cover his reaction, Reed took a deep drink of his coffee.

"I did a little background research on you," Alex said.

Despite expecting this, Reed stiffened. Forcing himself to relax, he nodded. "Then you know I spent three years in prison. Yes. For murdering my own brother." Staring the other man down, Reed crossed his arms. "Eventually I was acquitted for lack of evidence."

"So how have you been?" Alex leaned forward, his gaze shrewd as he studied Reed. "Are you finding it any easier transitioning from prison to civilian life?"

Careful to hide the flash of white-hot rage at the question asked by the man who'd not only put him there, but murdered his brother, Reed shrugged. "Not really. Why all the questions? I didn't come here to talk about me."

"I like to know who I'm dealing with."

The waitress brought their coffees. Alex took a drink of his, blotting the corner of his mouth with a paper napkin. "Let's cut to the chase. You know, of course, about the reward."

Reed nodded. "It's not enough."

To his surprise, Alex laughed. "Of course it's not. So tell me. Why do you think you can help me find Kaitlyn? Has she contacted you in any way?" His voice was casual. Too casual.

"No, of course not." Reed took a deep breath, meeting Alex's gaze directly. "But then, how could she, since she's been abducted?"

Alex's smile never wavered. Reed found himself wanting to wipe the smug look off the politician's face.

"Maybe the kidnappers let her make a phone call," Alex came back smoothly.

He was good, Reed would give him that. But this might just be Reed's chance to prove he was better.

Alex leaned back in his seat, elegant fingers curled around his coffee cup. A largish diamond ring winked from his pinky. "I agreed to meet you because you told me you had a good reason to believe you could find my Kaitlyn. Now let's hear it. You'd better not be wasting my time."

Taking another deliberately slow drink, Reed knew he'd have to be careful with what he planned to say next. The right delivery would be absolutely crucial. "Because I don't believe Kaitlyn was abducted. I think she ran off with someone."

The other man's entire expression hardened before he smoothed it back out. Still, rage flashed in the back of his eyes. "Explain." Cold death frosted together in his voice.

"I know Kaitlyn well. Very well." He swallowed, praying the lie slipped easily from his tongue. "After all, back when she was dating my brother, she and I were lovers behind his back. She always likes to have a guy on the side."

Alex stared at him, his patrician features a mask of ice. "She never mentioned anything like that to me."

Reed didn't reply, giving it a minute until the other man realized the implications of his words.

Cursing, Alex looked away. A muscle worked in his cheek. Reed waited while his enemy got a grip on his apparently powerful emotions.

After a moment, Alex pick up his coffee and took a long drink, as if the cup contained whiskey. When he finished, he set it down carefully and then met Reed's gaze. "What do you get out of this?"

Since Reed knew Alex would expect Reed to have a similar nature, Reed let a slow smile cross his face. "Payment, of course," he said. "More than that stupid reward. If I get Kaitlyn back for you, it's going to cost you."

Alex didn't even blink. "How much? Name your price."

Now for the game changer. It would either work or it wouldn't. If not, Reed knew he'd have to go back to plan B.

"I don't just want money." He spoke slowly and deliberately.

Narrowing his eyes, Alex stared him down. "Then what do you want?"

"Power and a steady revenue stream," Reed told him. "Before he died, my brother told me all about your operation. I want to be cut in on the action."

To give him credit, Alex didn't seem surprised. Nor did he waste time asking what Reed meant or deny anything. He simply nodded. "You'd have to be careful. With your criminal record, one misstep would land you right back in prison."

Reed flashed an icy smile. "Then I'll have to make sure I don't make a mistake, won't I?"

"Done." Apparently making an instant decision, Alex held out his hand. "You help me find Kaitlyn—and when I take care of her lover, I'm going to make it look like he kidnapped her—I'll get you set up in charge of your own area."

Deliberately vague. Reed decided not to press for specifics, especially since he knew there was no way in hell Alex planned to give him a single damn thing other than a bullet in the head when all this had finished. Reed would have become too big of a liability, especially to someone who was looking to broaden his political career.

Reed would have to be very, very cautious from this point on.

"Agreed." They shook hands.

"First thing I need to do is take a look at where she was living," Reed said, pitching his low voice with just the right amount of urgency.

The other man didn't even blink. "When?"

Bingo. Keeping his expression neutral, Reed shrugged. "I don't know. As soon as possible."

"How about now?"

Full of nervous worry, Kaitlyn didn't know what to do with herself. She'd played with Bentley, fed him and taken him outside. Twice. She'd rummaged in the tiny kitchen, put together enough ingredients to make a small pot of beef stew, which now simmered on the stovetop, filling the cabin with a delicious aroma.

She wasn't sure if she'd be able to eat it. Knowing Reed was meeting with Alex at this very moment made her feel queasy. In fact, she was pretty sure if she tried to force something down, her stomach would rebel and throw it right back up.

Once again, she felt as if she would suffocate, even though she tried to convince herself that being confined didn't equal being trapped. But that was what she felt like. A sitting duck. Even though she knew this place was safe.

She prayed Reed's plan worked. If he could get Alex to trust him enough to maybe video or tape a confession, they'd be on their way to winning.

Unfortunately, Alex didn't get to his position by being stupid or careless. Or nice. She knew it wouldn't be that easy.

Attempting to tame her agitation, she turned the tiny old television on. A talk show had just started, and she picked up Bentley and settled on the couch to try and watch.

At least this time, Alex Ramirez wasn't a guest. Petting her small dog, she sat up straight as they announced the topic of that day. Men—and women—who'd been falsely imprisoned and how this had affected them long after they'd been released.

Since this might help give her some insight into Reed's emotions, she paid close attention.

"Oddly enough," one of the women said. "I felt incredibly guilty, as if the entire thing was somehow my fault."

Kaitlyn shook her head. While she could identify and relate to what the woman felt, she doubted Reed felt the same way.

Next, the camera panned on one of the men. A tall, lanky man, he radiated calm confidence. When the talk show host asked him if he'd felt guilt, he said no. "I was angry. Furious, actually. Not only had the system dropped the ball big-time, but it felt like the entire world—my country, my family and my friends—had failed me. I refused to see anyone, talk to anyone. After the anger burned itself out, I wanted to be left alone." He swallowed, then lifted his chin and looked directly at the camera. "I wanted to die."

The host smiled sympathetically. "I understand," she said.

"No." He turned and glanced dismissively at her. "You don't. I had no criminal record, in fact, I'd never broken a law in my life. And then, due to sloppy law enforcement and a bad lawyer, I ended up behind bars, locked in with a bunch of hardened criminals. Talk about a wakeup call. I lost faith in everyone and everything. I've been out five years and honestly, I still don't trust anyone."

Leaning forward, the host kept an insincere smile plastered on her bright red lips. "How long were you in prison?" As if she didn't know.

"Too long." With a rueful grimace, the man uncoiled himself from the couch. Standing, he towered over the seated host and the other guests.

Kaitlyn held her breath. To their credit, none of the guests seemed alarmed, though he must have seemed menacing. Oh, wait, she spotted the tiniest tick in the corner of one of the polished host's heavily mascaraed eye.

The man removed the microphone clipped to the lapel of his shirt. Then, he held it in front of him. "I'm sorry. This was a mistake. I never should have agreed to do this." Then he handed the microphone to the host and strode off the set.

The show instantly went to commercial. Stunned, Kaitlyn reached for the remote and clicked the television off. She'd seen enough.

The man reminded her a lot of Reed. And now she understood a lot better the reason for his reluctance to trust.

She couldn't blame him. Especially since she herself felt much the same way.

Though Reed had known Alex Ramirez had money, he could not help being impressed at his first glimpse of the man's massive home. No, *home* was too small of a word. *Mansion* would be a better description.

First there had been huge, wrought-iron gates with

a scrolled letter *R* on each of them. Alex opened those with a remote control and, once they were inside, closed them the same way.

Alex had insisted Reed ride there with him. For security reasons, he'd said. Though Reed didn't like the idea—he wouldn't have an escape route—he had no choice but to go along.

Stopping the car for effect, Alex turned in his seat and eyed Reed. "Not only did I design it, but I had it built. I even had stone flown over from Italy, wood from Greece and various other materials from France."

Reed nodded, hoping he appeared suitably impressed. At first glance, the huge edifice resembled an ancient church. But the longer he looked at it, the place appeared to be something out of a horror movie set in Transylvania.

With an effort, he kept himself from laughing out loud at the thought.

"Very impressive," he said, since Alex appeared to be waiting for a response before putting the car back in Drive.

"It is, isn't it?" Sounding smug, Alex seemed satisfied. He drove up the long, winding drive slowly, as though he wanted to make sure Reed got the full impact of the perfectly manicured hedges and colorful flower gardens framing the massive, stone monstrosity of a house. There were statues and fountains interspersed with the plants. Oddly enough, it looked more like a presidential estate in a developing country than a wealthy politician's home. But then again, Reed supposed he had no idea what other politicians' homes looked like.

The instant Alex's Jaguar coasted up to the house, the front door opened and two men in uniforms rushed outside and down the marble steps. Exactly as if they were the doorman and bellhop at a luxury hotel.

One hurried around to open Alex's door, the other Reed's. Alex barely even acknowledged them. Instead, he bounded up the sweeping staircase and paused to wait for Reed, while indicating the double mahogany front doors with a dramatic flourish. *"Mi casa,"* he said, grinning proudly.

From that, Reed deduced Alex had not come from a moneyed background. If he had, he would have been blasé, acting as if all this grandeur was perfectly normal.

Instead, he was like a child eager to show off a new bicycle, except on a much larger scale. Reed wondered if Alex considered himself a self-made millionaire. He supposed he could, since drugs and money laundering, extortion and murder had all had a hand in obtaining his wealth.

When he thought of all this, the sight of the place made Reed feel queasy. Lifting his head, he tried his best to appear awestruck.

As they approached the heavy twin doors, they swung open as smoothly as if they were kept oiled. Two more uniformed servants stood at attention. Ahead of them, another staircase curved up on both sides of an open foyer. Reed half expected an entire crowd of domestic help to come swarming down them, welcoming their employer home.

Of course that didn't happen. Reed didn't know whether to be relieved or disappointed.

Alex glanced at his Rolex watch. "I can have someone show you around, if you'd like."

"Sure." Reed shrugged. "That'd be great."

Narrowing his eyes, Alex signaled to one of the male

servants. "Geraldo here will give you a tour. If you need anything, I'll be in my office."

And Reed was dismissed.

He turned to Geraldo, who stood at attention as though waiting for Reed to give him an order. Reed smiled, hoping to put the other man at ease. "I'd like to see Kaitlyn's room," he said, only to be met with a blank stare.

Then, while Reed watched, the other man took out a cell phone and made a quick call.

Chapter 10

Since Reed didn't speak Spanish, he couldn't follow the conversation. At least he recognized Kaitlyn's name, which meant the other man had to ask for permission to show Reed her room. Strange. Unless, for some reason, Alex had ordered that no one help Reed. This made no sense, but then in the man's bizarre world of delusions and lies, Reed wouldn't be surprised.

While Kaitlyn had told him exactly how to find her room, he couldn't just go upstairs, turn left and find the third room down the hall on the right. Especially since he had no doubt he was being watched like a hawk.

He'd just have to be careful not to do anything to attract interest. He had to get Alex to trust him. He imagined this would take a while, unless he could pull off something spectacular.

Geraldo ended his call.

"Well?" Reed asked. "Can you show me where Kaitlyn stayed?"

Glancing quickly over his shoulder as if to see if someone was watching him, Geraldo quickly nodded. *"Sí."*

After a second, narrow-eyed look, Geraldo complied, hurrying toward the staircase. Reed followed, noting the expensive-looking paintings hanging on the wall all the way up.

Once they reached the landing at the top, Geraldo turned right rather than left. Since he couldn't correct him, Reed had no choice but to follow along. This made no sense. If Alex wanted Reed to help find Kaitlyn, what was the purpose of keeping him from seeing her room?

Of course, if Alex was as warped as Kaitlyn claimed, he might enjoy watching Reed twist and turn for a while.

Paranoid? Maybe. Either way, Reed knew he'd have to be careful and watch his back at all times.

Geraldo led him to what appeared to be a guest bedroom. Utterly devoid of personality, there was nothing personal anywhere. No knickknacks or pictures, nothing to indicate anyone had spent time in the room.

Reed crossed to the closet and opened the double doors. Empty, as he'd expected.

"No." Turning and facing Geraldo, Reed shook his head. "This is not Kaitlyn's room."

Unsurprisingly, the other man appeared nervous. A fine bead of sweat glossed his upper lip. "No understand," he said.

"Fine." Reed decided to quit wasting his time. "Go away. I'll find her room myself."

A minute later, as if he had cameras on them (which he probably did), Alex appeared in the doorway. He glided into the room, his manicured eyebrows raised. "Is there a problem?"

Reed glared at him. "If you don't want my help, why not just say so?"

To give him credit, Alex didn't bother pretending not to know what Reed meant. Instead, he glanced at his employee and jerked his thumb toward the doorway. "Geraldo, you can go."

Head down, Geraldo hurried out.

Reed waited until the other man had left before speaking again. "What's up with this? I simply asked to see Kaitlyn's room. Instead, your employee takes me here."

Alex watched him closely. "How do you know this isn't her room?"

"This isn't anyone's room." Reed let his disgust show. "Clearly, it's a guest room or something. There's not one single touch of a woman's personality in here."

"Touché." Inclining his head, Alex gestured. "Follow me."

They went back toward the main staircase, crossing to the correct side of the building. Alex paused before the third room on the right and, digging a key from his pants pocket, unlocked the door.

Interesting. Reed didn't comment on why the other man felt the need to keep her room locked up tight. Instead, he waited patiently as Alex opened the door and stood aside for Reed to enter.

"Aren't you coming?"

Alex shook his head. "No. I find being in there among her things too painful. I'll leave you to look around. Once you've finished, just say my name and I'll come back and lock up."

"Say your name?" Reed frowned. Then he saw the

camera high up in the corner of the room. "Surveillance?"

"Exactly." Sounding satisfied, Alex left, closing the door behind him.

Slightly unnerved—but really, had he expected anything less—Reed slowly surveyed the space. There were bright spots of vivid color, interspersed with a lot of white. He guessed Kaitlyn had brought the color, while Alex or his interior designer, had wanted white.

The closet contained a full wardrobe of women's clothes. As far as he could tell, the outfits ranged from sexy to nearly naked, with nothing in between. Rows of shoes, mostly stiletto heels that appeared to be at least four to five inches tall, lined the bottom of the closet. No wonder she hadn't taken anything from here.

He moved to the dresser, opening the top drawer, half expecting to find a bunch of lacy panties or some other such thing. Instead, the drawer, along with most of the others, was empty. Only the long drawer at the bottom, filled with lacy negligees, remained full.

He got it. She'd left everything that made her feel like Alex's toy. He couldn't blame her. He also couldn't help picturing her wearing some of the frilly wisps of nothing.

No. Focus. He had to make Alex think he was trying to help recapture Kaitlyn.

A large, freestanding jewelry box occupied a place of honor against the wall between the bed and the bathroom. Opening one side, he discovered several sparkling necklaces, with matching bracelets and earrings in the top portion and drawers. Stunned, he stared. Apparently Alex had spent a small fortune in diamonds. Kaitlyn had taken none of them, even though Reed knew she could have used the money.

Bile rose in his throat. He swallowed it back, refusing to look at the camera, well aware Alex no doubt watched to make sure Reed didn't pocket any of the valuables.

"I'm just looking for clues," he said out loud, looking directly at the camera.

Crossing to the nightstand, he pulled open the drawer and gave the insides a cursory look. Socks, exactly as Kaitlyn had said. He didn't touch anything, just closed the drawer and opened the one below it. More socks.

Finally, he got on the floor and peered under the bed. Plastic boxes, packed neatly, took up every inch of available space. He slid one out, noted the sweaters and winter clothes packed inside, and put it back. Kaitlyn had left almost everything Alex had bought her. Reed couldn't help but wonder if the other man realized the significance of such an action.

Climbing back to his feet, Reed dusted his hands on his jeans and took one final survey of the room. Almost immediately, Geraldo appeared in the doorway, motioning him to follow.

Now what?

Geraldo led him to what appeared to be Alex's office. More dark wood, expensive-looking artwork and upholstered chairs. The man himself sat at a huge, mahogany desk and didn't at first acknowledge Reed's entrance.

So Reed waited. This was going pretty much the way he'd figured. No trust, and just enough rope to hang himself, if he so desired. Which he did not.

Finally, Alex looked up, his brown eyes flat and cold. "Did you find what you were looking for?"

Pretending not to notice the anger vibrating in the other man's voice, Reed shrugged. "I wasn't really looking for anything specific. Just hoping to find a clue, something to tell me where she might have gone."

"And did you?"

Reed got the distinct impression Alex was toying with him. But if that were the case, he figured he'd already be dead. Or imprisoned.

"No," he admitted, hoping he sounded sheepish. "But I'll find her. It would help if you had a list of her friends."

"She had no friends."

"Okay." Since he had to feign ignorance, he went ahead. "That's a little strange. Why is that?"

Jaw clenched, Alex shook his head. "She always used to tell me I was all she needed. You'd better find her."

"I will. Just give me time."

Eyes glinting, Alex dismissed him with a nod. "On your way out, make sure and leave your name at the gate. I'll approve you. That way you can come and go as you please."

Reed stifled a jolt of elation. "Thank you."

"Yeah." Looking up, Alex's hard stare wasn't friendly. "Just remember, you'll always be watched. Got that?"

"Got it."

Geraldo touched his arm and Reed turned to follow him back to the foyer. Two men waited. One of them opened the front door, the other took off where Geraldo had stopped and followed Reed outside and down the marble steps. He waited while Reed got in his truck and started the engine.

He continued to stand there as Reed drove off. Reed watched him in his rearview mirror, wondering if the man planned to wait until the front gates opened and Reed drove away.

Thoroughly paranoid now, Reed didn't go straight

home. Though he didn't see anyone following him, he wouldn't be surprised if Alex hadn't put some sort of tracker or bug on his truck.

What he couldn't figure out was why the other man had even asked him to help, when it was perfectly clear he suspected Reed of something.

Of course, trying to evade anyone following him made no sense, either. Alex would already know where Reed lived. In fact, that certainty was why he'd made sure Kaitlyn was tucked away someplace safe.

It was only the first day and even if he hadn't known the truth, he wouldn't have trusted the man.

Patience, he told himself. He'd known he would have to work to gain the other man's trust. It would be a simple matter of getting him to confess and recording it. Then it would be a simple matter of sending that video to every media outlet they could find. Once that happened, law enforcement would have no choice but to investigate.

Such solitude and the opportunity to commune with nature should have been a welcome respite. Kaitlyn knew she should use this opportunity as a chance to get her thoughts together and her priorities straight.

But now that Reed had gone, the restlessness plaguing her had intensified and changed. To her surprise, she really missed Reed. The thought of him at Alex's mercy made her skin crawl.

In her three years of captivity, she'd spent a lot of time planning what she'd do once she got free. Now, instead of longing to be free to come and go where she wanted, she ached to hear the sexy timbre of Reed's voice as they spoke over coffee, to see the way his eyes crinkled when he laughed, and more. So much more.

In a way, making love with him had healed her. With his touch, his kiss, he'd taken away the brutality she'd suffered at Alex's hands. He'd returned her to herself, and made her see she could still find pleasure at a man's hands.

Reed had given this back to her without even trying. For that, she'd be forever grateful.

Even though she doubted their coming together had meant as much to him, it didn't matter. Once this was over, Reed would never want to see her again. She couldn't blame him. For her, he was a symbol of the future. For him, she was a tie to the past.

A day went by, and then another with no word from Reed. Refusing to let isolation make her stir-crazy, she watched a lot of television and taught herself to knit. If she didn't have Bentley for company, she didn't know what she would have done.

At night, she cuddled her little dog and tried to sleep. She found it impossible, and she'd taken to writing in her journal, a spiral notebook she'd brought with her from her time in captivity. In it, she'd started out documenting all the horrible things Alex had done to her. She didn't dare go back and read those pages. Too much darkness there. She wanted to go forward instead.

That night, with the light of the full moon filling her room with silver, she tossed and turned for hours before finally falling asleep.

Bentley barked, a tiny yap of warning. Kaitlyn instantly came awake. Heart pounding, she sat up and listened. Had someone found her again?

Thunder rumbled in the distance and she realized a storm had awakened Bentley. Her little dog turned to look at her, then burrowed deeper into the sheets.

The wind picked up as the thunder grew louder. When the first drops of rain hit the tin roof, Bentley shuddered. But to Kaitlyn, the sound was delightful. She lay on her back, watching the flashes of light illuminate the room, taking comfort in the sound of rain and the ominous boom of thunder.

But then lightning struck, too close, the instant crack of thunder shaking the earth.

Then she smelled smoke.

"Oh, no." Grabbing up Bentley, she wrapped the sheet around herself and headed toward the front door. Praying lightning had just struck a tree, she pushed open the front door. Rain lashed her as she squinted out into the darkness, looking for a fire and seeing nothing but water.

A second later, another jagged bolt of lightning lit up the area. As far as she could tell in that instant of illumination, everything looked okay. If there had been something burning, apparently the rain had put it out.

She turned to go back inside and realized the cabin roof was on fire.

Heart pounding, she held on to Bentley and did a quick search for a fire extinguisher. She located one on the floor near the kitchen, grabbed it up and tried to make it work. But something jammed or it was old, she didn't know, and nothing happened. Instead, she grabbed her duffel bag, crammed her journal inside and headed for the door. Making sure she had her new cell phone tucked into her bag, she climbed on board the ATV and muttered a quick prayer it would start.

When she turned the key and the engine roared to life, relief flooded her. Even though the ATV had a headlight, the sideways sheets of wind-driven rain made visibility poor. Now she just had to hope she could make it down the hill without turning over her ride.

Luckily, years of four-wheeling as a teenager helped. Though she and Bentley were drenched and her dog had turned into a quivering lump of fear, she went slowly. Behind her, the cabin continued to burn. Apparently even the rain couldn't keep pace with the flames.

Now what? She couldn't call Reed, not with him trying to befriend Alex. Not only that, but she didn't have his number. Though the momentary impulse to simply disappear had her clenching her teeth, she knew she and Reed had come too far for her to do that to him.

She didn't want to call 911—assuming there even was such an emergency service out here in the country— because doing so might alert Alex or his henchmen. So her only choice would be to phone Brock and Zoe and see what they thought she should do. She pulled out her phone, trying to keep it sheltered from the rain with her hand, but she had no signal. Great. Just great.

The storm continued to batter her, refusing to abate even when she reached the paved road. She needed to find temporary shelter, but as far as she could tell, there were no other structures out in this vast, open space. Which meant she—and Bentley—were sitting ducks out in the open.

Keeping to the shoulder of the road, every time lightning flashed, she tried to scan the landscape for a shed, a lean-to, something.

Finally, she saw something. It appeared to be a rickety, abandoned barn. But part of it still had a roof and it sat tucked into a small valley between two rises of land. She drove the ATV right inside, killing the engine and briefly leaving the headlight on while she checked out her surroundings. She knew she didn't dare leave it on too long and risk draining the battery, but she had to make sure she wasn't sharing the space with a bobcat or coyote.

Satisfied, she flicked the light off. Still cradling her shivering, wet dog, she climbed off. Keeping her back against the ATV, she lowered herself to the ground and prepared to ride out the stormy night.

The storm continued eastward and by the time the sun made an appearance, the cloudless sky predicted a warm day. Standing, every bone in her body aching, Kaitlyn wrung out her clothes as best she could. She took Bentley outside, keeping an eye on him as the little dog toddled off to take care of business.

Now what? Her stomach growled, reminding her she hadn't eaten in a while. Cold, wet and hungry, but at least she was alive.

Checking her phone, this time she saw she had one bar of signal strength. Maybe that would be enough.

Praying silently, she punched in the number and hit Send. Static cracked on the line. Then, to her relief, Zoe picked up on the third ring. "I need help," Kaitlyn said. "Can you pick me up?"

"Sure." Zoe didn't even hesitate. "Same place?"

Kaitlyn glanced around. "No. I'm…I'm not sure where I am exactly. Down the road. There was a storm and lightning and a fire…"

Silence while Zoe digested this. "Are you okay?"

"Yes. I'm going to head back up there now. I'll meet you there."

"I'm on my way," Zoe said. "I just need to let Brock know. I'll make sure I'm not followed."

"Thank you so much. And, Zoe?" Kaitlyn swallowed. "Please be careful."

Aware Zoe would have to drive at least a couple of hours, Kaitlyn grabbed Bentley and started the ATV. She'd go back to the cabin and see if there was anything she could salvage while waiting.

Once she got out onto the road, she realized she didn't recognize any landmarks. Continuing slowly back the way she'd come, she almost cried out with relief when she spotted the rutted, pitted track going up the hill. Since the ground was wet, she had to be careful if she wanted to avoid getting stuck.

Somehow, she made it all the way to the top. As she'd feared, the cabin lay in charred ruins. While the rain must have finally put the fire out, enough of the place had burned to make it unusable.

Sad, she poked through the rubble, unable to locate anything even remotely salvageable.

Bentley found a spot in the sun and stretched out. After a moment, Kaitlyn decided to do the same.

She must have fallen asleep. The sound of a car horn and Bentley's barking woke her. Scrambling to her feet, she grabbed her dog and headed down the hill on foot. When she spotted Zoe's truck, she had to blink back tears.

"I'm so glad you're all right!" Zoe cried, enveloping Kaitlyn in a hug the moment she got out of the truck. "I am looking so forward to having you—and your pet—hanging out with us."

"I don't want to put you in danger," Kaitlyn protested.

"Nonsense. The FBI has already paid us a visit. No one else has any reason to think you'd stay with us. You'll be safe. Now get in."

Smiling, Kaitlyn complied. "I don't have my disguise," she said. "Reed didn't see any need for it out here."

"That's fine." Zoe gave her an appraising look before putting the truck in Drive. "Your hair color is different and if you just lay low and stay inside for a while, you should be safe."

Kaitlyn nodded, still unsure but deciding to keep that to herself. "Have you heard from Reed?"

"No." Gripping the steering wheel with both hands, Zoe focused on keeping the truck on the deeply rutted road. "But I'm sure he's fine. He's only been gone a few days."

"A few days with Alex is an eternity," Kaitlyn said. "I can't thank you enough for helping me."

Smiling, Zoe cast her a sideways glance. "That's what friends are for."

Once they neared the Anniversary city limits, Kaitlyn sunk down in the seat. "I'm going to put my head down while you drive through town."

"Good idea. No sense in taking any chances."

Once they reach Brock and Zoe's place, Zoe parked right next to the garage door. "Wait until I have it unlocked and then you and Bentley can dash inside."

Kaitlyn nodded. Despite glancing up and down the street and making sure the coast was clear, her heart was pounding madly as she ran from the truck to the house.

"There you go." Pride rang in Zoe's voice. "Let me show you where you'll be staying."

The guest room was decorated in a bright, cheerful motif. "I love it," Kaitlyn said, smiling at her friend. "Again, I can't thank you enough for—"

"Stop." Zoe shushed her with a touch on the arm. "There's a guest bathroom right down the hall. I bet you'd love a shower."

"That bad, am I?" Not waiting for an answer, Kaitlyn sighed. "You're right, though. I would love a shower."

"I've got to go back to the feed store," Zoe said. "There are sandwich fixings in the fridge, plus stuff to make a salad if you'd rather have that. Are you going to be all right?"

"Of course. Please don't let me keep you from anything."

"You won't. We've got to try and appear as normal as possible so no one suspects anything." Zoe eyed Bentley. "I'll bring home some dog food for him. Any particular brand?"

"Whatever you think is best. I've got a little cash, so I can pay you for it."

Shaking her head, Zoe walked away. "I'll see you later."

After getting cleaned up, Zoe ate a ham-and-cheese sandwich. She fed Bentley some ham, too, which thrilled him. She wasn't sure what time Brock and Zoe came home from working at their feed store, but she wanted to be as unobtrusive as possible.

Still exhausted, she thought she'd just take a nap. She took Bentley out back and then went to her room and closed the door. She stripped down to a large T-shirt. Sliding into the clean, crisp sheets felt like an unimaginable luxury.

Before she could count to ten, she went fast asleep.

When she next opened her eyes, the room was dark. A quick glance at her nightstand clock revealed it was after 11:00 p.m. She'd clearly missed Brock and Zoe coming home, and dinner too. Bentley woofed softly, staring at the bedroom window. Instantly alert, she scooped him up and held him close. "Shhh."

And then she listened.

A shower of pebbles gently rained on her window.

Pebbles? Pushing away her alarm, she shook her head. Bad guys didn't toss pebbles. Still holding Bentley, she threw back the covers and padded to the window.

Reed stood outside, about to toss another small handful of tiny rocks at her window. When he saw her, he waved.

Worried, she waved back. As she worked the locks and opened her window, she was glad her room faced the back of the house, away from the street.

"What are you doing?" she whispered. "This can't be safe."

"I need to talk to you. Come out," he urged. "And leave your little dog inside."

Immediately Bentley whined in protest, as if he understood.

"Just a minute," she told Reed. Placing Bentley on her bed, she patted his head and then gently covered him with the sheet. "You wait here, boy. I'll be right back."

To her amazement, the little dog huffed and turned a circle twice, before settling down with a sigh.

Good enough. Heart stuttering in her chest, worried and thrilled all at once, she hurried back over to the window. Swinging her bare leg over the sash and tugging her T-shirt to stay securely covered, she climbed out and dropped to the ground.

In the moonlight, Reed looked darkly mysterious and sexy as hell. She figured he had an important reason for driving all the way back to Anniversary and contacting her in the middle of the night.

"What's up?" Trying to keep her voice from quavering, she winced as she realized she was breathless. "Is everything all right?"

"I should be asking the same of you. Brock told me what happened at the cabin."

"I survived," she said, determined to downplay that. "What about you? How's your plan going with Alex?"

"He let me inside his mansion," he said, jamming his hands down into his pockets. "I need a little help, anything you can tell me that might make it easier. He still doesn't trust me."

"He doesn't trust anyone."

"Yeah. He has cameras everywhere. Not to mention all the large goons he calls his employees."

She nodded, unable to suppress an involuntary shudder. "Those men are the dregs of society. Some of them are bounty hunters, others criminals he's gotten out of prison in exchange for their loyalty."

"Good to know." He sounded pleased. "What about the household help? Most of them only speak Spanish."

"Family," she answered promptly. "Alex is a strong believer in helping family."

"I see." He nodded. "I've just got to come up with something that will make him consider trusting me."

"Tell him you heard from someone. Make up a name. Say they told you they'd seen me and you were going to check it out."

"And then what? How is that going to help?"

She considered. "I didn't take any of the jewelry Alex bought me, but I did take this." Slowly, she pulled a long chain from under her blouse. "It was my mother's. Alex knows I never take it off."

Holding out her hand, she dropped it into his palm.

"Take it. If you show this to him, he'll have no choice but to believe that you're on my trail."

"Thank you." He tucked the necklace into his pocket. "Anything else?"

Every time his gaze met hers, a shiver tickled her spine. She wished she had the right to ask him to hold her, to take what little comfort she could in his presence. Especially since she didn't know how long it would be before she saw him again.

"Are you cold?" He stepped closer.

Ashamed and not wanting him to realize her crazy, needy thoughts, she shrugged and attempted to feign indifference. "The breeze is a bit chilly, that's all."

Though the wind came from the south, he didn't comment. Instead, he dropped his gaze from her eyes to her breasts, already pebbled with unwarranted excitement.

Desire heated her skin. The breeze gently lifted the edge of her T-shirt, reminding her she was completely naked underneath. She waited for the familiar fear to paralyze her, but she felt nothing but an aching sort of need.

"Kaitlyn." Gently, he lifted a tendril of hair away from her face. Her breath caught in her throat. Every fiber of her being felt electrified as she waited to see what he'd do next.

Chapter 11

He moved his fingers to her shoulder. Kaitlyn fought the urge to arch her back to show him where she wanted his touch. He hadn't come for this, and they'd both admitted the other time had been a mistake.

Yet for the life of her, she couldn't find the words to tell him no. Truth be told, she didn't want to.

When he reached for her hand, she gave it willingly.

"Come, sit." He walked her around the backyard to a stone bench in the middle of a small rose garden. A six-foot privacy fence surrounded them, and she tried to relax, telling herself no one could see them.

He released her. "Please. Take a seat."

With a small nod, she complied. Again she took care to smooth her T-shirt down as she perched on the edge of the cool stone. The gesture gave away her nervousness, but she had to do something with her hands.

Reed remained standing, his broad-shouldered figure blocking out the moon.

"Believe it or not, I've actually sort of missed you," she said.

His smile flashed white. "Yeah, well. I actually kind of got used to having you around."

Which she guessed was as close as he'd get to saying he'd missed her, too. She nearly smiled back, then sensed she was treading on dangerous ground. He'd made it quite clear that their relationship would stay platonic, two people helping each other get what they wanted. The passion between them had been a mistake, and she knew he'd never understand how much his touch had healed her.

"Where's your truck?" she asked, trying to get back on normal footing.

"I parked a block over and walked here." His arch look told her he knew exactly what she was trying to do. "That way I knew for sure I wasn't followed."

Chest tight, she nodded. He'd never know how beautiful she found everything about him, from his shock of thick, dark hair, to the muscles that rippled under his T-shirt every time he moved. The inherent strength in his features, the calm confidence he carried with him made him devastatingly handsome.

And dangerous to her equilibrium.

"Why are you really here, Reed? Were you able to make any real progress with Alex?"

"Not yet." His voice rang with confidence. "But I will. It's only a matter of time."

She refused to allow herself to be swayed. "But you put yourself in danger. Both of us, not to mention Zoe and Brock. I don't understand why—"

"I wanted to make sure you were all right," he interrupted, sounding quietly furious. "I was careful. I took precautions. Kaitlyn, I don't understand, but I couldn't stop thinking about you. I… Oh, hell."

His mouth covered hers, his kiss hungry and hot as he pulled her up against him.

Then, just as abruptly as the kiss had begun, it ended. His expression fierce, he glanced away, swallowing hard. "No," he said. "That's not why I came here. Actually, I need to apologize to you."

Confused and aroused, she gazed at him. "Apologize for what?"

"For that. For what happened before."

Ah, now she understood. "You don't have to."

"I do. You deserve better." Taking a deep breath, he shoved his hand through his hair. He appeared to be struggling to find the right words. "Kaitlyn, all your life, men have manipulated you. They wanted to own you, to possess you."

She nodded, thinking it best to hold her silence until he got out everything he wanted to say.

"I will never do that to you. No matter what."

Then she realized what he meant. Though she felt it like a stab right through her heart, she managed to smile. "I think I understand. You want to make sure I don't get the wrong impression just because we…"

"Exactly."

And to think she'd nearly bared her soul, nearly told him how much he'd helped her find her balance, her confidence.

"No worries, then. I completely understand."

He met her gaze, a muscle working in his jaw. "You came to me for help. Instead, I took advantage of you. I manipulated you when you were weak." He stepped toward her, his hands clenched at his side. "And God help me, despite that, I still want you."

"I want you, too." She barely got the words out when he turned away.

"Coming here was a mistake, I see that now." He continued to look at her, but she knew he didn't really see her. "I won't contact you again until I have something concrete to relay."

And with that, he strode away. Leaving her aching and more heart-sore than she should have been.

The next morning when she greeted Brock and Zoe at the breakfast table, she didn't say a word about Reed's visit. She'd tell them—eventually. But right now, her emotions were too raw to bring him up and attempt to sound normal.

Being around the newly married couple was another education of sorts. Brock and Zoe clearly adored each other and showed it with soulful looks and frequent, loving touches. This was how a relationship should be— could be. Kaitlyn watched wistfully, her heart full even as she found herself longing for a relationship like that with Reed.

Which was all sorts of wrong.

After they left for work, the small house felt empty. Kaitlyn spent the morning reading. She made sure to take Bentley out first and fixed herself a cup of tea before settling on the couch with a book she'd borrowed from Zoe and Brock's shelves.

"Hello? Kaitlyn, where are you?" Zoe's voice. "I could use your help."

Kaitlyn put down her book and glanced at the clock, surprised to notice several hours had passed. She hurried down the hall to the kitchen. Zoe struggled to get through the back door, carrying a large box full of fresh vegetables.

Kaitlyn opened the door and took the box from her. "What's all this?" she asked, peering inside.

"I'm on my lunch break and I stopped by the farmer's market." Zoe laughed. "I got so much good stuff that I'm going to have to start cooking more. This box is the veggies. I have another in the car full of fruit." She turned around and hurried back outside.

When she returned, she carried another cardboard box, overflowing with apples, oranges, pears, peaches and other fruits. She set it on the counter, grinning while Kaitlyn closed the back door. Lifting a plump nectarine from the box, Kaitlyn inspected it. "All this looks amazing."

Zoe beamed. "Thank you. I got a little carried away, but we are going to be eating healthy for sure."

Nodding, Kaitlyn helped Zoe put away the produce, handing her the little plastic bags so she could stow in the fridge. When they'd finished, Zoe dusted off her hands and smiled at Kaitlyn. "Thank you for the help."

"You're welcome. I have to ask, though, is something wrong? Wouldn't you usually be at work right now?"

"Wel-l-l-l..." Zoe's smile widened. "It's been a little slow and I'm tired of taking my lunch at my desk. Since you're here, I think I might start coming home for lunch. It's got to be lonely and boring hanging out here all by yourself."

Kaitlyn blinked. The other woman's kindness touched her. "It is. But I don't want to inconvenience you."

"Pshaw." Zoe waved away her objections, her perfect red nail polish glinting in the bright light. "I can use a break."

"And I could use a friend." Impulsively, Kaitlyn hugged her. "Thank you so much. I appreciate you more than you know. To prove it, if you'll be coming home at the same time each day, I can make sure lunch is made."

Zoe's eyes widened. "Now that sounds amazing. I have a limited repertoire as a cook."

"I'm actually pretty good. Give me a minute and I'll put something together." Kaitlyn allowed her happiness to show. "It might be simple, but it will be tasty, I promise you."

Zoe followed her into the kitchen. "So you like to cook?"

Before Alex had captured her, Kaitlyn had considered making a career out of it. Now she just didn't know. "I love it. It's one of the few talents I possess."

Less than ten minutes later, Kaitlyn had put together a rudimentary lunch using ingredients she found in the cupboard.

"That smells fantastic." Pulling out a chair, Zoe dropped into it. "All the more so because I'm so hungry."

Kaitlyn dished up their tomato soup and grilled three-cheese sandwiches and took the seat opposite Zoe. "Me, too," she said. "Tomorrow I'll put together some salads."

Zoe took a bite and rolled her eyes. "This is amazing."

"Thanks." Kaitlyn dug in also. "I used all three of the cheeses you had, and that wonderful multigrain bread."

Both women went silent as they ate.

"Have you heard from Reed?" Zoe asked after finishing her sandwich and most of her soup.

"Actually, yes." Stirring her steaming soup, Kaitlyn

didn't bother to hide her despair. "He came to see me last night."

"What?" Zoe put down her spoon and stared. "When? Why didn't you say anything?"

Kaitlyn gave her an amended version of what had transpired, completely leaving out the kiss and Reed's vow that they'd never come together again.

"Wow." Zoe gave her a long look. "He sure went through a lot of trouble just to tell you he'd been inside Alex's house."

"I don't know. I was worried since it'd been over a week since he contacted Alex," Kaitlyn said. "I was about to ask you if he and Brock had spoken."

"They haven't." Zoe still sounded thoughtful. "Seriously, I think it's very interesting that Reed came to see you in the middle of the night like that. What time was it anyway?"

"After eleven. But he did it that way so no one would follow him."

"I see." Clearly unconvinced, Zoe picked up her spoon and tackled the rest of her soup. "Are you sure there's nothing else going on between the two of you?" Her casual tone fooled no one.

"I'm sure." Again, Kaitlyn struggled to remain expressionless. Time to change the subject. "I don't know if it's a good sign or a bad one that Alex hasn't been on the news or any talk shows lately."

Zoe laughed. "Be grateful for small blessings, right?"

"I guess." Kaitlyn worried her bottom lip between her teeth. "Though to tell the truth, his absence from the public spotlight makes me worry more about Reed."

Putting down her sandwich, Zoe eyed her closely.

"Despite what you won't say, you really care about Reed, don't you?"

Kaitlyn could feel her face heating. "I barely know him anymore," she hedged.

"That's not really an answer." Zoe smiled gently. "But in a way, I think it is. You do know him, hon. You knew him when you were dating Tim. I was in New York when all of that happened," Zoe said. "Tim's murder, Reed's conviction, all of it."

Kaitlyn gave a slight nod and took a sudden interest in polishing off her sandwich. Zoe's light touch on her arm startled her.

"Look, I know what it's like to want something you can't have. I nearly lost Brock." Zoe's caramel eyes filled with tears. She blotted them with her napkin, and continued. "I was afraid and I nearly let my fear ruin both our lives."

"Afraid?" Kaitlyn blinked. "I'm sorry, but what were you afraid of? Was it because you didn't want to leave your life in New York and move back to Anniversary?"

"Partly. And also, I believed Brock deserved better than me."

"Better than you? You two are perfect for each other. I don't understand."

Zoe took a deep breath. "I can't have children. A man like Brock deserves children of his own. I didn't want him to give that up for me."

Kaitlyn didn't know what to say. "I'm sorry."

"It's okay. I've learned to accept it. Especially since it turned out he'd rather have a life with me and possibly adopt." Zoe beamed. "Which is what we're doing. We've had our application in with an adoption agency for a month now."

"That's amazing." Kaitlyn took a deep breath. "I confess, I've had a few maternal yearnings myself. But since I'm not in a serious relationship, my focus is entirely on surviving this mess with Alex."

Zoe nodded, her expression curious. "What are your plans once all this is over?"

"Plans?"

"Yes. What kind of work do you do?"

The question stunned Kaitlyn, mostly because she'd never thought much beyond escaping Alex and making sure he paid for his crimes. But Zoe was right. Since Kaitlyn wasn't an heiress and hadn't won the lottery, she'd have to figure out a way to earn money.

"I haven't worked since Alex captured me," Kaitlyn answered slowly. "Before that, I was assistant manager in a retail clothing store in Town East Mall, over in Mesquite. My résumé is going to have a huge gap, isn't it?"

"That's okay. You can say you worked in our feed store. Brock and I will back you up."

Kaitlyn stared. So much kindness from a woman she hadn't known since high school floored her. In fact, for a moment her throat felt so tight she couldn't speak. When she did, tears pricked the backs of her eyes. "Thank you," she said quietly. "I can't tell you how much I appreciate everything you've done for me already, and then offering to do this…"

"No worries." Zoe waved off her thanks. "You can repay me by babysitting sometime. Once Brock and I find our child, that is."

Again, her words implied a level of trust the likes of which Kaitlyn hadn't experienced in years. The fact that Zoe believed in her, had such strong faith that she'd entrust her child with her, made Kaitlyn want to weep.

Which led to yet another revelation. Apparently, the verbal and physical abuse she'd suffered during her years with Alex had affected her more than she realized. Lifting her chin, she met Zoe's gaze. "You've given me a lot to think about."

Zoe sighed, pushing her plate away. "I didn't mean to turn this into a serious and deep, time-to-examine-your-life type conversation. I'm sorry."

"That's all right. I needed to hear this. I've been living in a cage these past few years. I needed a dose of reality."

"What do you like doing? Have you ever dreamed of having a particular job?"

"I always wanted to own my own bakery," Kaitlyn admitted. "Gourmet brownies or cupcakes or something."

"There you go. You love to cook, so it's right up your alley."

"Maybe," Kaitlyn said, considering. "But opening a bakery would take a lot of capital. And money is one thing I definitely do not have."

Zoe laughed. "So start small. Make up some gourmet brownies or cakes or whatever, and take samples around to local restaurants. Set up a web page. Take phone-in orders. If you concentrate on one item and really make it wonderful, I think you'd be a big success."

Again, the confidence this bright and energetic woman had in her humbled Kaitlyn. "Thank you. I'll start thinking about working up some sort of business plan."

"Great." Getting up, Zoe carried her dishes to the sink and rinsed it. "You know what? If you make brownies or cookies, I could try selling them at the feed store for you. Kind of like a test market. What do you think?"

Kaitlyn wanted to jump up and hug Zoe again. Instead, she settled for grinning at her. "That sounds absolutely wonderful. I'll get started today. That is…" Kaitlyn swallowed. "Is it okay if I used your kitchen? And I might need some baking supplies." She ducked her head, feeling ashamed. "I don't have money to buy much right now, but I can promise to pay you back as soon as I can."

"Don't worry about it," Zoe said, shrugging. "What are you going to bake?"

"Probably brownies, though I don't know for sure yet. Before I let you take any to the store and sell them, I should practice. You and Brock can be my guinea pigs."

Zoe grinned. "Now that sounds like my kind of deal." She walked over to the pantry and opened the door. "We have flour, sugar, cocoa, baking soda, baking powder and vegetable oil. I know I just picked up a dozen eggs yesterday, and there's plenty of milk. What else do you need?"

"I'll make you a list." Kaitlyn grinned back. "I see some miniature marshmallows. Is it okay to use those?"

"Sure. Take whatever you need. The only thing I ask is if you finish off something, write it on a list so I know to buy more."

"I will." Kaitlyn rubbed her hands together, eager to begin.

"Do you need cookbooks?" Zoe asked. "Because I don't have any. When I need to find out how to make anything, I just go to the internet." She gestured toward a laptop set up on a built-in desk in the corner. "Feel free to use it. It's not password protected."

"Thanks."

"I've got to go back to work," Zoe said. "Listen, I know you're bored and I would be, too, stuck in the house all the time."

Jumping up, this time Kaitlyn hugged her. "Now that

I have this, I won't be bored at all. Thank you so much again."

Zoe hugged her back. "Have fun." And with that, she left.

Feeling happier than she had in days, Kaitlyn began perusing recipes. Her first search—exotic brownies—turned up something that had nothing to do with cooking. She finally settled on one of the three biggest cooking sites and began scrolling through different brownie recipes.

She wanted her second batch to be simple, yet mouth-wateringly delicious. One of her favorite blog sites, *Pioneer Woman,* had a double chocolate recipe that seemed perfect. Especially since if Kaitlyn remembered right, Zoe was a chocoholic.

Humming to herself, she got busy assembling the ingredients.

Once the pan was in the oven, Kaitlyn sat down to figure out some sort of business plan. When all this was over, she hoped Zoe and Brock might let her stay a bit longer, at least until she was established. She'd talk to them about that, maybe.

Gradually it dawned on her that it was too quiet. Frowning, she went to check on Bentley, who'd been sleeping on the sofa. The little dog was nowhere in sight. Alarm mounting, she checked the hallway, the bathroom and bedroom before returning to the living room. "Bentley," she called for the tenth time. "Come. Bentley, please come."

Nothing. No sound of little claws on tile, no answering bark. Which made no sense. Her pet had to be around here somewhere. The only time the door had been open at all had been when Zoe had gotten home and again when she'd left.

Calling, her heart pounding, she searched the house again, this time peering in every nook and cranny, behind boxes, inside closets. She checked the backyard, the side yard, and even peeked out into the front.

Finally, she had to face the fact. Her little dog was gone.

Bentley must have slipped out when they'd carried in the boxes of produce. She took several deep breaths, pushing back her panic and calming herself long enough to figure out what to do.

She had to find him. Running to her duffel bag, she quickly put on one of her shapeless dresses and the big eyeglasses that made up her disguise. Just in case, she popped in the muddy-brown contacts. A quick look in the mirror told her she looked completely different, as unlike herself as she could get.

She grabbed her house key and went out the front door to search for her dog.

Taking care to act normal, she started off calling Bentley's name softly at first. After all, she'd only had the little dog a short time and she wasn't even sure he even knew his name was Bentley.

But after another quick search of the yard and the ones on either side failed to turn up a hairy little puppy, her worry and panic had her raising her voice. "Bentley! Here, boy. Bentley!"

Canvassing the street, she zigzagged from house to house. He had to be around here somewhere. A little puppy couldn't have gone too far. She hoped he hadn't made the main road with all its traffic.

When the police cruiser pulled up, her first thought was gratitude. Then, as the passenger-side window went down, her second was panic.

George Putchinski. Her heart sank.

"Well, well, well. Who do we have here?" he drawled.

There was no way he could have recognized her. Just in case, she kept her head down. "My little dog got out and I'm trying to find him."

He put the car in Park, got out and crossed around to her side. She could try like hell to bluff and hope he didn't realize who she was. Or she could run.

"What kind of dog is it?" he asked, his voice overly kind. "I can help you look."

Still keeping her gaze averted, Kaitlyn gestured toward the street. "He's a mix. Long hair, kind of scruffy. Maybe a sheltie mix."

"I see." Saccharine sweetness colored his tone.

Suspicious, Kaitlyn steeled herself and raised her head to meet his gaze. The instant she did, she knew he'd recognized her. He'd probably even known she was here, somehow.

Alex's reach went far and wide.

Run! Her inner voice screamed. But she hesitated, still needing to find Bentley. "I've got to find my dog," she said.

Slowly, never taking his gaze from her, George withdrew his service revolver. "Put your hands where I can see them," he ordered.

Pushing back the panic, again she hesitated before she finally did as he asked. "What are you doing? Why?"

His smirk told her not to waste her time. "You're a fugitive, my dear. And someone very powerful has been looking for you for a long time."

Her heart sank. Still, she tried to brazen it out. "I've done nothing wrong. You can't arrest me."

"Arrest you?" Laughing, he pulled out a pair of handcuffs, the metal glinting silver in the sunlight. "I'm just detaining you for questioning. Now put your hands behind your back."

She wondered if he'd shoot her if she took off running. She was pretty sure Alex would kill anyone who tried to harm her—he wanted the pleasure of doing that himself.

"No." She said, lifting her chin. "I need to find my dog. Now get out of my way."

This time his laughter had a hard edge. "Honey, I know ways to hurt people and make sure it doesn't show. Now you either do as I told you, or suffer the consequences."

The hell with it. She took off, praying he wouldn't shoot her in the back. Instead, he came after her, the pounding of his footsteps making her run faster.

She might have escaped him if she hadn't tripped and twisted her ankle. Down she went, crying out in pain and frustration. George yanked her to her feet, pushing her arms behind her and slapping on the cuffs. He gave her a shove. "Now walk."

The first step she took, her ankle gave way. She would have fallen, if not for George's iron grip on her arm.

"I think I sprained my ankle," she told him, wincing and trying not to cry.

"That's too damn bad." He shoved her again and then, when she didn't move, he dragged her the rest of the way to his car. He opened the door and pushed her into the backseat before going around to the front and getting behind the wheel.

"I hope you have dashcam video. Because you sure as hell are going to be in trouble when the sheriff see this."

He sneered at her. "I disabled that a long time ago. Those fools never check it. They trust me."

"Look, I have brownies in the oven," she began, then snapped her mouth closed, not wanting him to know where she'd been staying. But she also didn't want Brock and Zoe's house to burn down, either.

"Tough," George said. "Looks like they're going to be burned, because I'm not letting you go back to take them out."

Crud. Again, she tried to figure out a way to get away. She came up with nothing.

"Where are you taking me?" she finally asked, her ankle throbbing, unable to keep from still looking out the window to find Bentley. "Just wait, because once I tell the sheriff—"

"Oh, honey, we're not going to the sheriff's department." Putting the car in Drive, he grinned at her in the rearview mirror. "I'm taking you back where you belong. Alex is going to be very happy to see you."

Chapter 12

Kaitlyn supposed she should be grateful that George didn't take her directly to Alex. Instead, he took her to a deteriorating trailer house on a lot near the edge of town.

"Come on." Opening the back door, George yanked her out. "Get inside before someone sees you."

She stumbled and he pushed her, nearly sending her down onto her knees.

"Get inside," he barked again. Heart pounding, she hurried up the wooden steps onto his little porch, moving aside while he unhooked his screen door, then his regular door.

Inside, the place smelled like pizza and cat urine. It took Kaitlyn a moment for her eyes to adjust to the darkness.

"I'm gonna pat you down," he warned. She had to force herself not to cringe or comment as he did. He removed her cell phone and left the small tube of lip gloss she always carried.

"I'm surprised you're not armed."

She looked away and didn't even respond. She'd meant to ask Reed to give her a gun, but time and circumstances had prevented that. She'd never actually shot anyone. But she thought she could. Especially Alex. The thought made her grimace.

"How did you find me?" she asked.

"We have eyes on everybody. Every single person who knew you is being watched. Including and especially your friend Reed."

Her blood froze. Did that mean Alex knew what Reed was trying to do? Frantic, she tried not to show it. Somehow, she had to get a message to Reed. But how?

"This way," George said, pointing toward a narrow hallway.

For the first time she wondered if George operated on his own agenda, one not even remotely connected to Alex's. Did he plan to rape her, hurt her?

As she took the first footsteps on the dirty green shag carpet, he grabbed her arm, directing her into a small room on the left. "In here."

The room was empty except for a mattress on the floor. George flipped a switch on the wall and a light came on overhead. "Your new home," he told her.

She noted the window, and also the burglar bars on the inside. "I can't get out."

"Exactly." He smirked. "This ain't my first rodeo."

In lieu of her sanity, she decided not to ask him what he meant, even though she guessed he'd kept someone else prisoner in this room.

"There's a washroom right there." He pointed to a

second door. "I'll make sure and bring you something to eat later. Have fun."

When he closed the door, she couldn't help but notice the unmistakable click as he locked the handle. A moment later, she heard his car start and then pull away.

Great. Now what? Just to make sure, she crossed to the window and checked the burglar bars. They were sturdy and secure. She could only hope a fire didn't break out in this hellhole, as she'd be toast.

The washroom held a toilet and a sink, nothing else. It had no window. She spotted a closet and checked that out, too. Empty.

Great. She sank down on the mattress and covered her face with her hands. She needed to think, to try and come up with a way out of here. She had no doubt that once George had finished with her, he'd deliver her up to Alex.

That afternoon after lunch at home, Reed took his time leaving, pretending to be unaware of the man lurking on the sidewalk four houses down.

He almost pitied the guy. Except for the little belt of trees in the median, hiding places were in short supply, especially in such a tight-knit residential neighborhood. At least Reed had been right to send Kaitlyn away, no matter how much he surprisingly missed her.

Walking slowly out to his pickup in the driveway, Reed wondered if the other man planned to break in and do some more snooping around the place once he was sure Reed was gone.

Though he hated having his privacy invaded, Reed had expected no less. Alex wasn't the type to trust blindly, if he trusted at all.

Reed drove exactly the speed limit on the way to Alex's

estate, to make it easy on anyone who might have been assigned to follow him. He didn't spot a tail, but that didn't mean he didn't have one.

Finally, he pulled up to the massive front gates and pushed the button on the call box. As soon as he'd identified himself, the gates began to swing open to allow him to drive through.

Though the prospect made him inwardly wince, Reed knew he'd have to interview Alex Ramirez sooner or later. And it might as well be sooner, otherwise Reed would be floundering around the mansion like a fish out of water. If he was going to pretend to search for Kaitlyn, he'd need to get Alex to sit down and give him some details. Judging from what he'd seen of the other man's behavior thus far, Alex wasn't going to like that.

Oh, well. Tough. If the politician wanted to pretend he really cared about finding Kaitlyn, he was going to have to answer a few questions.

Straightening his shoulders, Reed made his way to Alex's office. The massive mahogany double doors were closed, so he knocked.

"Come in," Alex ordered.

When Reed opened the door, Alex was just hanging up the phone, a strangely satisfied expression on his patrician features. Something about that look sent a little prickle of warning up Reed's spine.

"I needed to talk to you," Reed began.

"Your services are no longer needed," Alex interrupted, his cold tone final. "One of my people will show you out."

Dumbfounded, Reed scratched his head. "I'm not sure what you mean."

"I have found my fiancée." Alex's malicious smile

hinted at what he planned to do next. "Ergo, I don't need you."

Found his...*Kaitlyn?* Reed went hot all over, refusing to acknowledge the possibility. "How? Where? When?" he asked.

"That's none of your concern." Alex pressed a buzzer and one of his large bodyguard types in a dark suit appeared. "Please show Mr. Westbrook out." He narrowed his eyes at Reed. "Fair warning. If I find out you helped her in any way..."

Reed got the point. Shaking off the bodyguard's hand on his arm, he marched out of the room, down the hall and all the way to his truck. Alex's goon stood, arms crossed, and watched as Reed started his vehicle and pulled away.

"Damn it," Reed cursed. Driving back down the drive, heart pounding in his chest, he tried to figure out what the hell had just happened. He itched to pick up the phone and call Brock and Zoe, but couldn't say for sure this wasn't a trap. Until he knew something, he didn't plan on doing anything to endanger anyone.

He checked his rearview mirror constantly and was absolutely certain he wasn't followed. When he reached the turnoff for his street, there weren't any other cars behind him.

Once home, he paced, then cursed and said the hell with it and dialed Brock.

No answer.

Next he tried Zoe. Again nothing. What the...? He swore. If Alex had touched one hair on either of their heads...

Reed ran to his truck and headed over there, still checking to make sure he wasn't followed. The fact that he didn't have a tail most likely meant that Alex had been serious. He had Kaitlyn. How or why, Reed didn't know.

As he pulled up to Brock and Zoe's house, he felt another frisson of alarm. There were no vehicles in the driveway and worse, the front door sat wide-open. Hurrying up the front sidewalk, he saw inside every light appeared to be on. And the place smelled like smoke, as if something had burned badly inside the oven.

He swore. He'd never forgive himself if Alex had harmed either of them. A quick search revealed the house was empty. A pan of charred brownies sat on top of the stove, which explained the awful smell.

As he headed back outside, Brock's truck pulled up. Brock jumped out and hurried over to Reed. "Something's happened to Kaitlyn," he said. "Zoe's out searching."

"Alex told me he has her." Realizing his hands were clenched into fists, Reed deliberately relaxed them. "What happened?"

"Zoe's pretty upset. She came home after work and when she got here, she found it like this, with the front door wide open and a pan of brownies burning in the oven."

"Any signs of a struggle?"

"No." Brock grimaced. "Though we're lucky the place didn't catch on fire. That's what makes this really strange. I mean, if they'd found her and took her, she would have put up a fight."

"Exactly."

Zoe's car rounded the corner. She pulled up, parked and jumped out. "I found Bentley running down the street." She held up the scruffy little dog. "And no sign of Kaitlyn anywhere."

"That's because Alex Ramirez somehow found her." Reed told them what Alex had said. "I'm not sure how, but he says he's got her back."

Still holding the wiggling animal, Zoe glanced at Brock and then back to Reed. Her horrified expression matched how Reed felt. "We've got to help her. What are we going to do now?"

"Not 'we,'" Reed corrected her. "I don't want you and Brock involved any more than you have been. Alex is too dangerous."

Zoe shot him a look that plainly said "we'll see about that." But instead of arguing, she nodded. "Okay. Then what are *you* going to do?"

Reed didn't even hesitate. "Rescue her, of course."

Zoe agreed to keep Bentley until Kaitlyn's return. Though Brock wanted Reed to come in and talk strategy, Reed left. He needed to get home and try to think this through.

Once inside his little house, he began to pace. The truth was, he didn't know where Alex would take Kaitlyn, but most likely it'd be to that ridiculous monstrosity of a house. Reed had only been there a couple of times, but he'd seen the setup and the security. Getting in there was going to be difficult, to say the least.

None of that mattered. He had to save Kaitlyn, no matter what. He could only imagine what she must be going through. His chest felt tight and he wished he could hold her and reassure her it would be all right.

The instant he realized this, he froze. What the hell? When had she come to mean so much to him?

He thought of the way he'd felt when they'd made love, the complete lack of walls she'd put between them. In everything, including this, she'd given herself to him with openness and candor, willing to trust despite what Alex had done to her.

And then he understood something else, something he'd known all along but hadn't been willing to admit. Kaitlyn was beautiful both inside and out. Her loveliness went all the way to the core of her. She deserved none of this.

Especially now. She'd finally found the courage to make a break for freedom and somehow Alex had managed to snatch her back in his evil claws.

Reed cursed again. He had to figure out a way to get back into that mansion and free her. From what he'd seen, Alex had a veritable army. Reed couldn't just go charging in there and think he could get Kaitlyn out. He'd get shot, maybe even killed. And then where would Kaitlyn be?

He'd given her his word he would help her. Now he admitted to himself that there was more involved than just his word. He wanted to help her because he cared.

He'd been home a little over half an hour—pacing— when he heard the sound of car tires on the gravel drive. He jumped up, peered out the window and groaned.

Of course. For the first time in over a week, George Putchinski had decided to pay him a call.

While biting back yet another curse and the urge to put his fist through the wall, Reed sensed he might just have found a way in. Since George worked for Alex, he might be able to give Reed some insight on how Kaitlyn had been captured. If Reed played him right.

Though dealing with that idiot was the last thing he wanted or needed right now, Reed had no choice. Just like he hadn't really had before. Except this time, he'd mention Alex's name and see what kind of reaction he got.

He had the door open before the other man had even

had a chance to knock. In fact, George had just gotten out of his squad car. With his mirrored sunglasses and his smug smile, he could have played a cop in an '80s television drama. He sauntered up the sidewalk toward Reed.

"Waiting for me?" he asked. "Then you must be guilty."

"Really?" Reed kept his tone mild. "Would you like to come in, George?"

Since this was a first, Reed knew George would be surprised. If he was, he didn't show it. Of course, he also didn't remove his sunglasses.

"Sure." George stomped inside. Once Reed closed the door, the other man had to take off his shades in order to look around.

After one quick glance, George faced Reed and crossed his arms. "Place looks nice," he said, his tone grudging.

"Thanks. Now can you tell me the reason for this visit?"

Eyes narrowed, George eyed Reed as if he'd spoken a foreign language. "What?"

"Why are you here, George? What crime that I didn't commit are you going to ask me about now?"

For once, the sheriff's deputy appeared at a loss for words. Of course, Reed had never invited him inside before, so maybe that had thrown him off a little.

Before George could answer, Reed pressed his advantage. "Did Alex send you?"

"Alex?" George gaped at him, not able to conceal his shock.

Reed smiled.

"You should know I saw Alex this morning. I've been doing a little work for him."

George's thick brows knit into a frown. "You have?"

"Yep." Reed grinned. "I was helping him find his woman. *Was* being the operative word."

Evidently, George wasn't as slow as Reed had guessed. "That's nice."

"Yeah, but some other hotshot beat me to it." Reed colored his tone with admiration. "Must have been sharp, that guy, whoever he was. Wish I was him. I bet he's getting all the money that was promised to me."

"Money?" George cocked his head and Reed knew he had him. "What kind of money?"

"Fifty grand," Reed lied. "Alex promised to give me fifty grand if I found Kaitlyn for him."

George swallowed hard, his Adam's apple moving. "Why would someone like him pay someone like you anything?"

Carefully casual, Reed shrugged. "Because men like him always reward people who do things for him. You should know that." He bet Alex had never paid ole George a dime.

A flush had begun to creep up George's thick neck, past his double chin, heating his face. "I got to go," he managed, looking as if he had just swallowed something unpalatable. Turning, he fumbled for the doorknob.

Once he was outside, Reed watched as he climbed into his squad car and peeled off. The instant George's taillights flashed as he rounded the curve in the drive, Reed sprinted for his truck. Keys in the ignition, *Start, start, start damn it.*

And he was off. Hot in pursuit of George Putchinski. He figured the other man would be too damn preoccupied to even notice he was being followed.

* * *

Time passed. Kaitlyn dozed and startled awake at the sound of car tires on gravel. George returning? Or Alex, coming to get the woman he regarded as his property?

A moment later, heavy footsteps entered the trailer. "You all right in there?" a voice called. George. Relieved, she answered in the affirmative.

"Good. I'll feed you in a little bit. Right now, I got a few things to do."

His cell phone rang and he answered that. Since the walls were thin, Kaitlyn could hear every word.

"Thank you for calling me back. Yes, you heard my message right. Like I told you before, I have Kaitlyn Nuhn."

Silence while he evidently listened to the other person—whom she suspected might be Alex—speak.

"Yes, I know I said I'd bring her to you. But I've changed my mind. For sure I'll take you to her." George cleared his throat. "For a price. I understand you pay other people a significant amount of money to bring you things. Earlier, we never discussed money. Now I want to be paid."

Kaitlyn could imagine how well that went over with Alex. She was surprised she couldn't hear him shouting on the other end of the phone line.

"Seventy-five thousand," George said, his voice stubborn. "More than you pay anyone else because I actually can deliver the goods."

Silence again. Then George spoke, his voice hard and flat and final. "You have twenty-four hours to think about it. You can call me again at this number when you decide."

Kaitlyn marveled at what was both foolhardy and

daring. Alex would squash him like an insect. Surely George knew this since he'd been doing business with Alex for years.

A moment later, George unlocked her door. His olive skin looked flushed, and his brown eyes gleamed. "You hungry?"

Slowly, she nodded. She wanted to be careful not to do anything to set him off.

"This way," he told her, pointing toward the front of the trailer. "I'll make us some tacos or something."

Walking, she kept her hands where he could see them and tried to case the rest of the trailer without him noticing.

When they reached the small kitchen, he pointed to a chair. "Sit."

The table and the front door were maybe twenty feet apart. She calculated her chances if she were to make a run for it. Not good. For now, she'd watch and wait. But she knew one thing for sure. No way in hell was she going back to Alex. She'd get away or she'd die trying. Because if she let George deliver her to Alex, she was as good as dead anyway.

Though she knew she shouldn't ask any questions or do anything to make George fix his attention on her, she had to ask. "Um, George? Does Alex know where you live?"

He swiveled so fast she thought he might backhand her. Instead, he gave her a hard look and a nod. "He does."

Her heart sank. That bit of information meant she had to get out of there sooner rather than later.

"But this isn't my place," he continued. "And Alex has no idea about it. I stay here sometimes when my friend

Barry is out of town. No one knows about this trailer house. And the phone I have is a disposable phone, so I can't be tracked."

Surprised, Kaitlyn nodded. Never in a million years would she have guessed George had it in him. Still, he'd managed to survive doing business with Alex all these years. Not too many people were able to do that.

Flattery couldn't hurt. She ventured a tentative smile. "I never knew you were so smart, George."

But instead of pleasure, his complexion flushed with anger. "Don't waste your time trying to butter me up. I care more about the money." Turning, he fished a video camera out of a bag, and then retrieved a tripod from the closet.

"I'm going to set this up and record us having dinner," he said. "It's more efficient than a cell phone video, and untraceable. I'll send that to Alex. That way he'll know I really do have you and that you're still alive. For now, at least."

That announcement made, George got busy cooking their dinner.

Aware he first needed to catch up with George's car and then fall back so he wouldn't be noticed, Reed accelerated. If George had gone to Alex's—or anywhere in the direction of town for that matter—he would have had to pick up the main highway.

Still, Reed didn't see a sign of the patrol car. Had he gone the wrong way, turning left when he should have turned right? Had he possibly guessed wrong when figuring where George would go?

Flashing lights appeared in his rearview mirror.

Damn. He glanced at his speedometer, noticing he was going at least twenty over the limit.

A siren let out a *whoop-whoop*. They wanted him to pull over. Seriously? It couldn't be George, could it? The sheriff's deputy had been too upset when he'd left to be worrying about using radar to trap speeders. Reed supposed it could be one of the other deputies, but in all the years he'd lived here, no one ever patrolled this area of the highway.

For one brief foolish second, he debated trying to run, but knew his elderly truck wouldn't be up to the task.

So he pulled over.

The man approaching his window addressed him by name. "Reed Westbrook?"

Trying not to grind his teeth impatiently, Reed nodded. The man handed him his badge without speaking. FBI. Special Agent Blake Kent.

As Reed tried to digest this, he noticed another man approaching on the passenger side. "Is this an ambush?" he asked, only partly joking.

"We just want to have a word with you."

And then shoot him and dump his body on the side of the road. Right.

"Do you work for Alex Ramirez?" he asked, figuring he might as well be blunt.

"No." The other man didn't even crack a smile. "But he's who we want to discuss with you. We think you can help us in our investigation of him." He indicated his dark, government-issue, sedan, dashboard light still flashing. "Do you have a moment so we can talk?"

Knowing George had likely gotten too far ahead to be followed, Reed finally nodded. If the feds were investigating Alex, that would only be to his and Kaitlyn's advantage.

But first, he needed to make them understand that she was in danger. He got out of his truck and got in their car. Speaking succinctly, he told them everything that had transpired, beginning with Kaitlyn showing up at his house and ending with her disappearance.

"And Alex claims he has her back again," he concluded. "If that's true, her life is in grave danger."

"Let me make a call." The younger of the two agents, got out of the car and stood outside, talking into his cell phone. After a moment, he pocketed the phone and got back in.

"We've just about got enough for a search warrant."

Immediately, Reed nodded. "What else do you need?" he asked quietly. "That man not only has held Kaitlyn a virtual prisoner, but he murdered my brother. Not to mention he set me up to go to prison for a crime I never committed."

From the way the two feds exchanged a glance, Reed knew they'd heard that particular line before from ex-cons. He didn't care. In his case it was true.

"Thank you for your cooperation." The agents got out again, holding the door open for him. "We'll be in touch."

Reed couldn't believe they were going to try and brush him off. "Are you going out there?"

"Out where?"

"We don't have time for games." Not bothering to hide his impatience, he ripped the words out. "Alex Ramirez's mansion. Are you going out there?"

"Eventually. The bureau is assembling a team right now."

"I'm going with you." Reed gave them a look to let them know this was nonnegotiable.

"That's not really up to us," one of the agents began.

Reed shook his head, heading back to his truck. "I'll meet you there," he said, ignoring the other man's protests.

Once inside, he turned the key in the ignition, put the shifter in Drive and headed toward Alex's estate.

It didn't take long until the smell of seasoned ground beef filled the room, making Kaitlyn's stomach growl. George filled a couple of corn tortillas and carried them over. He also grabbed a bag of precut salad and another of shredded cheddar cheese from the fridge and unceremoniously dropped that on the table, too.

"I forgot to get tomatoes," he said, turning back toward the stove to make his own plate. She watched as he dished up his own meat from the cast-iron skillet.

Cast iron. Heavy enough to knock a man out. Could she do it? It really didn't matter. This time, she'd have to find the strength. She was done being some man's prisoner. Finished hiding in the shadows. She'd get out of here herself and then she was through trusting anyone to help her. She'd go straight to the authorities and take down Alex Ramirez herself.

She ate all of her tacos, aware she was going to need her strength. Once she was done, she tried to calm her racing heart. Taking a deep breath, she grabbed her empty plate and pushed herself up from her chair.

George jumped up, too. "Where do you think you're going?"

Deliberately keeping her voice soft and her shoulders rounded, she showed him her plate and gestured toward the stove. "I was just going to get seconds. I can make you another plate first if you'd like."

He considered. She held her breath, well aware that men who liked to bully loved having women wait on them hand and foot like a kind of personal slave.

The second George's thick lips curled into a smile, she knew she had him. *Perfect.* "Sure," he said. "I'll take three more."

Dipping her chin, she grabbed his plate and carried it with hers to the stove. Her heart pounded and she prayed he didn't notice her hands trembling. She made his tacos first. Once they were made, she carried his plate to the table and placed it in front of him before returning to ostensibly make her own.

Instead, she grabbed a dish towel and, wrapping it around the handle, picked up the cast-iron skillet and quietly crept to stand behind George's back. Taking a deep breath, she swung. Hard. Spewing ground beef all over.

The skillet connected with the back of George's head with an awful thud. He went facedown on the table instantly.

Chapter 13

For a heartbeat, Kaitlyn stood frozen, still clutching the hot skillet. Then, when she realized George was out cold, she dropped her makeshift weapon and backed away, horrified.

Was he dead? She fumbled for his pulse, needing to make sure she hadn't killed him. She hadn't. He was still alive.

Still, she felt sick. Worried. She pushed the feeling away, her pulse pounding as she latched on to the rush of adrenaline. She'd done it. Opened up a chance to escape. Now she needed to get out of here.

Wiping her hands on the dish towel, she rushed to the door and yanked it open. George's police cruiser was parked outside and she realized she was going to need the keys.

Swallowing back nausea, she reached into his pants

pocket. Luckily, her fingers connected with his car keys immediately. She tugged them free and hurried back outside.

Aware that stealing a law enforcement vehicle was a crime, she started it anyway. George's actions while wearing his uniform definitely negated everything else.

Now, where to go? Briefly, she considered going to Reed. Even the thought made her chest ache. But no, the time had come to stand on her own two feet. She needed Bentley, though she had no way to know if her pup had been found. She could only pray he had.

As she continued to drive, she wished she knew which law enforcement agencies she could trust. She passed the Anniversary city limits, heading northwest, toward Dallas.

Driving a stolen sheriff's department vehicle, she felt like an actress in a movie. This didn't feel real. The fact that she'd been driven by desperation to act so irrationally shocked her.

Again she thought of Reed. Did he even know she was missing? And what about Zoe, and Brock? They must all be worried. But she had no phone and no way to contact them, so she continued on. Good thing the fuel gauge showed the tank was full.

Halfway there, she pulled over to the side of the road. What the heck was she doing? This had to end. By now Reed and Zoe and Brock had to know she was missing. She'd go back to town, find them and fill them in on what was happening. And warn Reed. Her only consolation was that at least Alex had no idea where she was or even that George no longer had her.

She'd need to ditch the cop car. As soon as she hit the city limits, she pulled in an alley behind a convenience store and parked. Wiping the keys off with her sleeve, she left them in the ignition. Let someone else steal the car. George could deal with trying to explain that.

On foot, aware she had no disguise, she kept her head up and her gaze straight ahead. No one paid any attention to her, and she guessed since her disappearance hadn't been featured in the news lately, she'd kind of faded from people's minds.

Finally, she reached the feed store that Brock and Zoe owned. Taking a deep breath, she pushed open the door and went inside.

The place was empty. Which wasn't so odd, this close to quitting time. If she remembered right, there should be an office in the back. She figured she'd find Brock or Zoe there.

To her surprise that, too, appeared empty. Surely they wouldn't have left their store open and unmanned, would they?

Unless something catastrophic had occurred. Like Kaitlyn's sudden disappearance.

Moving into the office, she picked up the phone and dialed Zoe's number. Zoe answered on the third ring.

"Kaitlyn! Where are you?"

Taking a deep breath, Kaitlyn answered. "I'm in your empty and unlocked feed store, watching over the place until one of you can get down here and lock it up." That said, she closed her eyes, waiting to hear Zoe's response.

"We're on the way. And, Kaitlyn, we found your dog."

Bentley. As she hung up the phone, Kaitlyn blinked back tears. The small pet represented so much, a start at things she'd never had. A home, friends and maybe someday a family—as she knew her gradual healing would become stronger each day.

She thought of Reed, ached to hear his voice. She debated calling him, too, but since she didn't know if he might be at Alex's, she didn't.

Instead, she went to the front of the store and locked the door, turning out the lights. She'd sit in the dark and wait until Zoe and Brock showed up.

Damn cell phone kept ringing. One hand on the steering wheel, Reed glanced at it. Caller ID showed it was Brock McCauley. No doubt he wanted to try and talk Reed out of doing something foolish. Doubts and warnings weren't something he was in the mood to hear. Brock called again, then Zoe. Finally, Brock flipped the ringer to Off, and stuck the phone back in his pocket.

The FBI agents' unmarked vehicle rode his tail, right behind him. Reed grinned, adrenaline making him feel savage. No doubt those agents were making frantic calls to get their warrant in place. At least he hoped so. Because he knew better than most that there was no way he would be able to get inside Alex's mansion without it.

Kaitlyn. Her name kept running through his head like a mantra. Right now, she'd have shut down, all the light gone from her bright blue eyes. The bastard better not have touched her, or there'd be hell to pay.

As he approached the massive gates, Reed pulled over. The agents parked right behind him.

The taller of the two got out, his black suit flapping in the breeze. "You need to wait here," he ordered. "Our team is on the way with the warrant."

Reed nodded. "She's in there somewhere. We've got to get her out."

Just as he finished speaking, gunfire rang out.

The agent shoved Reed to the ground. "Take cover.

Follow me." The two of them crab-walked, putting Reed's truck between them and the structure.

Reed pointed. "The house is too far away for anyone firing from inside to have a prayer of hitting us. I'm thinking this might be something else entirely."

"Maybe. But we're not taking any chances."

For the next moment, all was silent. The other agent spoke into his phone. Reed heard him say, "Shots fired."

The words had barely left his mouth when another round of gunfire erupted.

"Damn it," the first agent said. "We need our team. What's their ETA?"

"Less than five."

"Then we take cover and wait."

Headlights lit up the darkness as a car pulled into the parking lot. Overly cautious, Kaitlyn stayed hidden, peering out from in between the slats of the blinds. When she saw Brock and Zoe, she ran to unlock the door.

"Oh my gosh, you had us so worried." Zoe enveloped her in a fierce hug. "Why on earth did you go running off like that?"

Kaitlyn shook her head, blinking back unwanted tears. "I didn't," she said, and told them what had happened. "I checked to make sure I didn't kill George when I hit him with the skillet. He still had a pulse, but I don't know what kind of condition he's in."

Remembering the video camera, she winced. "And since he left the camera recording, whoever finds him will have a clear picture of me knocking him out."

"George deserves what he got," Zoe said. "The nerve of that man, wearing a uniform and pretending to be a real law enforcement officer. I can't believe he took advantage of his position and betrayed the public trust."

"That's it." Brock raged. "I'm calling Roger. He needs to know what his deputies are up to."

"Wait." Kaitlyn grabbed his arm. "What if the entire sheriff's office is on Alex's payroll?"

"Maybe some of them are, like George. But Roger Giles is a good man. He takes being a sheriff seriously. There's no way he'd get in bed with someone like Alex."

Kaitlyn glanced at Zoe, who nodded. "He tried his best to help me when Shayna disappeared, though at the time I didn't feel he did enough. He's honest."

"Maybe we should feel him out first," Kaitlyn said. Despite her best efforts, her voice shook a little. "Just to be safe. You never know about some people."

"I'm calling him." Brock took out his phone. "But if it makes you feel better, I'll scope him out first."

Slowly, she nodded. This, too, was part of the growing part. Learning to trust others.

"Do you know where the mobile home is located?" Brock asked.

"Yes. I drove to town from there." She gave him a quick set of directions, which he jotted down.

Punching in a number, he asked to speak with the sheriff and moved away to have his conversation with a modicum of privacy.

"Where's Bentley?" Kaitlyn asked, looking around for her pup. "I was so worried about him."

"He's out in the truck. I left the AC on, so he'd stay cool. I'll go get him and bring him in." Zoe went out. A moment later, she returned carrying the squirming bundle of fur. She placed him on the ground. He yipped once and launched himself at Kaitlyn.

She laughed as she caught him midleap. Whimpering, he licked her nose, her cheek, her chin. "He missed me," Kaitlyn said, amazed and delighted.

"He knows you're his mama." Zoe smiled. "It kinda warms the heart."

It sure did. Kaitlyn smiled back, still tussling with her dog. "I won't lose you again, little guy."

Brock returned. "Roger is pissed. He had no idea. He tried to get a hold of George, but no answer. I told him George is probably still unconscious. He sent a patrol car out to the location you mentioned. He also sent a couple of guys to retrieve the squad car. I told him where you'd left it."

Suddenly nervous, Kaitlyn nodded. "Now what."

Brock sighed, dragging his hand through his hair. "I've been trying to call Reed, but he doesn't answer. I've left him a message, though, so I'm sure he'll get in touch when he can."

"I'm worried about him," Kaitlyn confessed. "I don't think he understands how ruthless Alex can be. Worse, I think Alex might be on to him."

"Reed can take care of himself," Brock said, patting her shoulder in reassurance. "We've got to keep our focus where it belongs. Taking down Alex Ramirez. That's what Reed wants. To get justice for Tim's murder and to clear his name."

She nodded, though right now she'd trade Reed's safety for Alex's arrest. She couldn't shake the feeling that something had gone very wrong.

More gunshots rang out, tearing up the side of the government-issue vehicle. Reed cursed, not entirely sure what the hell Alex was up to.

Finally, the SWAT team and their armored vehicle came rolling up. They stopped, acknowledged the two agents with Reed, and then crashed through the gates, heading toward the mansion.

Reed and the other agents jumped in their bullet-riddled car and followed behind.

As the SWAT vehicle reached the front of the mansion, the vehicle's back door swung open and armed men poured out. Normally, Reed supposed they would have stopped and contacted the homeowner to inform him of the warrant.

The fact that they'd been fired on changed all that.

Using some sort of makeshift battering ram, the SWAT team crashed through the double doors, splintering the expensive mahogany and shattering leaded glass.

"Stay back with us," the FBI agents told him. "We don't go in until the place is cleared."

"Gotcha." Reed looked around. "At least they've stopped shooting."

"For now," the man agreed. "Let's hope it stays that way."

The team fanned out, leaving one agent to stay with Reed. Babysitting. It pissed him off to no end, but there was absolutely nothing he could do about it.

He was forced to stand in one place, fuming, while the agents searched.

Finally, one of the men returned.

"She's not here." The FBI agent didn't look too happy. In fact, judging from the grim set of his mouth, the man was downright furious. "And Alex Ramirez is saying he has no idea what you're talking about. He claims his fiancée is still missing."

"That's bull." Teeth clenched, Reed shoved his fingers through his hair. "Just this morning he told me he had her back."

"Yeah, that's another thing. Mr. Ramirez claims you're a disgruntled employee. Are you—or were you—working for him?"

Reed didn't even bother to answer. This agent hadn't been with the two who'd come to him asking for his help. This guy clearly didn't know what was going on.

Brushing past two more people with FBI on their black jackets, Reed hurried up the staircase. When he reached Kaitlyn's room, he entered and remembering, turned and shot the camera the bird.

A sound behind him made him freeze. Straightening, he turned.

"What are you doing in here?" It was the agent who'd hassled him downstairs.

"Just looking around," Reed said easily. "Hoping to find clues."

The man tilted his head. "How did you know this was Kaitlyn's room? And that there was a camera in the corner for you to flip off?"

The hair on the back of Reed's neck rose. "You work for Alex, don't you?"

Instead of answering, the FBI agent pulled his gun. "One move, and I'll shoot you. I can always say you tried to grab my weapon."

Except for the camera. Reed resisted glancing up at it.

"Whatever," he said. "Since you work for the bureau, you should know Alex is under investigation. Getting rid of me isn't going to help him at all." He took a deep breath. "If you're going to shoot me, you might as well do it now. Otherwise, I'm going to walk away."

The other man stared at him, his gun still raised. Reed

shook his head and brushed past him, his heart pounding hard in his chest. He made it to the door when the agent shouted at him to stop.

Instead, Reed leaped around the corner. The bullet hit the door frame. Reed cursed. He couldn't believe the idiot had really fired at him.

Instantly, two agents appeared, the two who'd first asked for Reed's help. They ran down the hall toward him, weapons drawn. Reed pointed, legs shaky.

Just as they reached the doorway, another shot rang out.

Followed by a thud.

Exchanging glances, one of the men asked the other to cover him and, leading with his pistol, swung around the corner.

"Clear," he shouted. "He's dead."

Reed followed the other agent into the room. The blood spatter and brain matter made him feel like he might puke.

Damn. The man had shot himself. Reed could hardly believe it. "I don't understand," he said.

"You need to leave." The first agent took Reed's arm, steering him toward the door. "This is a crime scene now. Can't let you accidently contaminate the evidence."

"Evidence? This clearly was a suicide."

"We still have to investigate it. Now get out."

Slowly, Reed nodded and began backing away. He had to figure out who he could trust. And most important, find out where the hell Alex had stashed Kaitlyn. Clearly, she wasn't in the mansion.

He made it to the front door before someone stopped him. The man wore a suit but had the look of either a federal agent or a drug kingpin. Reed instantly suspected he was another one of the agents in Alex's employ.

"Reed Westbrook?"

Wary, Reed nodded an affirmative.

The man twisted Reed's arm behind him, whipped out a pair of handcuffs and slapped them on Reed. "You're under arrest. Anything you might say can and will be used against you."

Dumbfounded, at first Reed couldn't move. "On what charge?"

"Kidnapping and extortion, to begin with. We know you took Kaitlyn Nuhn and tried to extort Alex Ramirez. We also know a deputy sheriff has disappeared and you're considered a prime suspect."

Set up. Once he'd been booked, he was strip-searched, his belongings taken from him, and assigned an orange jumpsuit. Next Reed had been dumped in a holding cell until his court-appointed lawyer arrived.

It all felt way too familiar. And the sinking feeling in the pit of his stomach told him that this time, too, there would be no true justice. Not for him, not for Kaitlyn.

As far as he could tell, he'd been locked up in some county jail, not Dallas county, but smaller. Maybe Kaufman County, since that was on the way toward Dallas. Which made absolutely no sense.

If the FBI had brought him in, he would be in FBI custody, wouldn't he? Reed didn't know, as he'd never been arrested on federal charges before.

He'd asked his court-appointed attorney, when that person finally showed up.

Instead of the lawyer, one of the dark-suited feds came into the room, his expression sober. "I can't believe you tried to play us. Don't you realize we find everything out sooner or later?"

"Play you?" Reed grimaced, pretty damn sure whatever he said was going to fall on deaf ears. "I'm not the one doing that. Alex Ramirez is."

The agent began shaking his head before Reed even finished. "We have you on video, Reed. We have you boasting to a sheriff's deputy that Alex was paying you fifty thousand dollars."

Reed bit back a groan. "If you bother to listen to the entire conversation, you'll hear I said that for information. George Putchinski is actually on Alex's payroll. I told him that to try and find out who had Kaitlyn. That morning, Alex told me he'd located her and had no more need for my services."

The man stared at Reed, tapping his pencil on the table in staccato fashion. "You do realize, the more elaborate the story, the easier it is to trip yourself up?"

"It isn't a story." Frustrated, Reed wanted to lash out. This interview reminded him uncomfortably of the one after which he'd been wrongfully convicted of armed robbery.

"What about the gunshots?" he asked, trying not to sound as desperate as he felt. "Alex's people shot at federal agents when we pulled up to his estate."

"He showed us the gate camera. He saw you and two men. He felt threatened. He says he shot you in self-defense."

"That's bull," Reed protested hotly. "All of this is. Don't you see what he's doing?"

"Reed." The agent leaned close, fixing Reed with a hard glare. "We also have you on tape asking Alex Ramirez for money. Any one of these things alone is enough to make an arrest. All three of them? A surefire conviction. And with your previous record…"

Realizing everything had been heavily edited, Reed asked for a lawyer. Unfortunately, he'd come to accept the truth in what Kaitlyn had warned him about.

He had no idea who to trust. And worse, no idea where Kaitlyn was or who actually had her.

Kaitlyn had never actually met Roger Giles, the sheriff. From the faces she made when his name came up, Zoe didn't seem to like him much, but Brock was all smiles as he welcomed the man into the feed store.

Roger listened without interrupting until the entire story was out. In the silence that followed, Kaitlyn found herself silently praying that he, too, wasn't on Alex's payroll.

"Our only hope is the media," he finally announced.

"But what if Alex owns people there, too?" Kaitlyn couldn't help but ask.

"He can't have every station in his pocket. We'll alert the NBC, CBS, ABC and FOX affiliates in Dallas. I'll also make sure the story is picked up by the Associated Press."

Kaitlyn glanced at Zoe to see what she thought. Zoe nodded. "That makes sense. I take it you're going to call a press conference?"

"Yes."

"How will you protect her until then?" Brock asked, sounding protective.

Roger smiled to show he appreciated the concern. "First off, I'm not going to give them much time. They can either use their choppers to get their reporters here, or miss out on the story. Second, I'm going to state the press conference will be held at the sheriff's department, so anyone looking to silence you will go there. Once everyone is assembled, I'll bring them here."

"Sounds good." Brock glanced back at Kaitlyn and winked. "You've just got to stay hidden a little bit longer."

She nodded. "What about Reed? We need to make sure he's safe."

Before anyone could answer, Roger's cell phone rang. He listened, grunted a thanks and ended the call. "Alex Ramirez has just announced a press conference of his own."

Kaitlyn's heart dropped all the way to her feet. "For what? What could he possibly have to say?"

Roger flashed a grim smile. "I don't know. But since he beat us to the punch, let's hear him out. Once we find out what he's up to, we'll have a better idea how to proceed."

"Where's it at? His mansion?"

"No. Surprisingly, he's asked to have it here in town. At Sue's Catfish Hut." He shrugged. "No idea why."

Kaitlyn knew why. Even now, Alex the ultimate politician, was motivated by votes. "He's seeking a warm, homespun environment to spin whatever lie he's planning." She took a deep breath. "Try Reed again."

Brock did, grimacing. "The call went straight to voice mail. Like his phone is turned off." He met Kaitlyn's eyes. "Hopefully he'll call when he can and let us know what's going on."

Though she tried to fight the panic, she couldn't shake the sense that something had gone majorly wrong. But seeing the concern in everyone's face as they watched her, she managed to nod.

"Maybe you folks ought to come with me," Roger said.

"No." Brock, Zoe and Kaitlyn all spoke at once.

Roger cocked his head. "Okay. Then tell me, what are ya'll planning to do?"

"We'll stay holed up here," Brock told him. "With the door locked and the front lights off. No one will look for Kaitlyn here."

"And we have a television in the back room, so we can catch Alex's press conference." Zoe looked grim. "Thanks for your help." She sounded anything but thankful.

"I'll be back in touch," Roger said on his way out the door. "Call me if you need anything."

After he left, Zoe let out her breath in an audible hiss. When Brock shot her a look, she grimaced. "Sorry. I just have trouble forgetting the way he didn't take Shayna's disappearance seriously."

Again trying not to panic, Kaitlyn eyed them both. "Can he be trusted?"

"Yes," Brock said firmly. "Zoe just doesn't think he did enough when Shayna vanished. But even if he'd done anything differently, I don't know that would have made a difference. Shayna's friend killed her. It wasn't some drifter or criminal."

Pain flashed across Zoe's expressive face. "It still hurts," she said quietly. "But you're right, we'll never know. Now let's go get settled in the break room. I think we've got some microwave popcorn we can make to munch on while we wait for Alex to have his news conference."

By the time the television flashed the words *Breaking News,* they were trying to relax and were passing around a huge bowl of popcorn.

Instantly, everyone froze.

"Turn up the volume," Zoe ordered.

Once Brock complied, they all leaned forward to watch, popcorn forgotten.

After the introductions, Alex dipped his head with what Kaitlyn knew was mock humility. "I'm happy to say that the FBI has captured my darling fiancée's kidnapper and he is in custody at this very moment."

The assembled reporters went crazy, erupting with questions, competing with each other to be heard. Alex ignored them all, standing with bent head, the very expression of grief.

Puzzled, Kaitlyn gripped the edge of the table and waited. Once the crowd had fallen silent, Alex lifted his head and continued. "One of the local deputy sheriff's, a George Putchinski, was found deceased earlier today."

"I swear, he was alive when I left him," Kaitlyn cried.

But Alex hadn't finished. "Unfortunately, we believe Kaitlyn is also dead. All that remains is for us to find her body."

Staring at the man who'd all along tried to destroy her, Kaitlyn gasped as a chill stabbed through her. In that moment, she knew the truth. "He means to kill me," she said, shuddering. "As soon as he can."

Chapter 14

The court-appointed attorney made it clear to Reed that he couldn't have cared less about hearing his side of the story. He began yawning as soon as Reed started speaking, and Reed found himself wanting to throttle the young man, who appeared to have just passed the bar exam.

Finally he stopped talking, waiting until the lawyer looked up. "Am I keeping you awake?" he asked as politely as he could with his teeth clenched.

"What?"

At that moment, a commotion out in the hall had them both looking up. A huge man wearing a suit burst into the room. "He's coming with me."

Of course the attorney didn't protest. Why should he, when he clearly would rather be anywhere else besides there.

Reed knew there was no way in hell he was going anywhere with this guy. Everything about him screamed "hired goon." Without a doubt, Alex had sent him to make sure Reed didn't convince the wrong people of the truth of his story.

Tough.

Reed remained standing and shook his head. "I'm in a meeting, with my attorney. With whom I have a legal right to confer. Now go away and let me have my time."

From the look on the huge man's face, he wasn't used to being refused. Reed didn't care. He'd fight tooth and nail if he had to. "Unless you're prepared to drag me down the hall kicking and screaming," he said, meaning it.

Glowering at Reed, the man backed out of the room.

Reed's attorney looked green around the gills. "Who was that?"

"Damned if I know." Reed leaned closer. "Now I need you to listen to me. I'm innocent. I'm being framed. I know you've heard that before, or if you haven't, you've seen it on TV. I need you to contact the sheriff of my hometown, Anniversary, Texas. His name is Roger Giles. Let him know I'm here."

The young man squinted at Reed, his thick wire-rimmed glasses magnifying his eyes. "Why?"

"Because he's possibly one of the few people who can help me clear my name. And we both want that, right? I mean, since you're my lawyer, after all."

Hesitating a moment, the attorney finally nodded. "I'll do the best I can."

"Not good enough," Reed barked. "I need you to do it, no matter what. Do you understand?"

Face flushed, the other man nodded. "Are we finished?" he asked, swallowing hard.

Reed glanced at the door, wondering where Alex's goon had gone. "Not just yet. Tell me about your credentials."

For the first time since he'd arrived, the young lawyer brightened. Reed tuned out the rest, while he tried to figure out what the hell Alex was up to.

"We've got to counter this," Brock exclaimed. As Kaitlyn looked at him blankly, feeling numb, he grinned at her like a wild man.

"It's a chess game," he said. "Alex has exposed his queen. Now it's up to us to capture her."

Since Kaitlyn didn't play chess, she had no idea what he meant.

"We can't let him win," Zoe said, chiming in, nearly as animated as her husband. "Imagine the stir if you go on the air and expose him."

"I'd love to." Kaitlyn took a deep breath, desperately hanging on to the last shreds of her courage. For Reed. Not for herself. But for Reed. Wherever he might be.

"Good." Brock beamed at her with approval. "I'm going to call Roger and make sure he gets the second press conference set up ASAP. Especially since all the reporters are here already."

It crossed Kaitlyn's mind that Alex might try to have a sniper take her out or something. Of course, things like that took a while to set up, didn't they?

"I want the press conference to be inside," she said. "Just a few reporters, those from the major networks and one from the Associated Press. Tell him that, will you, please?"

Slowly, Brock nodded. "I'll get it going. Are you sure you're ready?"

One more deep breath, and then she smiled. "As ready as I'm going to be."

Teased with the promise that this second press conference had something to do with Alex Ramirez and his startling announcements prior, coupled with the presence of the Anniversary Sheriff's Department, the reporters showed up in droves. In fact, peering outside, Kaitlyn thought the number had increased.

Which made her very, very nervous.

Still, true to his word, Roger only allowed five inside. A representative of ABC, NBC, CBS, FOX and the Associated Press. Someone from CNN practically begged for entrance, so after a quick consultation with Kaitlyn, that reporter was also allowed in.

As he'd promised, Brock made sure cameras were rolling and they were live before he ushered Kaitlyn out.

"Ladies and gentlemen," he announced, sounding for all the world like a carnival hawker. "I present to you Kaitlyn Nuhn."

All of the reporters began talking at once, asking questions. Roger called for silence and then informed them that she wanted to make a statement.

At first, Kaitlyn thought she'd be terrified, but by keeping Reed's handsome face in her mind, she found the necessary courage to face the bright lights and the cameras. "After hearing Alex Ramirez earlier, I felt the need to confirm to you all that I most assuredly am not dead. Nor was I kidnapped. I left of my own free will."

Immediately, the questions started again. But since the group was smaller, this time Kaitlyn easily waved them away. Once they'd again fallen silent, she continued.

She held nothing back. She told them everything, including the fact that she had been a witness to Tim's murder, among others.

As she spoke, eyeing the red camera lights which meant she was being broadcast, she could imagine Alex's reaction—if he was watching, which she had no doubt he was—cold hard fury, followed with an immediate desire for vengeance.

When he got like that, nothing could stop him. She hoped like hell Roger Giles and his local sheriff's department were up to protecting her. Because she wasn't trusting anyone else. Not until Alex had been locked up. And even then, she knew she'd have to be watching over her shoulder until he was convicted.

For the third time, Reed stood at the bars of the holding cell, trying to get someone's attention. His attorney had left, promising to file something with someone and see about getting Reed out of there.

Here being, according to his attorney, the Kaufman County Jail. Apparently, all federal prisoners were the custody of the U.S. Marshals, who utilized local jails for holding. Eventually, he would be transferred to Dallas.

Unless a miracle happened.

Though he knew he shouldn't, a tiny spark inside him refused to believe this was hopeless. Kaitlyn was still alive. She had to be. And this time, she wouldn't let him down.

Again, he banged on the bars, asking for his one phone call. So far, his plea had fallen on deaf ears. No doubt Alex had ordered them to make sure Reed had no contact with the outside world.

Just as Reed dropped his hands, about to turn away,

a uniformed officer appeared. Her expression had that world-weary look worn by so many longtime law enforcement officers. "Is there a problem here?" she asked.

Reed hadn't seen her before. And surely, not everyone who worked in this county jail worked for Alex. "I haven't gotten my one phone call."

Her brows rose, indicating surprise. "Let me check the logs. If that's the case, I'll be back."

Finally. Energized, he paced, waiting for her to return.

Instead, two men in suits appeared, the female jailer right behind them. They stepped aside to allow her to unlock his cell.

"You'll get your phone call, I promise," she said. "But you need to speak to these FBI agents first."

Resigned, Reed followed them down the concrete hallway toward what had to be another interrogation room. He hadn't seen these two before. Maybe they were genuine. After all, how many people could Alex Ramirez have on his payroll?

"Some interesting news has come to light," the first man said, as soon as the door was closed and before even telling Reed to have a seat.

"What?" Reed asked, crossing his arms.

"We found the body of George Putchinski, a deputy sheriff in Anniversary, Texas."

"I know who he is," Reed snapped. "What happened to him?"

"He was shot. Two bullets right in the head."

Stunned, Reed could only stare. Any minute, he expected them to try and pin the murder on him.

"What's more, we have video. He had Kaitlyn Nuhn, but she hit him with a frying pan and apparently escaped. Sometime later, Alex Ramirez himself showed up with another man. At Alex's direction, the other man shot George dead. They mustn't have known about the camera."

Then, as Reed struggled to process this news, the agents exchanged glances. "There's more. Kaitlyn Nuhn herself gave a press conference. Live, from an undisclosed location. She claimed Alex Ramirez was actually holding her prisoner for three years and that she was never his fiancée. She also stated she personally witnessed him murder your brother, Tim."

"Did she?" Reed brightened at that. Kaitlyn was not only alive, but safe. "How long ago was the press conference?"

The man shrugged. "I think about thirty minutes ago. Apparently the sheriff's department in your hometown has her in custody."

"The sheriff's department?" Which meant Roger Giles. Reed wasn't sure if Roger was up to the task of keeping Kaitlyn safe. He sure hadn't had a good handle on George, his own deputy.

"That's about it," the agent flashed a fake smile and opened the door. "As of right now, we have no basis for holding you. You're free to go."

Reed didn't move. "What about Kaitlyn?" he asked. "Are you sure she's safe?"

"We've got men on the way to assist the sheriff." The agent looked confident. "We'll put her in protective custody once we have her. It's only a matter of time."

Protective custody. Reed took a deep breath. "Have you arrested Alex Ramirez? She won't be safe until he's locked up."

"Not yet." The agent grimaced. "We sent a team to do that, but he's disappeared. We've got to find him first."

"Disappeared?" Reed took a step forward and stopped himself. He wanted to throttle the man. "You do realize he wants to kill Kaitlyn, right? Her life is in danger."

"Mr. Westbrook, I've asked you to leave." The agent held the door open wider. "We know our jobs, believe me. Now please let us do them."

As soon as she finished speaking, Kaitlyn declined to answer any questions. Flanked by Roger and Brock, she slipped away, stepping into an unmarked police car, which then sped away.

"Wow." Placing her shaking hands against her burning cheeks, Kaitlyn struggled against a rising tide of panic. "That went okay, right?"

"You did very well." Smiling at her, Roger patted her shoulder. "Now we need to get you into hiding."

"You're right about that." She managed a weak smile. "Until he's arrested, Alex will be after my blood."

Brock's cell phone rang. Glancing at it, he flashed a grin. "Finally! It's Reed."

He answered, listened a minute, and then said, "Sure. I'll be there as quickly as I can."

As soon as he ended the call, Kaitlyn grabbed his arm. "Is he all right?"

"Yes. He's at the Kaufman County Jail. They've just released him. I'm going to head over there now and pick him up."

"I want to go with you."

Both Brock and Roger instantly shook their heads. "Not a good idea. It's best to keep you hidden, under guard, where we can keep you safe."

"No one will expect me to be riding with you to pick up a man at a jail," Kaitlyn insisted. She couldn't articulate why it was so important that she see Reed immediately; she just knew it was.

"I'm afraid I'm going to have to insist that you remain here," Roger said.

She smiled at him. "And I'm afraid I'm going to have to insist on going. Unless you're arresting me, which I believe you're not, I'm a free woman."

Shaking his head, Roger mumbled something that sounded a lot like "Women." He grimaced at Brock. "You do something. She's your friend."

"Looks like she's going with me," Brock said, laughing as Kaitlyn widened her smile into a grin. "Come on, Kaitlyn. Let's get you two lovebirds back together."

Lovebirds? Following Brock out back to where he'd parked his truck, she pondered the moniker. *As if.* Except, part of her, most of her…okay, *all* of her wished that were true.

"Wait here," Brock ordered. "We need to check out the parking lot and make sure no one's here who isn't supposed to be."

Roger motioned to two of his men. "Do a sweep of the area. If you see anyone who doesn't belong, chase them off."

Standing in between Brock and the sheriff, Kaitlyn wondered if Reed had been successful in getting her cell phone with the all-important video. She'd made sure not to mention it to anyone else, not even people she trusted, like Zoe and Brock. The less people who knew of its existence, the better.

Finally, the two uniformed deputies returned. "The parking lot is clear," one said. "And most of the media that was camped out in town is gone. So you ought to be safe driving through town."

"Great. Thank you." Roger turned, eyeing Kaitlyn before facing Brock. "Would you like me to go along? Just in case you need some firepower."

"No, thanks," Brock replied. "I have a license to carry, and my pistol is in my truck. We'll be fine."

As they drove away, Kaitlyn couldn't contain her nerves. She kept turning to look behind them, worried someone might be following.

"Hey, if you're this nervous, why'd you want to go?" Brock finally asked, his tone a bit exasperated.

"I have to see Reed," she said. "And I can't really explain why I'm a bundle of nerves. Hopefully it isn't some sort of premonition."

"I don't believe in those." Brock gave her a reassuring smile. "Zoe does, but every time she thinks she's having one, it turns out to be nothing. It's almost over, Kaitlyn. You have to trust that this thing will work out."

Trust. Easy for him to say. Every single man she'd ever known had betrayed her trust. Until now. Until Reed.

Heading toward the highway, each of them fell silent, lost in their own thoughts. The closer they got toward the turnoff that lead to the main road, the more Kaitlyn began to relax. After all, there wasn't a single other car anywhere behind them.

At the stop sign near the graveyard, Brock glanced at her. "Are you okay?"

Slowly, she nodded. "You know, I think I am. I'm ready to put all of this behind me."

"Good." He smiled as he lightly squeezed her shoulder and began driving through the intersection. "Reed's a good man. I'm happy to know you're giving him a chance."

A chance? Kaitlyn realized Brock definitely had the

wrong impression. As she opened her mouth to tell him so, a speeding car came flying over the hill, T-boning them and sending Brock's truck spinning out of control.

For the fifth time, Reed checked his watch. What the heck was taking Brock so long? Though he really didn't want to pressure his friend, well over an hour had passed. The drive from Anniversary to this jail was thirty minutes, thirty-five at best.

And he really wanted—no *needed*—to see Kaitlyn with his own eyes.

A car pulled into the parking lot, coasting slowly to a stop in front of Reed. Reed stepped back. While he didn't think Alex Ramirez would mess with him, he knew he couldn't be too careful.

The window went down and Reed froze. Alex. He had to say, the man had brass balls to show his face around here.

"Get in the car," Alex ordered.

"No." Reed gauged how far he could jump to put the mailbox between them as it was the closest thing to shelter anywhere near. He expected his nemesis to pull out a gun and start shooting. Revenge would have to be the only motive. He guessed Alex wanted to go out in a blaze of glory.

"Your game is over," Reed said, muscles tensed as he prepared to make the dive. "You might as well give it up. Go on inside and turn yourself in."

"I have Kaitlyn."

About to leap for cover, instead Reed froze. "No, you don't. You already tried that one on me once. Don't bother a second time. Despite being locked up, I'm aware she was on TV. I also know the feds are looking for you."

Alex smiled, the white flash of teeth that of a shark about to bite. "Let's call her," he said. "Right now."

Disgusted, Reed turned away. "Give it up. The game is over."

"Wait. I'll do it." Was that a trace of desperation in the politician's voice? "I'll put it on speakerphone."

He dialed. The phone rang once, twice, and then someone picked up. "Hello?" a masculine voice said.

"Put the woman on," Alex ordered. "And put it on speaker."

"Okay. Here. Alex Ramirez wants to talk to you."

"What do you want?" Kaitlyn's voice sounded shaky and stressed. Or worse, in trouble or hurt.

"Kaitlyn. It's Alex," Alex's smug tone made her stomach clench. "I'm here with your boyfriend, Reed Westbrook. Why don't you tell him where you are and what's going on with you?"

"No." Though she felt on the edge of tears, steel threaded Kaitlyn's voice. "Run, Reed. Run away as fast as you can."

A sharp slap, and then Kaitlyn's scream. Hearing that curdled Reed's blood. He stood frozen, rage filling him, as Alex continued to smile. "Now, Kaitlyn dear," Alex said sweetly, "let's try that again. Tell your friend what's happened."

Silence.

"Don't make him hit you again," Alex drawled.

Reed took a step toward the man, gripping the edge of the passenger door. "You touch her again, and I'll kill you," he promised.

"Brock," Kaitlyn screamed. "Alex, please help him. He's bleeding. It looks serious."

Brock? What the… "I think you'd better start explaining," Reed said. "What have you done to my friends?"

"Get in the car."

Reed didn't move.

"Get in the car if you want me to give the order to help Brock McCauley."

Reed got in the car. Once inside, he tried to ignore the pistol Alex had pointed at him. "What have you done to Brock and Kaitlyn?"

The smile spreading across Alex's face was pure evil as he punched the off button on his phone. "They had a little accident. Kaitlyn's injuries aren't serious, though they could be with a little help from my men. Now your friend Brock McCauley…he's pretty badly hurt."

Reed swore. "I got in your damn car. Now tell your men to help Brock."

"All in good time," Alex said. "All in good time."

"Why are you doing this? Revenge?"

"Partly." Alex narrowed his gaze. "But I refuse to let you pieces of trash ruin my political career and my life. The damage you've done can be repaired. And you're going to be the one to repair it."

Was the other man delusional? Because Alex had Kaitlyn and Brock, Reed knew he had no choice but to play along for now.

"Even if I can fix things for you, why would I? You've already lied once to me. You said if I got in the car, you'd get help for Brock."

With a tilt of his head, Alex acknowledged Reed's point. Keeping the gun trained on Reed, Alex hit Redial on his phone.

"Get the injured man some medical help. Yes, I know he'll have to go to a hospital. Drop him off at the nearest emergency room and leave. And make damn sure the woman doesn't escape. There," Alex said, ending the call. "Your friend will get help. And I still have Kaitlyn. And that, my friend, is why you're going to help me."

"I'm not your friend," Reed responded. "Furthermore, do you really think I believe you will let Kaitlyn go, even if I do what you want?"

"You don't have to worry about that." Alex's lip curled in contempt. "Once my good name is restored, my enemies will be watching me closely. I'll need to distance myself publicly from her, of course. But if something were to happen to her, I'd be the first place they would look."

While he had a point, Reed still didn't entirely trust him.

"What choice do you have anyway?" Alex echoed Reed's thoughts. "Nothing will change for me if I kill Kaitlyn now. Nothing."

And in the end, that's what it all came down to. Reed couldn't let Kaitlyn die at Alex's hands. Not only had he promised to protect her and failed miserably, but he loved her.

Even though he knew she deserved better and if they got through this, she'd likely move on, leaving him in the dust, he wanted her to live more than he cared about his own safety.

Reed wasn't fooling himself. He figured once he did whatever Alex wanted, he'd be a dead man.

Apparently taking Reed's silence for consent, Alex continued. "Here's what I want you to do."

After the accident, Kaitlyn must have blacked out. She remembered absolutely nothing after the moment of impact. When she opened her eyes again, she was lying in the back of a windowless van. Her hands had been bound behind her back, and her cuts and scrapes still bled onto the old blanket cushioning her.

Gingerly, she tried to move, needing to see if anything was broken. As far as she could tell, she'd been lucky. Her face throbbed, which meant she had a gash on one cheek. Her arm had been sliced open—not too deep. The way she'd been lying, she'd inadvertently been putting pressure on it and the bleeding had slowed.

Dizzy and weak, she licked cracked lips and tried to figure out what had happened.

A moan from beside her made her slowly swivel her head. Her eyes widened with horror as she took in Brock. The impact had been all on his side, and one leg was twisted at a crazy angle which meant it had to be broken. He had cuts and gashes and looked so battered it tore at her heart.

"Brock," she said. "Can you hear me?"

Apparently still unconscious, he didn't move. Her heart sank. While she couldn't catalog all of his injuries, the ones she could see appeared to be serious.

Turning her head slightly more, she realized she was indeed in a van, and a man sat in the driver's seat with another in the passenger. They were moving. Hopefully, to a hospital.

The van pulled over. Again she tried to raise her head, to push herself up on to her elbows, but lacked the strength. Then, to her disbelief, the man in the passenger seat turned around and held up a phone.

"You're on speaker," he said. "Alex Ramirez wants to talk to you."

The instant she heard Reed's voice, her only thought

was for his safety. When the man slapped her, it felt like a thousand fireworks exploded inside her head. She screamed, unable to help it.

And then Brock coughed. It sounded as if blood bubbled up in his throat. She realized he would die—might die—if he didn't get help immediately.

So she'd begged for him and heard Alex use her plea to make Reed get in the car. Before she could say another word, the call ended. The driver pulled the van back onto the road, and they were again moving forward.

She must have drifted in and out of consciousness. She heard the cell phone ring, the passenger answer. The two men in the front began to argue, but she heard the words *hospital* and *emergency room*. While she didn't know for sure what Reed had done to make this happen, she was grateful.

Now all that was left to do was pray they weren't too late to save him.

After Alex informed Reed what he wanted him to do, Reed swallowed back bile and listed his own conditions. "I'll do it with one condition. I need proof Kaitlyn is safe. Before I open my mouth and say a single word."

"No can do," Alex replied promptly. "I'm well aware she's the only leverage I have. Once I let her go, you'll simply step into the crowd and disappear."

Personally, Reed thought Alex's idea would never work. Even if people believed it—and that was a big if—too much damage had already been done to Alex's reputation for him to ever be able to consider a career in politics. Plus, did the man really think the FBI investigation would simply go away? Who knew, maybe he had so many feds on the payroll he thought he could accomplish that.

Reed didn't trust the man at all. Not for one second did he believe—no matter what he did or didn't do—there was any way Alex would let him get away alive.

However, Kaitlyn still had a chance. She deserved it. She'd suffered enough at this bastard's hands. If Reed could gain her freedom, that would have to be enough.

Yet, Alex had asked the one thing that Reed had sworn he'd never do again, even if his life depended on it. Take the blame for something he hadn't done. Ruin what was left of the reputation he'd worked so hard to build back up.

But what did any of that matter now? Of course he'd do it. For Kaitlyn. As long as he could make sure she was safe. Because never mind the very real possibility that Alex would kill him. Reed couldn't live with himself if he didn't save the woman he loved.

"Proof she's safe or it's a no go." Crossing his arms, he glared at the other man, daring him to argue.

When Alex shrugged and capitulated, Reed let out a breath he'd been holding. "If you can do that, I'm in. Tell me what you had in mind."

The scenario seemed elaborate, speaking to Alex's desperation to regain that which he deemed most important: respect and adulation. As he listened, Reed realized even with Alex leaving out the most important part—Reed's death—it was crazy enough that it might work. If not, it was a hell of an attempt.

Staged as carefully as any movie, the security cameras would be set up to record Reed as he taunted a tied-up Alex and one of his men. Reed would be given a gun with blanks and would brandish this threateningly as he confessed to everything—from coercing Kaitlyn to falsely testify against Alex, to having his own brother murdered, and setting up Alex to take the fall.

Disbelief mounting, Reed listened without saying a single thing. Finally, as Alex went on and on, warming to his story, Reed had to interrupt. "I refuse to say I had my own brother killed. That's off the table."

Alex's smirk infuriated Reed. "I figured as much. I just threw that in there to see how far you'd be willing to go for your whore."

Another deliberate taunt. Clenching his teeth, Reed met the other man's eyes. "Keep it up and I'm beginning to think you really don't want me to do this. Is that what it is? You're just amusing yourself before the feds come and lock you away?"

Though a muscle moved in Alex's jaw, Alex refused to acknowledge the comment. "You left prison and came straight here to get your revenge. And you'd better make this believable. Kaitlyn's life depends on this."

Reed couldn't imagine a scenario where Alex could make him believe Kaitlyn was safe. Finally, he said this out loud. "Because there's no way I'm going to take your word for it," he finished.

Alex raised his brows. "It appears we're at a stalemate. I refuse to let her go until you do what I ask, and you refuse to do it unless I let her go."

"Exactly."

"Then I have no choice." Turning to one of his men, he handed over his phone. "Call them and tell them to kill Kaitlyn Nuhn."

Chapter 15

Though injured and in pain, Kaitlyn was clear-headed enough to understand that if she didn't figure out a way to get away, she was dead. Alex wanted revenge, and in the entire time she'd been his prisoner, she couldn't remember a time when Alex hadn't gotten what he wanted.

Alex would use her to make Reed do something, and then he'd kill them both. That was how he operated. She'd heard him boast about this very same thing too many times to count.

The fact that her guards believed she'd been badly injured was the only thing in her favor. They'd pulled the van around to the back of some building, judging from the huge pole lights shining inside. They'd even killed the engine and both appeared intent on separate tasks—one playing games on his phone and the other texting.

Now or never. She didn't know if she could run and

if she tried, how far she'd get. All she knew was she had to try.

The sliding side door seemed beyond her current capabilities. Plus, in the time it would take her to open it, all one of the men had to do was reach around and grab her. No, she'd have to try the back.

Slowly, painfully, she managed to inch toward the back. Her every movement agonizing, she clenched her teeth and forced herself to go on. She'd either die trying or get away, but she refused to perish at Alex's hand.

Glancing up front, she made sure both men were still engrossed in their phones. They were. And since neither was expecting anything from her, they never once looked back.

Tap, tap, tap. She froze. Someone was knocking on the driver's window.

The driver pressed the down button. "Can I help you officer?"

A policeman. For a split second, she debated calling out for help, but knew they'd shoot him before he had time to react.

No, her best bet would be to use the diversion to her advantage.

"I'm sorry, but this is a no parking zone," the officer said. "I'm going to have to ask you to move."

"No problem, sir." Courteous and pleasant, the driver started the ignition.

Now. Wincing with pain, she crawled to the back door, flipped it to unlock and pulled the handle to open.

The van lurched forward. As it did, the back door flew open, sending Kaitlyn sprawling on the pavement. In agonizing pain, trying in vain to crawl away, she saw the uniformed officer staring at her in amazement.

"They've got guns!" she shouted, as the brake lights flashed on and the van began to reverse. She rolled toward the cop car. The police officer leaped into action, grabbing her arm and yanking her toward his car just as the van careened back over where she'd been.

"Get in," the cop ordered. Ignoring her pain, Kaitlyn managed to do exactly that.

Her savior got on the radio, requesting backup. He'd barely finished when the first shots rang out.

"Get down," he ordered, returning fire. "More units are on the way."

He didn't have to tell her twice. She huddled on the passenger-side floor, in pain and unable to stop shaking.

Sirens wailed in the distance.

"Here they come," he told her, grimly confident as he fired off another round.

Evidently realizing reinforcements were about to arrive, her captors changed plans. They gunned the accelerator and tried to speed away. Two squad cars, lights flashing, pulled in and blocked them.

Another marked car came from the other direction, blocking from the back. Kaitlyn attempted to raise her head to see, but it hurt too much to move.

"Out of the van with your hands above your heads," someone shouted.

"How many are in there?" Kaitlyn's rescuer asked her.

"Two," she managed. "Both armed. And they work for Alex Ramirez, so they know if they're arrested, they're as good as dead. Plus my friend. He's badly injured."

He shot her a surprised look, then nodded before moving away.

Beyond that, Kaitlyn remembered nothing.

When she came to, she opened her eyes to bright lights

and beeping machines. A hospital room. She must have passed out, but her first concern was for Brock. He'd been hurt because of her.

Pressing the call button, she waited impatiently until someone answered. "I need help," she rasped. "Please."

Almost immediately, a uniformed nurse appeared. At this point, Kaitlyn trusted no one, especially since she had no idea how far Alex's reach extended. She wouldn't put it past him to have people in the hospital masquerading as medical personnel.

"My friend. Brock McCauley. Is he here?"

"Who?" The young woman's bright smile faltered.

"My friend. He was dumped off on the curb outside the emergency room." Kaitlyn realized she didn't even know if this was the same hospital. "Please. Can you check?"

"Certainly." The nurse moved away, her sneakered feet soundless.

Once she'd gone, Kaitlyn let her head fall back on the pillow, having already exhausted what little strength she had. She hated that she was so weak. Not only did she not know what had happened to Brock, but Reed was out there somewhere with Alex. And he most likely had no idea she was safe.

She must have slept. When she opened her eyes again, two men in dark suits stood alongside her bed. A shudder of terror nearly paralyzed her. "Did Alex send you?" she croaked.

"No, ma'am," the taller of the two answered. "We're with the FBI. We need to ask you a few questions."

Relieved, she managed a wobbly smile. "Okay. But first, can you tell me what you know about Brock McCauley and Reed Westbrook? Are they all right?"

The men exchanged a glance. "McCauley's here in ICU. He has some pretty serious injuries. His wife is with him."

She nodded. "Thank you. What about Reed? Brock and I were on our way to the Kaufman County Jail to pick him up when we were broadsided."

Surprise registered briefly on both their faces. "Is that so?" one man asked. The other excused himself and went into the hall to make a call.

"You haven't found him yet?" Kaitlyn asked, unable to hide her terror.

"Not yet. But what you've just told us should help tremendously."

A moment later the other agent returned. "We're pulling the prison parking lot video as well as surrounding traffic camera video." He allowed her a slight smile. "It shouldn't take us too long to find him now."

As Alex ordered Kaitlyn's death, Reed knew he was next. Alex had no reason to keep either of them alive if they were no use to him.

Quietly and unobtrusively, Reed pressed the record video button on his phone and placed it next to him. He couldn't believe no one had taken it from him. Maybe, just maybe, he could get Alex to confess.

"Wait," Reed said.

Alex motioned to his man to stop. "What?" he asked, one elegant brow raised.

"I'll do it." Reed kept his voice level. Right now, he needed to stall for as much time as he could. Because he had no doubt how this scenario would play out. He'd do what Alex wanted, and somehow end up shot dead when it was over.

And right now, more than anything, he wanted to live. Despite the mess his life had been recently, Kaitlyn had made him realize his life was worth living. Enough so, he now wanted nothing more than to explore the chance of sharing the rest of it with her.

If they could both survive, that is. He was determined to somehow make this happen. Even if he had to confess to crimes he hadn't committed. "Tell me what you want me to do."

A slow smile spread across Alex's face. "I thought you'd come around to my way of thinking," he said. Turning to the driver, he ordered him to get everything ready.

"First, call your men and tell them not to kill Kaitlyn," Reed ordered.

"Not until we're done," Alex replied. Which meant he had no intention of letting either of them live.

"Also, one more thing. I want to know why you killed my brother."

Cocking his head, Alex flashed him a smile. "Because he had something I wanted. Kaitlyn."

Reed stared. "You killed him over a woman?"

"*My* woman. I knew the instant I saw her. Plus, Tim was skimming off the top, taking my drug money. That alone would have earned him a cement shackle in the lake. Kaitlyn was the icing on the cake."

Bingo. Not only had Alex confessed to the murder, but he'd mentioned drugs and the fact he'd been holding Kaitlyn hostage.

Alex turned away, peering out the window. Reed took that time to slide the phone closer, and then shoved it into his back pocket, leaving it still recording. Even just the sound, without the visual, would help.

"What are you doing?" Alex snapped, staring at him.

Reed stared back, his heart racing. "Getting ready. Where are you going to tape my fake confession?"

"Outside. We're parked in an alley behind a deserted warehouse." Tone dismissive, Alex appeared to be sending a text message. "It'll make everything more authentic."

Authentic. Again, Reed felt like shaking his head in disbelief. Instead, he said nothing, sitting back and waiting, as if he'd become completely resigned to his fate.

"All right," Alex finally said, looking up from his phone. "We're ready to start rolling." The driver passed back a pistol, which Alex handed to Reed. "It's loaded with blanks. Now get out from the car and wait for instructions."

Every nerve on alert for the tiniest opportunity, Reed did as he'd been told. The instant he stepped out, a spotlight illuminated the car.

"FBI." A voice shouted, using what sounded like a bullhorn. "Put your hands in the air where we can see them."

Reed did one better. He tossed the gun away and threw himself on the ground, hands behind his head. If he knew Alex, the other man would go down in a blaze of gunfire.

But no, instead Alex emerged from the car, his hands in the air and a grateful smile creasing his aristocratic features. "Thank goodness you people arrived," he began. "This hoodlum was about to shoot me. He'll have a full confession for you."

Three agents converged on them, weapons drawn. "Don't move." One barked out.

Another one hurriedly cuffed Alex and his driver. The third helped Reed to his feet. "Are you all right?" he asked.

Reed had barely nodded when an infuriated Alex began shouting. "Cuff that man. He's a criminal, with a record, and he threatened me and my man. He needs to be arrested."

No one even responded, other than to bundle Alex and his driver into the SWAT vehicle, reading them their rights as they did.

More relieved than he could say, Reed turned to the agent. His heart still pounding in his chest, he took a quick gulp of air. "I need to find Kaitlyn Nuhn. I have reason to believe her life is in danger."

"It's okay, buddy." The man clapped his hand on Reed's shoulder. "She's safe. She's in the hospital."

"What about Brock McCauley? He was driving her to come pick me up in Kaufman."

The agent's face sobered. "He's there, too, but in worse shape. He's in the ICU. His wife is with him."

Swallowing, Reed said a quiet prayer for his friend. "Can you take me there?"

"I'm sorry." He handed Reed his card. "I'm Special Agent Brown. We've got to question you first, and then I'll personally make sure you get to the hospital. Would that work for you?"

Since he didn't see he had any other choice, Reed nodded. "I have some questions for you, too. I'm really curious how you found us."

The other man grinned. "A combination of info your friend Kaitlyn gave us and traffic cams. That, plus luck. You can't hope for more than that."

Since he was absolutely correct, Reed managed to smile back. "Let's get this show on the road, then. I've got to finish up here so I can go check on my friends."

* * *

Kaitlyn tried to stay awake in case there was any news of Reed, but her eyelids were so heavy they defeated her. Evidently her battered body needed sleep to heal. And while she slept, she dreamed.

At first, the dream didn't make sense. Even when she woke at the end of it, itching to write it down, which she couldn't since she had no paper. Instead, she kept her eyes closed and relived it, hoping to decipher the meaning.

In her dream, she'd been holding a baby. She'd known the baby wasn't hers, but holding her gave her such joy, that it didn't matter. Two people stood back, their faces obscured by mist, but the way they held hands showed they were together. Someone came up behind her, someone beloved, and put his hands on her shoulders as if trying to give her strength.

And in that instant she knew. Someday yes, she would have a baby with this man, but for now the baby she held belonged to someone else. Joy filled her, because this particular child had never been hers, she'd only been asked to hold it for a moment.

She'd awakened before seeing any of their faces, including that of the infant.

Finally, tired of trying to puzzle out the dream, she'd let herself drift back to sleep.

When she next opened her eyes and saw Reed's handsome, worried face, she thought she might still be dreaming. She reached out a hand, even though he was too far to touch.

"Kaitlyn." The deep rumble of his voice brought tears to her eyes. He took her hand, and she held on as if he alone might keep her from drowning.

"I was so worried about you," she said, blinking back unexpected tears. "After I heard Alex order you to get in his car, I didn't know what he planned to do to you." Aware she was probably babbling, she closed her mouth and waited for him to say something.

"They got him, Kaitlyn." He squeezed her hand. "Alex has been arrested. Though the FBI tells me he's already assembled a team of high-powered lawyers to defend him."

Her throat felt tight. "Finally."

When he covered her hand with his, her heart turned over. Aching and confused, she cleared her throat. "Have you seen Brock? Is he all right?"

When he nodded, the relief that flooded her made her feel almost giddy.

"He's going to make it," Reed reassured her. "Zoe hasn't left his side."

Again Kaitlyn battled the urge to cry. Somehow she managed to nod, trying to hide the yearning for more. She wanted him to hold her, to smooth her hair back from her face, and whisper words of comfort or endearment in her ear. Her face heated, glad he couldn't read her mind.

She knew she craved something she could never have. Nor was she even sure she wanted it. She needed to learn how to stand on her own two feet and make her way in this world. Without yet another man wanting to suffocate her.

Yet with Reed gazing so intently at her, she could hardly even think. The shadow of a beard gave him an even more ruggedly masculine look.

"Do you have any update on Brock's condition?" she asked.

"He's definitely improving. They're even moving him up from ICU to a regular room today."

"I'd like to see him," she said immediately.

Reed stood, his dark hair gleaming in the fluorescent lights. "Let me go ask if that's okay. If so, I'll find a wheelchair and push you down there."

He left the room. After he was gone, Kaitlyn tried to sit up straighter, suddenly woefully aware of her lack of clothing. The stupid hospital gown tied in the back at the top, but if she got up she'd have to hold it together with one hand or her entire backside would be exposed. And she wasn't sure she had enough balance to do that.

Still, she needed to try and test her strength. Now would be the perfect time to do it, while no one else was around.

It took a few seconds, but she was able to not only maneuver herself into an upright position, but swing her legs over the side of the bed. When she first saw them, all bruised and scratched up, she winced, understanding the pain better. As her doctor had told her, she was lucky she hadn't broken any bones.

Now to see if she could stand on her own. Gripping the edge of the hospital bed, she worked her feet down toward the floor. One foot, a moment's hesitation, and then the other. Flat-footed, she stood, swaying slightly, her hand on the bed rail her lifeline. After a moment, she allowed herself to breathe. She'd done it.

By the time Reed returned, she'd managed to turn herself around, so that she faced outward rather than the bed. She'd taken care to make sure her hospital gown was as closed in the back as she could make it.

Reed stopped in the entrance to her room, staring. "Look at you," he said, before crossing the room and taking her arm. Even now, she felt the heat of that touch all the way to her core. "Maybe you should sit down and conserve your strength. The nurse has asked for an aide to bring a wheelchair, but you know how long that type of thing can take."

Since she had no idea, she nodded. Though she hated to admit it, the simple act of standing had exhausted her. Easing back until the edge of the mattress touched the back of her knees, she sat. The entire room tilted for a second. She closed her eyes until it passed.

"Are you all right?" Reed again, his husky voice sounding concerned.

"I'm fine." She gave him a rueful smile. "But I'm going to need that wheelchair if I intend to go anywhere."

He waited another couple of minutes, maybe five total, and then took off, telling her he was going to go hunt it down himself.

When he returned, he pushed a heavy-duty wheelchair in front of him. She eyed him, her confusion and sadness gradually replaced by a warm glow. She didn't know what kind of meds they had her on, or even if they were responsible, but right now, in this moment, she felt blissfully, achingly alive. She had some healing to do, sure. As did Brock. And she knew, right up until the moment he was convicted, Alex could somehow manage to go free.

But with Reed gazing at her, his hazel eyes full of light, she felt as if she could do anything. Except walk, that is.

His large hands were gentle when he lifted her, his expression tender, which deepened her sense of contentment. Once she was settled, he took the small blanket off the hospital bed and placed it over her lap, tucking it in for her.

"Let's go say hello to Brock and Zoe," he said. And then he wheeled her out of the room and down the hallway to do exactly that.

Brock looked a lot better than he had the last time she'd seen him. He was sleeping, so Kaitlyn didn't speak. Zoe got up from the chair next to Brock's bed and hugged Kaitlyn, then Reed. "He's so much better." Zoe swallowed, her caramel-colored eyes filling with tears. "For a while, we weren't sure he was going to make it."

Kaitlyn nodded, trying to speak past the lump in her throat. Again, the wild mood swings. Though this time, she knew her guilt and sorrow were completely justified. "I'm so, so sorry," she whispered.

Immediately, Zoe crouched down so she could look her in the face. "It's not your fault, Kaitlyn. Alex Ramirez did this, not you. Please don't blame yourself."

Wiping at her eyes, Kaitlyn nodded. All of the energy she'd felt earlier had vanished. "Tell him I apologize anyway," she told Zoe. A quick glance at Reed told her he understood. But the sympathy in his gaze was too much, again making her want to weep.

"Are you all right?" Concern darkened his eyes.

"I'm fine. Must be the meds," she said by way of explanation. "I can barely keep my eyes open. Reed, do you mind taking me back to my room? I need to sleep." And to be alone, so she could try to puzzle out the confused tangle of emotions plaguing her.

Once he'd gotten Kaitlyn settled back in her bed, a nurse came in to administer meds. After informing Kaitlyn that a physical therapist would pay her a visit later, the nurse told them both it was time for Kaitlyn to take a shower.

Reed took that as his cue to leave. He went home, where Zoe had left Kaitlyn's little dog—at his insistence. He'd told Zoe to focus on getting her husband well enough to return home. He'd take care of Kaitlyn's pet.

The instant he walked in the front door, the little mongrel began barking furiously. As if Reed was an intruder in his own house. Nevertheless, since Kaitlyn loved her pet so much, the least Reed could do was take care of him. "Hey, Bentley." Crouching down at floor level, Reed kept his voice soft and nonthreatening.

Damned if the rodent dog didn't back up, growling and bearing his pointy teeth. Any second now, Reed expected the dog to rush him and chomp down on his leg or arm.

"Fine." Backing away, Reed went into the kitchen and poured the little guy a bowl of kibble. Bentley came running at the sound. This time, his ears were up and his scruffy little tail was wagging.

Moving slowly and deliberately, Reed placed the dog bowl on the floor and stepped back. He watched the dog eat, and he waited for Bentley to lick the bowl clean, before he crossed to the refrigerator and got a beer.

When he looked back, he was startled to realize Bentley had followed him and was sniffing his leg. Now what? Surely Kaitlyn's pet didn't intend to lift his leg on Reed's pants, did he?

Not wanting to take a chance, Reed hustled to the back door and threw it open. "Here, Bentley," he called. "Let's go outside and go to the bathroom."

With a happy bark—at least he thought is sounded happy—the little dog rushed past him and out the door.

Reed watched while Bentley watered his shrubs. Once

the animal had taken care of business, he came back inside without even being called. For such a small dog, even Reed had to admit Bentley made a good companion.

After fixing himself a sandwich, Reed settled on the couch to watch the news. To his surprise, little Bentley jumped up and snuggled right next to him. Smiling broadly, he thought of Kaitlyn's reaction when she saw this. He couldn't wait.

The doctor had said she could go home tomorrow, as long as she had someone to help her. Though he suspected Kaitlyn would be appalled, of course Reed promised to take care of her. The only other alternative would be Zoe and Brock, and not only did they have a business to run, they'd have enough to do getting Brock well.

Reed took Bentley out before going to bed, and locked up. When he woke up in the morning, he stretched and his hand connected with something small and furry.

Bentley. Stunned, he realized the little dog had climbed into bed with him. Grabbing his cell phone, he took a picture to show Kaitlyn, then picked the dog up and carried him outside.

After Bentley had been fed, Reed showered and dressed. He felt a bit anxious, like a kid on his first Christmas morning after his parents have divorced.

He wanted Kaitlyn—and her pet—in his life for good. But she'd belonged to a man for so long, he knew she wanted to stand on her own two feet. It would be up to her to decide if she wanted Reed to be a part of her life. He'd have to fight his own battle of restraint.

The warm ache of desire was always with him, even now when she was in the hospital. The heat would only intensify once they were under the same roof. The strong yearning between them wasn't only one way. They both felt the connection.

But passion alone wouldn't be enough. There had to be more. There had to be trust.

Reed headed to the hospital after breakfast. When he arrived, he popped in to visit Brock first. This time, Brock was awake and sitting up. He seemed alert and smiled a welcome.

"How are you feeling?" Reed dropped into the chair normally occupied by Zoe. She must have run out for coffee or something.

"Better." Brock's smile slipped a little. "Though I'd really like to go home. They're wanting to transfer me to a rehabilitation hospital. I told them I want to go home. I'll continue with my physical therapy from there. Zoe says that's what Kaitlyn is doing."

Reed nodded. "True. They're releasing her today. But she wasn't as badly hurt as you."

"Don't give me that." Shooting Reed a look of disgust, Brock sat up straighter. "You sound like Zoe."

"She only wants what's best for you."

"True. But I'm going home." Brock stared, practically daring Reed to disagree.

"Your choice, man. I'm on my way to take Kaitlyn home."

Brock nodded. "Good. I think Zoe can use the company."

Crap. "I'm not taking her to your place. Zoe's got enough to deal with. She's coming home with me."

Instead of responding, Brock studied Reed's face. When he did reply, it wasn't what Reed had been expecting. "Good. Make sure you don't hurt her. She's already been through enough."

Time for truth. "I plan to make sure she's never hurt again."

The declaration was out there in the open. Both men understood what it meant.

"Good luck." Brock stuck out his hand.

Reed shook it. "Thanks." He allowed himself a wry grin. "I have a feeling I'm going to need it."

Chapter 16

When Reed got to Kaitlyn's room, she was dressed and waiting in the armchair near the window. The wheelchair he'd used the day before sat nearby.

"About time you got here," she said, her voice weak and slightly cross. "Now all we need is to get the doctor to show up and sign those discharge papers."

"Are you all right?" he asked, searching her face. Her alabaster skin seemed paler than usual, and her beautiful eyes were rimmed in red.

"Sorry." She exhaled. "I'll feel better once I get out of here."

He figured now was as good a time to tell her as any. "I'm taking you back to my house with me."

She froze. Her bright blue gaze met and held his. "Why is that?"

Reed guessed he knew what she was thinking, most

likely some kind of convoluted, flawed logic involving holding her prisoner. "Zoe's got enough on her plate dealing with Brock," he said. "So unless you've got somewhere else you'd rather be, I'm afraid you're stuck with me."

"Or vice versa." She swallowed, the movement in her graceful throat drawing his eye.

Forcing himself to look away, he smiled. "You know I don't mind. I've enjoyed having you at my house. Plus, I think Bentley misses you."

At the mention of her little dog, she brightened. "Is Zoe bringing him over?"

He shook his head. "Nope. He's already there." He decided to tease her a little. "I might have to keep him. He's starting to get used to me now."

She knew him well enough to laugh. The lighthearted sound made him smile. "I can't wait to see him." Another glance toward the doorway. "Where are those discharge papers? They said I'd be out of here by ten."

Recognizing and understanding her impatience, he told her he'd go check.

When he got to the nurses' station, the lone occupant was on the phone. She held up a finger, asking him to wait. Once she'd finished her call, he told her what he wanted.

"Going home today?" she asked, sounding surprised. "Let me check her file." Once she'd located the manila folder, she opened and read a sheet of paper. Looking up, she shook her head. "That's what I thought. She was scheduled for release today. But that's been changed. The doctor has ordered more tests."

"What kind of tests?"

Her expression changed, the friendliness becoming a sort or brisk professionalism. "And you are?"

"Her friend."

"I'm sorry, sir, but we can't discuss her medical information with you. We're prohibited by law."

This he understood. "There's a solution for that. Ms. Nuhn is in her room, dressed and ready to go. Why don't you come with me and explain to her what additional tests are needed."

Though she nodded, she made no move to leave her spot behind the counter.

Something wasn't right. The hair rose on the back of Reed's neck. Alex? Even though he was currently in custody, he still had minions willing to do his bidding.

"I'll wait for you in the room," he told the nurse, turning and hurrying back to Kaitlyn.

When he reached the room, he closed the door. "Grab your stuff. We're leaving."

She stared at him. "Did you get the discharge papers? I thought I had to sign something."

"Nope. Something's not right. I'll explain later. Can you walk or do you need the wheelchair?"

"I can walk, but I'm slow." She didn't question him, for which he felt grateful. "It might be faster for you to push me."

Unable to contain his rising agitation, he helped get her settled. "Just act like everything is normal," he said. "No one in the place knows what's going on everywhere. For all anyone knows, you've already been discharged. Getting past the nurses' station will be the only hurdle." Especially since it was on the way to the elevators.

"What about my doctor?" Speaking calmly, she looked over her shoulder at him as he pushed her out the door.

"We'll call him once we're safe. You need to talk to him and find out exactly what's going on. I'm not sure how this works, but I'm guessing if he really ordered more tests, he would have told you about it."

Like all hospitals, this one was busy and no one noticed them leave. They reached the elevator and he pressed the button, doing his best to appear to be waiting patiently. Kaitlyn had gone silent, too, though he couldn't help but notice how she occasionally darted glances over her shoulder.

Inwardly cursing Alex for the long tail of destruction that had started so many years ago and continued to this day, Reed exhaled in relief when the elevator doors opened. Then they were inside, the doors closed, and finally they were on their way to freedom.

Once they reached the front lobby, he fought the urge to push the wheelchair faster. Normally, in an ordinary situation, he would have had her wait while he went and got his truck. Since this was far from normal, there was no way he was going to leave her by herself. Not for even a second.

"How far can you walk?" he asked. "My truck is in the lot, second row back."

"I can do that," she said, her voice ringing with confidence. But when he helped her stand and she went to take the first wobbly step out of the wheelchair, it became apparent she couldn't.

"Sit," he ordered. "I'll just wheel you out to the truck, load up the wheelchair in the bed, and drive it back to the front door."

And that's exactly what they did.

Reed took a roundabout way back to his house, just

in case. He hated to be paranoid, yet he knew what Alex was capable of, even while in police custody.

"I'm thinking we'll go stay at the ranch," he said. Kaitlyn smiled. "I'd like that."

On the way home, Reed's cell phone rang. It was Zoe calling from the hospital.

"They're in a bit of a tizzy here," she said, "trying to find Kaitlyn. I'm guessing you spirited her away?"

"Yep." And he told her about the potentially fake doctor's orders and the sense of danger both he and Kaitlyn had felt.

"Ah, now I understand." She sounded relieved. "Her doctor is here in Brock's room and he'd like to speak to you."

"Okay." That was so unusual that Reed couldn't help but wonder if it was really her doctor or one of Alex's men pretending to be. This frustrated the hell out of him, as he didn't want to go through life seeing Alex's dirty hand in every single person he dealt with.

"Hello?" A male voice came on the line. "May I please speak to Kaitlyn Nuhn? This is Dr. Newberry calling."

Reed handed her the phone. She spoke, listened a minute, then thanked the man and ended the call. When she handed the phone back to read, she appeared about ready to cry. "Dr. Newberry said he didn't change the orders. Someone got into my file and falsified the info. Even worse, if I'd been given those drugs in that quantity, he said it probably would have killed me."

Once Reed had Kaitlyn settled back in her old bed in the guest bedroom, with an ecstatic Bentley beside her, he pulled out the business card he'd been carrying around and called Agent Brown, the one FBI agent he felt he could trust. He relayed what had happened at the hospital and the other man promised to look into it. Meanwhile, he offered to provide a protective detail for Kaitlyn or even move her to witness protection if necessary. While Reed hated the idea, it might be the only way to keep her safe, so he told the agent he'd check with her and let him know.

But when he went back into her room to discuss it with her, Kaitlyn had fallen asleep.

Such a major decision could wait for an hour or two. But Reed paced the living room, wishing he had an outlet for his frustration. No matter what he and Kaitlyn did, he knew they weren't safe. It wouldn't surprise him if the next thing to happen was Alex getting off on a technicality.

Except…Reed had the cell phone video. Time to upload it to the internet and send copies to all pertinent law enforcement agencies, as well as the media.

After finding the USB charger, he plugged it into the phone and to his laptop, and got ready to end Alex's reign of terror once and for all.

Forty-five minutes later, Reed's phone began to ring. Both his cell and his house phone, the one no one ever called anymore and which he'd been meaning to disconnect. They rang and rang, sometimes in unison. He didn't answer, and watched in disbelief as the voicemail messages began mounting.

When his cell showed he had sixty-two new messages, he began to play them back. Most were from various media outlets—the big ones like CNN and FOX, as well as local news stations and newspapers.

Agent Brown had phoned, too. Five times, each call sounding more and more agitated.

Reed took a deep breath and called him back.

"Why didn't you turn that evidence over?" the agent nearly shouted. "That is tantamount to a taped confession and will result in more charges being brought against him."

"No offense, but we weren't sure who we could trust." He explained what had happened during the raid on Alex's house, and about the local sheriff's deputy George who had also been on Alex's payroll. When he'd finished speaking, Agent Brown had gone quiet.

"I think you and I need to have another chat," he finally said.

Reed agreed. "Just not right now. The media is blowing up my phone and I need to watch over Kaitlyn. I would like to take you up on your offer of providing us additional security, if you don't mind." He cleared his throat. "Just make damn sure whoever you send isn't on Alex's payroll."

There was a distinct edge to the other man's voice as he replied. "Will do."

After days of being in the hospital, where it seemed as if she was woken up constantly for tests or blood work or meals, Kaitlyn slept like a baby in Reed's quiet spare bedroom. Even with the lumpy old sofa bed, she felt at home in his house, an odd sort of feeling since she was only a guest.

Sunlight warm on her face woke her. Stretching, she winced at the twinges of pain. It took a moment to register why she felt so battered and bruised, another that she was no longer in the hospital.

"Are you finally awake?"

Reed. A hot flush suffused her entire body and she

looked to see him standing in the doorway. At first, she felt a flash of panic, wondering if he'd been watching her while she slept. But then, she relaxed. This was Reed. Her friend. They needed to figure out the logistics of their relationship. He was the man she loved and wanted to be with for as long as she lived.

"I am." She smiled brightly, unable to keep from tugging down the hem of the oversize T-shirt she slept in. "I could really go for a shower and then a cup of coffee."

"I can't help you with the first, but I can make some coffee." Gaze intense, he returned her smile. "You're going to have to walk." He indicated the crutches leaning on the wall next to her bed. "You can use those. We don't have a wheelchair."

Pushing her hair away from her face, she nodded. "That's a good thing. My physical therapist told me I need to start walking. A little bit at a time, to build up my strength."

Light smoldered in his eyes as he studied her. "Sounds good. Take your time. I'll wait for you in the kitchen."

Once he'd gone, Kaitlyn pushed herself to a sitting position. Slowly, she swung her legs, one at a time, wincing at the aches and pains. Overall, she'd been lucky. No broken bones, just some messed-up tendons and a sprained ankle. In time, all of this would pass.

Gingerly, she lowered herself to the ground, good ankle first. With some maneuvering, she was able to grab the crutches. Then, feeling extraordinarily proud of herself, she hobbled into her bathroom to get ready to start her day.

When she emerged thirty minutes later, having showered, brushed her teeth and blow-dried her hair, she felt like a new person. The pain had subsided to a dull ache.

And the delicious scent of freshly brewed coffee wafting her way from the kitchen made her smile.

As she went toward it, the sight greeting her made her stop and stare. Throat tight, heart full. Reed stood at the stove, his back to her, his broad shoulders straining the cotton T-shirt he wore. He appeared to be cooking. She sniffed. "Is that an omelet?"

Turning, he grinned, a flash of white in his tanned face. "Yep." He handed her a mug. "Here's your coffee. One cream, one sugar. Exactly how you like it."

She took a sip and nearly moaned with pleasure. "Have I died and gone to heaven?"

His grin widened. "Wow, you really know how to thank a guy."

She hadn't realized she'd spoken out loud. Though she knew she'd turned red, she shrugged it off. She liked this new easygoing, friendly Reed. Pushing aside a pang of longing, she hobbled over to the table and awkwardly lowered herself into a chair. A minute later he brought her a plate with a perfectly cooked ham-and-cheese omelet.

"Wow." Inhaling deeply, she smiled at him. "This looks wonderful. Thank you."

Their gazes locked. Her heart turned over, even though she willed herself not to react. She needed to get used to thinking of Reed as a friend, nothing more. Even though he'd always be more to her.

He pulled out the chair across from her, watching as she ate. "I bet you're glad to be out of the hospital."

"Yes." Swallowing the last bite, she blotted her mouth with the paper napkin and then took a deep drink of her coffee. Though she tried to relax and enjoy the moment, she couldn't keep from frequently glancing at the front window and front door.

"Are you all right?" he asked, noticing.

"Ever since the hospital confirmed someone changed my orders, I'm even more nervous." She decided to be honest. "Since I'm the only witness, I guess I'm going to be spending the rest of my life looking over my shoulder, aren't I?"

"Maybe, maybe not. But..." His smile widened. "I got a taped confession out of him. I've already sent it to every media outlet I could think of. The FBI also has a copy. So even if you weren't able to testify, there's enough incriminating evidence to put him away for a long time."

Stunned, she wished she could jump up and hug him. "How did you manage that?"

"I just hit Record on my cell when he wasn't paying attention and asked him a few questions." He shrugged as if it was no big deal. "The media is going nuts. I'm sure the craziness will fade once Alex is convicted. A few months after that and no one will even remember who he is."

Almost afraid to believe, she waited.

"I don't know how long it will take to uncover his massive web of deception," he continued. "Or for his trial to come up on the docket. The main thing we need to hope for is that they'll consider him a flight risk and refuse bond."

Bond. She hadn't even thought of that. The idea made her shudder. "If they let him bond out, he'll come after me for sure."

"The FBI has promised extra security." He gave her a long look. "Meanwhile, instead of worrying about him, why don't you start thinking about making plans for your future? It's wide-open now, full of possibility and potential."

Without him? She managed a tentative smile back. "I like the way you put that."

"Do you?" He leaned forward, a lock of dark hair falling over his forehead. "Do you have any ideas? Any thoughts about what you might want to do?"

"Zoe and I were talking about that. I'm a pretty good cook," she put in, hesitating despite herself. "I'm considering starting a gourmet brownie business. I could start out local, and then set up a website and ship orders all over the country."

He nodded. "Great idea." Every time his gaze met hers, her heart skipped and her stomach did a flip.

His cell phone rang. Frowning as he glanced at the caller ID, he answered and listened for a moment.

"What?" Reed's voice echoed with fury. "You can't be serious."

Something, a premonition, a shiver of disaster, had her turning. When she caught sight of the stark fury on his face, she froze.

"I'll let her know," he said, still staring at Kaitlyn. "And yes, we would appreciate whatever extra protection you can provide."

As he ended the call, she waited, heart pounding in her throat. "What is it? What's happened?"

"Alex has escaped." Crossing to her, he wrapped her tightly in his arms. "They're looking for him now. But until he's found, both of us are in grave danger."

Her entire body started shaking, something which she realized she had absolutely no control over. "Oh crap."

"Shh." He crossed to her, pulling her in close and stroking her hair. "I'll protect you."

For one wonderful second, she allowed herself to melt into his embrace. And then, when she realized she'd reverted to her former pattern of letting a man take care of her, she pushed out of his arms. Refusing to meet his gaze in case she'd hurt him, she grabbed her crutches, climbed to her feet and hobbled into the living room. There, she picked up the television remote and clicked the TV on.

"A massive manhunt is underway," the reporter said, panning to a shot of a chopper with a spotlight. "Suspected killer and former congressional hopeful Alex Ramirez has escaped and is on the run. This is not looking good for someone who, until now, has steadfastly maintained his innocence."

Kaitlyn could only stare at the screen. She felt hollow, almost resigned.

"Resigned to what?" Reed asked, his expression thunderous.

She sighed. "I wasn't aware I'd spoken out loud. This has to end. Now. I have no doubt Alex is on his way here."

"That's what the FBI thinks, too. I can promise you this. If he comes here, there's no way he's going to get you."

Eerily calm, she turned to face him. "Why do you say that? What kind of guarantee do you have?"

His expression hardened. "The FBI have assured me. They've got men all over the place outside. There are even snipers hidden somewhere."

"And of course the FBI has such a good track record." She didn't bother to hide her bitterness. "You do realize what he'll do to us once he finds us, right?"

"He won't get that far."

She inhaled, using her crutches to pivot and survey the room. "We need to arm ourselves."

"What?" Staring, he didn't move.

"Yes. Open your gun safe. I need that .38. The one I used before."

Eyeing her, he appeared to be considering her plan. Hands in a white-knuckled grip on the crutches, she clenched her jaw and struggled to contain her agitation.

"I can handle that pistol," she told him, just in case there was any doubt. "And if Alex makes it in here, I deserve a chance to defend myself."

She had him there. She knew the instant when he realized. Without another word, he turned and went to his gun safe to retrieve weapons so they could arm themselves.

Once Reed returned and handed her the pistol, Kaitlyn checked to make sure it was loaded. "More ammo?"

He handed it over. She saw he held another, larger pistol. Seeing her look, he shrugged. "Just in case, like you said."

The news report had gone to commercial.

Kaitlyn glanced at the front door. "I want to sit on the floor, with my back against an interior wall," she told Reed. "But I have to be able to see the front door."

"He's not going to make it that—"

"Stop." She held up her hand, grimly determined. "Humor me. Let's plan as if we know he will."

"Fine. What about the back?" he said. "If he manages to get past all the law enforcement personnel stationed outside, I think he'd be more likely to come in through the back."

"You might be right," she allowed reluctantly. "Is there somewhere we can sit and have a view of both doors?"

"Maybe." He looked as grim as she felt. She couldn't explain the feeling, but she was absolutely certain Alex Ramirez would soon be bursting through one of the doors. He'd want his revenge, and wouldn't care if he died getting it. Especially not now, with his political career in tatters and every ounce of respect he'd once had kicked into the gutter.

"He has nothing to live for," she said. "That's why I think he'll come in through the front. Blaze of glory and all that."

Something akin to pain flashed across Reed's face. "You really know him well, don't you?"

"Unfortunately, I do."

Reed gestured to a spot near the entrance to the kitchen. "Here. If you lean forward, you can see the front door and if you lean back, you can see the back. It's good because it's not a direct shot from either place, so if he comes through shooting..."

"Perfect." Still skirting the windows, she took a seat. Reed sat down next to her.

"You know we're going to feel pretty foolish when he's captured," he said, in what she suspected was clearly an attempt to tease her out of her black mood.

"Maybe," she allowed. "But at least if that happens, we'll still be alive. And if it doesn't, we have a fighting shot."

The news show had returned, but they were no longer talking about the search.

"Let's turn that off," Reed suggested.

Startled, she looked down to see she still had the remote. "How about we just turn it down? I want to hear if there's any news on his capture."

She pressed the volume button without waiting for his response. As she moved, their upper arms bumped. Instead of giving in to her first impulse, which was to scoot away, she did the opposite and moved closer.

"Are you all right?" he asked, the huskiness in his voice making her heart ache.

"No." He deserved an honest answer. "I know I'm being pessimistic, but I can't shake the feeling we're—or at least I'm—not going to get out of this alive."

"Listen to me," he ordered, cupping her chin and making her look at him. "Evil doesn't always win."

Gazing into his eyes, so close if she leaned forward a few feet their noses would bump, she couldn't stop feeling that this was it—the end. She'd been lucky before, always keeping ahead of him, but this time her luck seemed to have run out. She had no faith in law enforcement right now. The only people she had faith in were herself and Reed.

In that instant, she knew there was one thing she had to do before she died. Tell Reed the truth.

"Reed." Even speaking his name, her voice trembled. As she gazed at him, his pupils dilated. When he leaned in to kiss her, she held up her hand to stop him.

"I love you," she said, putting her heart into words.

"Don't say that," he groaned. "Not now. I understand, believe me. And know this—I don't ever want you to feel like you have to pay me back."

Crushed and hurting, she couldn't respond. He understood? Once again she'd managed to make a complete and utter fool of herself. She loved him. He understood. Clearly, Reed didn't feel the same way.

To her humiliation, a tear rolled down her cheek. Wiping her eyes with her fists, she twisted away in order to hide her pain.

"Kaitlyn, don't be like that," he said, his deep voice full of sympathy. "Listen to me. You're special to me, I promise."

Special. Next he'd say the same thing she'd once said about him, before she'd realized the true depth of her feelings. If he dared to say he thought they would always be friends, she didn't know how she'd react.

The sharp report of gunfire outside made her freeze. Reed pushed away, motioning at her to stay low as he crawled to a spot on the wall opposite her. "I've got the back door," he said, his voice low and urgent. "You watch the front."

After a quick nod, she checked her weapon, making sure the clip was in place. Then she removed the safety and raised the pistol, pointing it toward the door. She braced her arm on her knee to keep her aim steady.

Tense, she sat up straight, keeping her back against the wall. Now she'd be as ready as she was going to get to defend herself against whatever—whoever—came in through the front.

Which her intuition told her would be the way he came.

As long as she'd known Alex Ramirez, he'd never lost. Though she wanted to, she couldn't bring herself to believe this time would be any different. Except this time, she didn't plan on going down without a fight.

More gunshots, a sharp *rat-ta-tat-tat,* like in a mob movie.

"Sounds like a friggin' AK-47," Reed said, his voice grim. "If he comes in here spraying gunfire, promise me you'll dive for cover."

Still intent on watching the door, she nodded. She would, but first, she intended to put a bullet through the bastard's head.

A siren screamed, a quick *whup-whup,* cut off in mid-squawk.

She and Reed exchanged glances. But she couldn't tear her focus away for long, so she returned to watching the front entrance, her pistol steady and unwavering.

Yet another round of gunfire, and then someone screamed, the sound high and desperate and awful. Immediately, the back of Kaitlyn's throat began to ache, though she knew she couldn't afford to empathize. Not right now. Not just yet.

As if a movie played in her head in slow motion, the front door burst open. A shout from outside, a shot, and the figure briefly silhouetted in the doorway jerked up, the outline of the assault rifle ominous as it pointed up, firing a round into the ceiling before the man who carried it crumpled.

Chapter 17

Kaitlyn didn't have time to react, and yet she did. She crumpled in on herself, shielding her body and firing off a shot of her own, much too late. The opposite of what she'd intended, yet she registered relief that it hadn't been her shot that had taken him down. She'd never killed anyone and was grateful she wasn't starting now.

More voices. Shouting. A spotlight shining in the doorway, blinding her. Reed's arms around her, his deep voice reverberating in her ear, telling her it was going to be all right, that she was safe.

Telling her Alex Ramirez was dead. And despite believing that someone else had killed him, she'd also shot him. When she started to shake, she closed her eyes as if she could escape it all.

Reed carried her outside, handing her up to a waiting paramedic, who sat her down in the ambulance.

"Was she hit?" he asked.

"I don't think so." Reed sounded worried. No, more than that. Terrified. She didn't understand why. She wasn't hurt.

The tears came. She couldn't stop crying. From relief? From anguish? From what…she didn't know, her tangled emotions had her tied in knots. She was on the verge of becoming hysterical, but she didn't know how to stop it from happening.

Luckily, one of the paramedics did. "You're going into shock," he said. "Now you need to slow your breathing down and quit hyperventilating, or you're going to pass out."

Now the shudders came, wracking her body so violently her teeth chattered. "I can't," she moaned, praying he could give her something to help.

When she saw him lift the needle, she exhaled with relief.

Reed stood by helpless, watching as Kaitlyn fell apart. Alex Ramirez was confirmed dead—one of the snipers had taken him out before he'd been able to do any more damage. Two federal agents and one local police officer had lost their lives, and four others were wounded.

Once Kaitlyn had been sedated, the paramedic insisted she be transported to the hospital for observation. Though Reed knew he might be paranoid, he refused to allow this. He didn't know how many more of Alex's men might be out there, still tasked with getting Kaitlyn. Until they were rounded up, exposed and arrested, he couldn't take the chance.

He hoped once Alex's apparently vast army learned

of their leader's demise, they'd drift away into their own lives and leave Kaitlyn alone.

More than anything, he wanted her to be free to have the life she'd always been missing. Even if he had to rip a chunk out of his own heart to do it.

With the reluctant paramedic's help, Reed managed to get Kaitlyn into his truck. She was pretty out of it, but they were able to use the portable wheelchair to move her.

Then, despite the FBI's insistence that he remain for questioning, he took Kaitlyn home to the ranch they both loved.

On the drive, she opened her eyes and gave him a drowsy look from half-lidded eyes. "Where am I?"

"On the way to the ranch. We're almost there." Ignoring the sharp stab of desire, he managed to give her a reassuring smile. "Go back to sleep. I'll wake you when we arrive."

To his relief, she did exactly that. As he drove, he kept stealing glances at her. Even in sleep, she enchanted him.

When he pulled up in front of the ranch house a few minutes later and parked, she was still sound asleep.

He took one final moment to gaze at her, the spotlight a few feet away putting her profile partly in shadow. Her beauty—both inside and out—made his chest ache. He loved her, loved her more than he'd ever thought it was possible to love someone. Loved her so much, he'd give her the gift of letting her go. No matter how badly it hurt him.

The first few nights Kaitlyn had been back in Reed's ranch house, she hadn't been able to sleep. Even though Reed had given her his bed and had taken the couch. Every time she started to drift into slumber, she kept seeing Alex framed in the doorway, his AK-47 ready to mow her down, and then his body jerking as he was riddled with gunshots.

Reminding herself that she would have been dead if someone hadn't taken Alex out was a thought she held on to like a lifeline.

By the third day she felt as though she'd gotten herself back. She could walk without the crutches and her body no longer felt as if it had been run over by a steamroller. She celebrated by taking her car into town by herself for shopping and then some ice cream. It felt amazing not having to hide, and she was surprised by the friendliness of everyone she met. Since her story had been on the news for so long, everyone acted as if they knew her, even if Kaitlyn was just meeting them for the first time.

Initially, she'd been a bit startled. But as the day wore on, she found it charming. Amazing how much more she'd come to like the town of Anniversary now that she was able to get out and about in it.

Since Reed had offered to let her stay with him until she could get on her feet, she pushed away the constant, nagging hurt that he hadn't been able to tell her he loved her back. She told herself she was okay, that she enjoyed his company, and despite the fact that her insides turned to mush every time he looked at her, she realized she'd been a fool to expect more than friendship from him.

Eventually, she supposed the pain would go away.

Focusing on her new business helped to distract her. She'd started small. Every day, she baked a huge batch of gourmet brownies. She individually wrapped a dozen and took them to the feed store, where Zoe and a recovering Brock sold them for two dollars each. The rest, she carried to Sue's Catfish Hut. Sue had added them to the dessert menu and claimed they were a big hit with customers.

Kaitlyn had purchased a domain name and hosting service, and had started the process of building her own website. Eventually, she hoped to take online orders and ship her brownies to various locales.

Someday. For now, she was doing what she loved, and making money. For the first time in a long time, she was happy. The only thing that would have made her happier would be for Reed to want to be more than just a friend.

Ah well, maybe with time. Life was so good, she felt greedy wanting everything.

Now it was Friday, and Kaitlyn had been looking forward to her lunch date with Zoe all week.

After putting the finishing touches on her makeup, Kaitlyn dug her car keys out of her purse. At least now she no longer had to hide her car. Circumstances had certainly improved now that Alex was gone and she no longer had to constantly look over her shoulder.

Humming all the way, she drove into town. As she crossed the long bridge over the lake, she relished the way the water sparkled in the sunlight. A few boats were out, fishermen mostly, though she spotted a speedboat idling near the bridge.

When she arrived at Sue's and walked in, Zoe was already seated in one of the booths. Kaitlyn grinned at her friend, who looked happy enough to burst. Practically bouncing up and down in her seat like a child, Zoe jumped to her feet and gave Kaitlyn an impulsive hug.

"Sit, sit," Zoe gushed impatiently, trying to hide an impish grin. "I have the best possible news."

"Tell me!" Kaitlyn ordered, lowering herself into the booth. "Your excitement is contagious."

"It should be. Brock and I are going to be parents! The adoption agency called, and we're getting a baby girl." As soon as Zoe finished speaking, she began to cry, smiling a watery smile as tears ran down her cheeks.

"Are you all right?"

"Happy tears," Zoe said, waving away Kaitlyn's attempt to hand her a napkin.

Kaitlyn's own eyes filled, remembering her dream. "That's fabulous," she said. "I'm ecstatic for you two."

The waitress came, bringing Kaitlyn a menu and an iced tea without being asked. Kaitlyn didn't even glance at the menu. She knew what she wanted. The catfish lunch special. Two pieces of crispy fried perfection, tater tots and cole slaw, along with a couple of hush puppies. Nothing made her feel more at home than this quintessential Southern-style meal.

"I just can't believe I'm going to be a mother." Zoe sat back in the booth, her expression both dazed and elated.

"When?" Kaitlyn asked.

"Next week." Zoe drank deeply. "Just enough time to get a nursery set up. Will you help me shop? I'm planning on heading to Dallas for a day."

"Of course." Kaitlyn felt honored. And excited, too. It wasn't every day that her best friend had her deepest wish granted. "How's Brock?"

Zoe's smile barely dimmed. "He's still doing physical therapy three times a week. He just started walking, using a cane, and insists on going to work. He won't be able to hold the baby yet, at least not while standing. But he's over the moon and ready to be a dad."

They ordered, and chatted some more about baby clothes and what theme to use in the nursery.

When their meals arrived, they both fell silent and dug in.

Finally, with plates mostly empty and bellies full, in unison they leaned back in their seats and sighed in contentment. Kaitlyn felt a bit queasy, which she figured was due simply to overeating.

"How's Reed?" Zoe asked casually.

Not fooled, Kaitlyn shrugged. "He seems fine. We're kind of roommates."

"Ooh."

Since this was Zoe, Kaitlyn leaned forward and leveled with her. "It's driving me crazy. He treats me like he thinks I might break if he touches me."

Zoe winced. "I think he's trying to give you time to make up your mind."

"Make up my mind about what?"

"Kaitlyn, for the past three years, you've been a prisoner, completely controlled by a domineering man. Reed's trying to give you space, and let you make the choice. I'm pretty sure he's not going to be the one to initiate anything. He wants you to feel secure and to be absolutely certain."

Stunned, Kaitlyn didn't know what to say. When she finally found her voice, it came out shaky. "That's not it, Zoe. You see, right before Alex was killed, I told Reed I loved him."

"Seriously? What did he say?"

Glancing away to try and hide the hurt, Kaitlyn grimaced. "Something about how he didn't want me to feel like I owed him. And that I was special to him."

"Well, there you go."

Kaitlyn blinked. "Zoe, he didn't say he loved me back.

He acted like I was telling him my deepest feelings out of a sense of gratitude."

Zoe started shaking her head before Kaitlyn had even finished speaking. "Don't you see? That's because that's how your life has been up to now. Men give you things, and they think they own you. Reed doesn't want that for you. He wants you to stand on your own feet and when you do give your love, it needs to be without any strings attached."

Strings. "All of life is made up of strings. Everyone— you, me, Brock, Reed—we're all connected by a web of strings of one sort or another. No." Jaw set, Kaitlyn shook her head. "If he truly loved me, he would have said so."

Zoe leaned forward, her expression serious. "Sometimes, love is letting go."

"No greeting card poetry, please."

"I mean it," Zoe continued. "And I'm not quoting you meaningless rhymes. I believe Reed does love you. Brock thinks so, too. But he's afraid if he tells you, you'll feel obligated to stay with him, and then you'll always wonder if you missed out on something in your life."

Truth resonated in Zoe's voice. Her words hit home. Kaitlyn attempted to act unfazed, but she began trembling and no matter how hard she tried to will herself not to, she couldn't stop. She finally clenched her hands together, hoping Zoe wouldn't notice.

"You're right—he's right," she managed, choking on the certainty, though her voice came out clear and strong. "I've never been given a chance to decide before. Anything."

Despite her resolve, to her consternation, her eyes filled with tears. Again. She'd been doing that a lot lately.

"Are you all right?" Zoe asked, clearly concerned.

"It seems I'm full of emotion these days." Kaitlyn summoned up a watery smile. "And I've learned a few things on my own during all this. Walking my new path alone won't give me strength. Walking it with the right partner just might. With Reed, my life just seems to get better and better."

"Then the answer is simple." Wrinkling her nose, Zoe flashed an impish smile. "Go after what you want. Prove to him that he's a necessary part of your life."

Taking a deep breath, Kaitlyn lifted her chin. "You know what? I'm going to do exactly that."

But a few days passed while Kaitlyn tried to gather up her courage. Zoe called, excited beyond words, and let her know that the adoption agency had notified them that she and Brock were getting their baby daughter in a couple of days. Kaitlyn rejoiced for her friend. When she told Reed, he grinned and said he needed to buy Brock a cigar.

While making brownies, Kaitlyn rehearsed a dozen different scenarios, wishing she had more courage, aware that whenever she chose to talk to him, the outcome would affect the remainder of her life.

On top of that, she'd realized she was over a month late on her period. She bought an at-home pregnancy test, not really surprised when the stick showed she was pregnant.

Now she had not only her own happiness to think about, but her unborn child's. *Their* unborn child's. She decided she wouldn't tell Reed until she learned how he felt. Even if he didn't want her, she'd make sure he had

access to his child. But she didn't want him to feel obligated in any way.

Another week went by. Still she procrastinated, though
the anticipation was making her tense. Yet every time
she thought about putting everything on the line, she felt
sick. She called Zoe for encouragement, and ended up
inviting Zoe and Brock over to show off their new baby
and have dinner that night. Despite the long drive, they
agreed to come.

"You'd better have told him by then," Zoe threatened.

Kaitlyn gave an uneasy laugh. "I will," she promised.
"Though it will be an extremely awkward evening if it
turns out he doesn't share my feelings."

"I don't think you have to worry about that," Zoe said.
"Now get out there and do your thing, girl."

"I will. See you tonight."

Since her nerves were getting the better of her, Kaitlyn
did what she did best—baked. She made a batch of her
best brownies, the ones with double chocolate, caramel,
marshmallows and nuts. According to Zoe, whenever
she'd made these, they sold out within hours.

Reed walked into the kitchen as she was slicing them.
"Smells wonderful," he said, his easy smile making her
entire body clench.

"Try one." Heart racing, trying to act normal, she offered him a gooey brownie on a paper napkin. "I hope
you don't mind, but I invited Zoe and Brock to dinner
tonight. I'm dying to meet their new baby."

He shrugged. "Sounds good. Do I need to run to the
grocery store or anything?"

The easy camaraderie of the scene floored her. Doing
her best to sound casual, she shook her head. "Nope. I've

got enough supplies to make spaghetti and meatballs, plus a salad and garlic bread."

He studied her and finally smiled. "You seem quite comfortable in the kitchen."

Now or never. Trying to ignore her racing heart, she nodded. "I am. I really appreciate you letting me stay here with you."

Reed considered her, his gaze smoky. "You know if you stay here too long, the locals are going to consider you tainted by proximity. My bad reputation will spill over to you. That could hurt your business."

Was he hinting that she should leave? Deciding to focus on the positive, she managed a smile. "Your reputation is about to get a dramatic overhaul. Once the rest of the news story reports on Alex, everyone will know you were wrongly convicted. I've already sent a letter to the governor asking for a full expunge of your records."

At her words, he swallowed hard. "You did that? For me?"

"Of course I did. All this time, the years of your life that were lost because of Alex…" Blinking back tears—again!—she swiped at her eyes. "This is the least I can do for you."

The least she could do. If only he knew, she wanted to do so, so much more. And might, if he'd let her, now that she'd overcome her fear of becoming lost in a man's shadow. Reed wasn't the type to keep her in darkness. She knew he'd support her, be there for her and help her grow.

Reed didn't speak, not at first. Head bowed, he turned his cowboy hat over and over in his hands. When he raised his gaze to hers, the gratitude and pain in his eyes nearly undid her.

"Thank you," he said, his voice thick with emotion. "I really appreciate that."

She ached to reach for him, to hold him, to press her body and her lips to his. Instead, she kept herself still, telling herself she didn't want to use her body to distract him.

Now would be the time to let him know how she felt. Until now, fear of rejection had kept her from speaking the truth. Even now, the possibility that he could turn her down made her insides quake.

She had nothing to offer but herself. All of her, body, soul and heart. And if she didn't at least try, she'd spend the rest of her life wondering what might have been.

"Reed," she began, swallowing hard. She knew she had to be careful—too much and she'd scare him off, too little and he might not even want to try. "I'd like to stay here with you indefinitely."

"You would?"

Aware he didn't understand the full meaning of her statement, she continued. "Yes. I enjoy your company. And if you agree, I'd like our relationship to…" She stopped, trying to find the right words. How could she tell him she wanted them to make love again, without sounding needy or worse, crass?

Knowing if she hesitated, she'd never regain her nerve, she blurted out the words. "I'd like to make love again."

There. She'd said it.

Reed didn't respond, though his gaze had darkened.

"So," she finished, probably sounding a bit lame, "I was thinking we could give it a shot, if you'd like. Having a real relationship. More than just roommates. On a trial basis, of course."

He stared at her, his gaze dark with emotion. "A trial basis?"

"Yes." She rushed on, aware she probably was making a mess of things, but too nervous to figure out how to correct it. "That is, if you want to."

"I do. But since we're being honest, you should know I want more," he said, reaching out and capturing her hand in his. "I'd like to give us a fighting chance." He looked away. "But I'm not sure I'm up for a trial basis, open-ended thing. I understand that would be best for you, but I'd rather just wait until you're certain."

She gaped at him. "I'm not sure I understand. What are you trying to say?"

"I'm a one hundred percent kind of guy," he said quietly. "All or nothing for me. I'd much rather wait until you're positive, until there's not a single doubt that I'm the one for you."

"I—"

"I know." He met her gaze and held it. "You might not ever reach that conclusion. I understand how important your freedom is to you. You could easily see a better life on the horizon, something so richer than anything you could ever have with me. In that case, I'll respect your decision and watch you walk away."

Excuses? Couched in pretty lies and vague phrases? If so, she was having none of that.

"It's time to cut through all the nonsense," she told him, pulling her hand from his. She kept her chin held high and her voice unwavering. "If you don't want me, just say so."

"Don't want you?" Incredulous, he took a step toward her and stopped, hands clenched into fists at his side.

"Kaitlyn, how could you even think that? If anything, I want you too much. But I don't think my heart can stand a trial anything."

The tightness in her chest eased. He wanted her too much. What about love?

As if she'd spoken out loud, something intense flared in his gaze. "I love you, Kaitlyn. I know you said you love me, too, but I need to be sure you mean it."

He loved her! Her heart sang. "All or nothing, then?" she asked, loving him so much she thought she might burst.

"Exactly." The sadness in his voice told her what he believed she would choose.

Lifting her chin, she caught and held his gaze. Heart pounding so hard she thought it might burst from her chest, she took a deep breath. Going for the gusto was harder than she'd thought it would be, like baring her soul.

"And, if you're really serious about all or nothing," she continued, "I'd like to ask you if you want to get married."

Time stopped. Frozen, she couldn't move, couldn't think, couldn't breathe. If he turned her down, if he didn't really mean what he'd said, then she'd have no choice but to leave. Forever.

Hope warred with uncertainty in his unwavering gaze. "I need to know one thing, Kaitlyn. Are you absolutely sure that this is what you want?"

"I've never been more certain of anything in my life. I want a life with you." Conviction lent her bravery. "With love. Supporting each other, no matter what. All or nothing."

The fact that she'd thrown his own words back at him wasn't lost on him. A smile tugged at Reed's mouth. A very sensual, loving smile.

When he reached for her and covered her mouth with his, she had her answer. But, even though the passion of his kiss set her aflame, she knew she needed to hear the words. She had to know, could not assume.

All or nothing.

Gently, she pulled herself back. "Well?" she asked, aware she sounded like a breathless girl. "I need an answer."

Grinning, he pulled a small, black velvet box from his pocket. "I've been carrying this around for over a week. It was my mother's, and she left it to me when she died."

"Why?" Kaitlyn could hardly believe it.

"Just in case I ever got the slightest sign from you that you might want me. Permanently."

And then, while she stood shocked, filled with relief and joy, he removed the sparkling diamond ring and slipped it on her finger, murmuring, "My answer is yes."

They met halfway, his mouth covering hers in a hunger she shared. His kiss sang in her blood, and she gave herself freely, finally safe in the certainty of his love.

Later, much later, the doorbell chimed. Breaking off from what had started out as cuddling after and turned into a deep and passionate embrace, Kaitlyn took a deep breath. "Reed, I have something else to tell you."

"Save it for later when we're alone." He reached out and tucked a strand of hair behind her ear.

Suddenly, she realized she might be a mess. "Do I look okay?" she asked.

Eyes dark and full of passion, his proud grin was her

answer. "You're always gorgeous to me, no matter what." That said, he went to the front door and opened it.

Zoe and Brock stood on the front steps, both beaming. Zoe stepped forward, Brock's hand on her shoulder. She tenderly held a tiny infant in her arms. "Meet April," she said as they came inside. "Our daughter."

Transfixed, Kaitlyn moved closer. "She's beautiful."

"Would you like to hold her?"

Taking a deep breath, Kaitlyn nodded and held out her arms. Gently, Zoe transferred the baby. Inhaling the sweet scent, Zoe marveled. "She smells like powder and sunshine."

Zoe laughed. "Yes, she does."

Kaitlyn's eyes filled with tears. She tried to blink them away, aware she'd been far too emotional recently. But who could blame her? Lately it seemed like her every dream was coming true.

And now this. Her best friend, Zoe, had gotten her prayers answered, too.

April opened her eyes. "Oh!" Kaitlyn exclaimed. "They're caramel. Just like yours."

Zoe nodded. "When I bathe her, her skin practically glows."

Reed came up behind Kaitlyn, peering down at the newest addition to the McCauley family. "She is a pretty little thing," he said.

"Would you like to hold her?" Kaitlyn offered.

Immediately, Reed backed away. "Uh, no. I'm afraid I'd drop her or something."

"Come on, man." Grinning, Brock lightly punched Reed's shoulder, gripping a stylish cane with his other hand. "You can do it. Sit on the couch with her if that makes you feel better."

Reed shot Kaitlyn a look of pure desperation. She returned it by pouring every bit of love and joy inside her into a soft smile. "Sit," she said. "I'll take a seat beside you. I'll be right there if you need help."

Still appearing uncertain, Reed dropped onto the couch. Carrying her precious cargo reverently, Kaitlyn carefully sat next to him. "Are you ready?"

Hesitating, he finally nodded. Meanwhile, Brock cracked up and Zoe watched them with a mother's nervous eye.

"Here. She's not very heavy." And Kaitlyn transferred baby April to him.

At first, Reed looked as if he'd rather be anywhere else, holding anything but a tiny newborn. But as he nestled little April against him, a look of wonder came over his rugged face. "Wow," he said. "Just wow."

Apparently Brock understood his guy talk. "I know, man. Right?"

Without taking his gaze off April's café-au-lait complexion, Reed nodded. When he finally spoke again, awe reverberated in his husky voice. "You must be so proud."

"We are," Brock said, grinning. Zoe beamed, too. "We barely had time to get her nursery ready before she arrived."

At that moment, baby April scrunched up her face and let out a wail. Reed jumped. Immediately, Zoe moved in, speaking soothing nonsense as she took her daughter from him.

"She's hungry," Zoe said. "I need to go warm her bottle. Kaitlyn, do you want to go with me?"

"Sure." Kaitlyn hurried after her friend.

Once they were alone in the kitchen, Zoe expertly heated the premade bottle in the microwave and tested it on her wrist, before feeding it to her hungry baby. Kaitlyn watched with amazed happiness.

"Life is good," she finally said.

"Yes." Zoe's bright smile confirmed the statement. "It is. Now, do you have something you want to tell me?"

Kaitlyn grinned. "I was going to wait until after dinner," she said. "But since you noticed, Ms. Observant, yes." She held out her left hand, letting the ring sparkle in the light. "Reed and I are engaged."

Zoe gave a satisfied squeal. "Look at that rock! It's gorgeous!"

"Thank you." Though Kaitlyn ached to tell her friend the rest of her news, she knew she owed it to Reed to tell him first. After all, she wasn't entirely sure how he'd react.

Everyone gathered around the kitchen table. The baby slept while they ate. Reed opened a bottle of red wine for the occasion. Kaitlyn carried her glass to the sink when she went to bring the big bowl of spaghetti and poured most of it out, not wanting to make an issue of being unable to drink it.

They would all know soon enough anyway.

After the meal, Reed tapped on his wineglass, grinning. "Kaitlyn and I have an announcement to make."

Since Brock was the only one at the table who had no idea what Reed meant, Kaitlyn sent a silent prayer to Zoe to act surprised.

She needn't have worried.

Reaching over for Kaitlyn's hand, Reed gazed into her eyes. "Kaitlyn and I have decided to get married," he said, his expression tender and still amazed.

"Congratulations!" Brock sounded surprised.

Zoe responded with the exact same squeal she'd done

in the kitchen. "Fabulous news. I'm so happy for you two."

Reed smiled. "Thank you. And if we're lucky, someday we might be as blessed as you two have been, with a child of our own."

Nodding, Brock replied. "Sooner or later, I'm sure you will be."

Now? Swallowing, Kaitlyn looked around at the faces of the people she loved and decided, *Why not?* All or nothing, right?

"About that, Reed." A deep breath, willing her voice to sound steady. "It might be sooner rather than later."

He cocked his head, his gaze sure and steady and full of love. "What are you trying to tell me? Remember what we decided. Together in everything."

Right then she knew. Reed would welcome this baby into his life with as much joy and love as he welcomed her.

"What?" Zoe shrieked, as the truth dawned on her. "Are you saying you're—"

"Pregnant," Kaitlyn finished, grinning from ear to ear. "Of course, I just took an at-home test. I haven't been to the doctor's yet."

She met Reed's gaze. The excitement and love in his eyes, made her want to weep.

"We'll go together." Reed got up, went behind her chair and encircled her in his arms. "I hope it's a little girl, who will look just like you."

Kaitlyn tried to smile past the tears that suddenly filled her eyes. "I want a little boy, with your eyes and chin."

Later, she found out she was carrying two, possibly one of each, though it was too early to tell.

"You're starting your family out in a big way," the doctor commented. Kaitlyn and Reed just looked at each other and shared a secret smile.

All or nothing, after all.

* * * * *

If you loved this novel, don't miss other suspenseful titles by Karen Whiddon:

A SECRET COLTON BABY
THE MILLIONAIRE COWBOY'S SECRET
THE COP'S MISSING CHILD
TEXAS SECRETS, LOVERS' LIES

Available now from Harlequin Romantic Suspense!

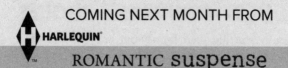

COMING NEXT MONTH FROM

HARLEQUIN®

ROMANTIC suspense

Available April 7, 2015

#1843 CAVANAUGH FORTUNE
Cavanaugh Justice • by Marie Ferrarella
Tech-savvy officer Valri Cavanaugh must track down a ring of hackers causing major destruction to businesses in Aurora. She's partnered with detective Alex Brody, an incorrigible flirt who keeps his distance because of her name. Will they find love even as the danger escalates?

#1844 SECRET AGENT BOYFRIEND
The Adair Affairs • by Addison Fox
When long-buried secrets surface for an American royal family, society princess Landry Adair and too-handsome FBI expert Derek Winchester must pretend to care for each other to trap a killer. But fake romance turns very real while they work to solve a decades-old kidnapping.

#1845 JOINT ENGAGEMENT
To Protect and Serve • by Karen Anders
Special agent Kinley Cooper and NCIS special agent Beau Jerrott don't work well together, but when a boat is found adrift with all personnel aboard dead, they must learn to trust each other, putting their careers—and their hearts—on the line.

#1846 McKINNON'S ROYAL MISSION
by Amelia Autin
Not a chance. Government ultrasecret agent Trace McKinnon won't babysit. He nearly refuses the assignment to guard Zakhar's princess Mara Theodora, but his fluency in the Zakharan language is what the State Department needs...to spy on the targeted—and far too appealing—princess!

HRSCNM0315

REQUEST YOUR FREE BOOKS!

2 FREE NOVELS PLUS 2 FREE GIFTS!

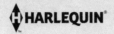

ROMANTIC suspense

Sparked by danger, fueled by passion

"Won't Detective Brody feel resentful, being paired up
with a beat cop?" Valri Cavanaugh asked.

"Possibly," the chief acknowledged, his tone stern.
"Which is why I'm issuing you a temporary promotion to
detective for the duration of this investigation."

"Promotion? To detective?" she repeated in an awed
whisper, never taking her eyes off the chief.

"Tell me—and think carefully—are you up for this?"
he asked her.

There was no hesitation in Valri's voice this time as she
gave him her answer. "Yes, sir."

"Good." He nodded, appearing pleased for a split
second then once again stern. He hit the button on his
intercom, connecting him to his administrative assistant
out front. "You can send him in now, Raleigh."

"Right away, sir," the feminine voice on the intercom

HRSEXP0315

promised.

The next moment the door to Brian Cavanaugh's inner office opened. A tall, broad-shouldered detective with dirty-blond hair that was slightly longer than regulation dictated walked in as if he owned every square inch of space he passed.

Sparing an appreciative glance at the officer sitting in front of the chief of detectives—Brody was not one who didn't note beauty wherever he came in contact with it— he then focused his attention entirely on the chief.

Alex had spent his morning with a dead man in a dingy apartment that desperately needed a thorough cleaning and a massive dose of fresh air. The chief's immaculate, spacious office was a very welcome contrast. He stood behind the only empty chair in the room, waiting to find out if this was going to be something he needed to sit down for, or just a quick, "touch base" sort of a meeting.

"You sent for me, sir?" he asked the chief.

Brian smiled then gestured for the young detective to sit down. "I did indeed, Detective Brody."

What came next, Alex knew, would test him to the limit. He hadn't spent years in the trenches for this. But then, you didn't say no to a Cavanaugh…

Don't miss
CAVANAUGH FORTUNE
by USA TODAY *bestselling author*
Marie Ferrarella.
Available April 2015 wherever
Harlequin® Romantic Suspense
books and ebooks are sold.

www.Harlequin.com